CUT OFF

CUT OFF

ADRIANNE FINLAY

Houghton
Boston

hmhbooks.com

The text was set in Sabon LT Std.
Design by Mary Claire Cruz
Logo by Joel Tippie
Texture (interior) © Apostrophe/Shutterstock

Library of Congress Cataloging-in-Publication Data
Names: Finlay, Adrianne, author.
Title: Cut Off / by Adrianne Finlay.
Description: Boston ; New York : Houghton Mifflin Harcourt, [2020] |
Summary: When something goes horribly wrong during the
filming of a new virtual reality show, teenaged contestants
question how much of the game is real.
Identifiers: LCCN 2019012438 (print) | LCCN 2019016650 (ebook)
| ISBN 9780358237358 (ebook) | ISBN 9780358006459 (hardcover)
Subjects: | CYAC: Survival—Fiction. | Virtual reality—Fiction. | Reality
television programs—Fiction. | Science fiction.
Classification: LCC PZ7.1.F536 (ebook) | LCC PZ7.1.F536 Cut 2020
(print) | DDC [Fic]—dc23
LC record available at https://lccn.loc.gov/2019012438

Manufactured in the United States of America
DOC 10 9 8 7 6 5 4 3 2 1
4500799724

For Ginny and Hattie

Brandon McCay is going to die.

That's what he thinks as he stumbles, gasping and bleeding, through the forest. But he's determined—that's what's important. He's got grit, and willpower, and no *way* will he let a reality show be the thing that kills him.

Everything was fine until the earthquake.

Everything was *fine*. He was surviving, no doubt better than anyone else on the show. He'd caught fish, built a great shelter, and actually had a decent shot at winning this whole thing. He'd already started planning what to do with the money after the show. Buy a new car, pay off his parents' house, maybe backpack to exotic destinations. Have adventures, live it up, embrace his inner adrenaline junkie.

He's over that now, though. The next trip he takes, there'll be feather pillows and room service. There'll be hospitals. He'd trade every cent of the million-dollar prize for a morphine drip right now.

He clutches his side. The blood on his fingers is thick and sticky.

Was the earthquake only yesterday? It seems longer.

He was ascending a rock face when it happened, trying

to get to higher ground, have a look around. He balanced on a scraggy bit of ledge, figuring he looked pretty good on the Skym camera hovering just above his head. The Skyms were sophisticated, and definitely expensive—top-of-the-line drone cameras that did all the filming for *Cut Off*, creating a 3-D virtual-reality experience for the folks back home. Brandon's climb gave them a pretty sweet panorama. Those viewers who dropped the nine hundred bucks on the *Cut Off* virtual-reality visors were sure getting their money's worth.

Not that Brandon was simply performing for the camera. He had plans, like signing a first-class endorsement deal with a sporting-goods company or an energy drink. Eventually he'd have his own show. Getting picked for *Cut Off* was just the start for him. High on that cliff, it all felt inevitable, a sure thing.

Then the world shook, and knocked him right off the side of it.

He dropped twenty feet to the ground and lay there dazed, staring into the blue sky, waiting for the rest of the mountain to crash down on him. When it was over, he sat up to find that a branch as wide as his finger had torn through the side of his t-shirt. For a second, he couldn't make sense of it, and then his mind clicked together that it hadn't ripped through his shirt, it had ripped through *him*—his muscle and flesh. That was when the pain hit, and he screamed.

Lying there, pierced through the gut, a swelling knob on his head and blood soaking into his clothes, his first thought was about the damn show and how he couldn't win now. The producers would swarm him, pull him from the game, and that was it. Over and out for Brandon McCay.

He'd barely lasted three weeks. That wasn't enough time for fame and endorsements, not enough time to become a household name. He was hurt and yeah, scared, but mostly he was pissed.

Even though it was obvious he was out of the game, for the sake of the drama he yelled up at the fluttering Skym, "Hey! Come get me, I'm tapping out!"

While he waited, he used the time to his advantage, chatting with the camera, putting on a steadfast, heroic front. There was an audience behind that dead glass eye, and it'd be his last chance to connect with them, perhaps turn his bad luck into something that would look gutsy and badass.

The first hour passed, and then another. Where were they?

He reached for his bag, the wound screaming at him as he drew his body off the branch. He dug out the beacon and pressed the red tap-out button. He didn't know how it worked, but it was supposed to send out his GPS location, alert the producers that he was quitting. They were supposed to answer.

Instead, he was met with silence.

When darkness came, he knew something was wrong.

Really wrong.

That all happened yesterday, when he still thought the camera was sending a signal to the audience, the producers, the crew. Now he doesn't know what to think. He wasn't about to lie there rotting in the woods, so he's been walking since morning.

As if things couldn't get worse, he's pretty sure something's following him. Something big, a wolf or a wild boar. He can hear it in the bush. It smells the blood that soaks his pant leg, and there's nothing he can do to stop it. He needs to lie down, rest a minute, that's all, but every time he slows, the trees rustle with a noise like a creature stalking through dry leaves.

His limbs tingle, and some distant part of him knows that's bad.

A low growl rumbles from the darkness.

Brandon walks faster, but he can't keep going like this much longer. Just as the darkest thoughts, the ones he's held at bay all morning, threaten to tumble forward, hitting him like an avalanche of rocks, he sees a trailer. A sound escapes him that he doesn't recognize as his own. Part whimper, part laugh. The relief is so strong and sudden he feels like throwing up.

The trailer is white and broad, a relic of the civilized world in the middle of nowhere. Among the blue design swirls decorating the side and under the windows, someone has slapped a decal of the show's logo: **CUT OFF**, with an image of the earth within the O, and bows, arrows, and fierce animals bordering the perimeter. It's the producers' trailer, like a base camp. Brandon doesn't care anymore that they didn't show up right away. They're here, he's found them, and everything will be okay. The earthquake knocked out his Skym signal, killed his beacon's GPS, but everything is okay now. He's safe.

With a groan, he pushes the door open and falls to the floor, the Skym flitting in after him. He lifts his eyes to find . . . no one. It's empty.

Terrified of whatever beast has been tracking him, he kicks the door shut and turns the lock.

"Hello!" he calls, his voice wet with pain and desperation. "Hello?"

Brandon drops his pack and drags himself across the gray carpet. With his last bit of strength, he hauls himself into a chair at a bank of computer screens.

There's a smartphone on the desk next to a half-eaten tuna sandwich and a partially full water bottle. Brandon guzzles the water and shoves the sandwich in his mouth. The tuna tastes sour. He doesn't care.

Where is everyone? What happened here?

Blood smears the buttons of the console as he presses them, at first methodically but then with increasing panic. The computer boots up to reveal the show's logo, but there's no signal, no internet, no sign of anyone or anything. The console phone is silent. The cellphone has no signal. One of the computer monitors flickers on, and a black-and-white screen glows to life. Twelve scenes divide the screen, seven of them blank and five showing the remaining contestants, footage from their Skyms. One of them is building a fire, another's fishing. And there he is, Brandon, in the image on the bottom right, hunched over the desk.

At first glance, he doesn't recognize himself, and for a moment he thinks, *That guy's screwed.* His face is drawn, and his blood shows black on the monitor. How can that be him?

His hopes of winning the show might be over, but if that

Skym is still filming, he's giving it a goddamn story, a *drama* is what he's giving it.

"Hey!" he yells at the footage of the four other people. "Hey, someone! I need help!"

The contestants don't react. They can't hear him, of course. He lays his head on the desk and cries long enough to come back to himself, and then he cries some more.

Rolling the chair across the trailer, he brings himself to the couch. As he eases onto the pillows, his wound oozes more blood, but it doesn't hurt as much now. It's a throb, constant and relentless, but no longer piercing. As the pain retreats, he finds himself using it as a gauge to make sure he's alive.

Suddenly he wishes he could see the outside. After so many days, he thought it'd be a relief to finally be indoors, out of the forest, on a soft couch. But he's always been happiest outside. He craves fresh air, the clear space of a cloudless sky, the rush of a breeze. The somber trailer, with its dingy carpet, plastic chairs, and moldering smell—it isn't what he wants in this moment.

There's a poster tacked on the wall: mountains with snowy crests, green fields below, a spray of wildflowers—yellow, violet, iridescent blue. In the black border on the bottom is the word **ESCAPE**. Brandon lets his gaze settle on the image while he rests, just until he can figure out what to do next. He needs to find the main camp. Surely someone will be there.

He imagines what the crisp air would taste like on top of that mountain. The pain has slipped away entirely now, and that's nice. His fingers grow numb. Then colors drain from the wildflowers until they, and everything around them, turn gray.

Brandon's hand drops from the couch. The Skym bobs overhead for a long time, its signal transmitting to the screen three feet away, until at last its battery wears down in the gloom-ridden room. It settles gently to the carpet and its red eye blinks off.

THE
SHOW

CHAPTER 01

HITCHENS: Now is the time in our interview when you can ask any nagging questions you might have for us.

RIVER: How much longer will all this take? I figured since you guys came to me, asked me to apply, there wouldn't be this whole process.

HITCHENS: Well, there's another interview, and the psych eval, and if you're selected you'll have the wilderness survival training. Though you hardly need it, you'll have to participate in the training if you're selected. Liability and all that. It's fundamentals – fire starting, shelter building, that kind of thing. Should be a piece of cake for you. Otherwise, the selection process is variable. So, I'd guess another week and then we'll do some paperwork.

RIVER: My uncle is the one who really wanted me to do this. I'm not so sure.

HITCHENS: He told us you'd be perfect for this when we spoke to him. And I have to say, your application is the best of the bunch. It's good stuff, River. You're not second-guessing, are you?

RIVER: I don't know. We're on camera the whole time?

HITCHENS: That's right – our Skym cameras will follow your entire journey on the show, transmitting the whole thing in 3-D on a virtual-reality platform.

RIVER: So they're, what, like a drone camera?

HITCHENS: Yes, but much more sophisticated. The Skym recognizes your face, your clothes, it zooms in and out with changes in your expression, and it's programmed to stay with you at all times, no matter what.

RIVER: And the cameras are self-sustaining?

HITCHENS: They require very little maintenance. You only need to change out the solar battery chargers once a day, and charge the supplemental battery. They do the rest of the work.

RIVER: That contract said something about the show possibly taking a year. It's a lot to think about.

HITCHENS: Yeah, there's no set time frame. We're not a traditional television show, we don't have a network to answer to. We plan to stream on every media platform for as long as you kids stay out there surviving. And it'll be hard, but think of the payoff. Not just the money – you'll have great exposure. You'll be famous.

RIVER: I don't care about money. My parents had insurance. And I don't want to be famous.

HITCHENS: I won't lie, River. We want you on the show. But you're right, it's a commitment, and you need to figure out if it's what you really want. You filled out the application, and you've come this far in the process. Why do all that? You must have your reasons.

RIVER: Why kids?

HITCHENS: Why what?

RIVER: Why kids? Everyone you recruited is under eighteen.

HITCHENS: Well, you're not *kids*, exactly, are you? You'll be eighteen in less than a year. But it's part of the experiment. To observe what happens when young people are removed from civilization. Not only from the comforts and conveniences of the modern world, but also from the difficulties that society, and older people – people like me – created. Also, while the content of the show will be available traditionally, on televisions and computers, the audience also has the option of streaming the show on our new virtual-reality platform. The technology we'll implant in the contestants means that their brain waves – yours, if you're selected – will be transmitted through our new app. The audience won't just be able to watch the show, they'll be completely immersed in the experience – they'll see what you see and hear what you hear, with our special cameras that record everything in 3-D. Frankly, the technology is most effective with a certain plasticity in the brain. The younger the recipient, the better it works. We cast young contestants, but only those mature enough to give it a go by themselves in the wilderness.

RIVER: Transmitting my brain waves sounds . . . invasive.

HITCHENS: It's completely safe, nothing to worry about. Once you tap out, the ions will be neutralized. What they do, however, is give the audience a fully immersive experience. Your visual and auditory perception will be transmitted, through our 3-D application, into our Cut Off Experience visors. People wear these things, and let me tell you, River, it's amazing. They get so caught up in the experience, they actually start thinking they can touch the world around them. It's a real trick of the brain. We're also expecting that a young audience is more likely to adopt our new technology, really live with it, you know? Your experience out there, in the wild, it'll make them feel like they're living it too. Groundbreaking stuff, River. So what are you thinking?

RIVER: Can I do it alone?

HITCHENS: Of course. Other contestants will end up working together, probably. It'll give them an advantage. But there's nothing that says you have to, if you don't want.

RIVER: Yeah. I work better alone.

END RECORDING

EVALUATION:

River Adan is thoughtful, but reserved. That's where the risk in casting him lies. He's not forthcoming, and unlikely to share his journey with the viewers in a way that allows them to emotionally connect. Honestly, his interaction with the Skym will likely produce more dead air than anything.

Our observations and psych profile, however, suggest something interesting beneath the surface that we're hopeful will come out in the tense conditions the show will produce. The death of his parents has led him to become isolated. When he encounters other contestants (and of course we'll ensure he *will* encounter others, despite his desire to work alone), we envision some entertaining outcomes.

Otherwise, he's extremely competent. With his skills, there's a better chance of him keeping the show going than some of the other contestants we've chosen so far. I'd put money on him sticking it out for the long haul. He is genuinely interested in the wilderness experience and will be an asset both as a contestant in the game and, with the right influences called into play, as a driving narrative force.

Recommendation: Accept and advance to final interview screening.

—G. Hitchens

■ ■ ■

The frigid water of the ocean seeped into River's bones, dragging him down. He'd made a string of bad decisions, and now here he was, sinking.

It was his own fault. He should have changed the Skym battery yesterday. One minute it had been fluttering high above the water, then it had dropped several yards from shore, splashing like a stone. He'd instinctively plunged after it. Within minutes the Skym had floated out of reach, and a rogue wave crashed on top of him. He was in over his head, and had no idea which way was up.

He'd been overconfident. He was weak, tired, pretending the past few weeks of sparse diet and sleepless nights weren't affecting him. For the first time, he regretted the deal he'd made with Uncle Jim: stick it out on the show until the end, or at least six months, and Jim would give it a rest about the military academy and pay for a year of travel. This time next year, River expected to be backpacking the Appalachian Trail, taking as long as he liked. No cameras, no audience, no show. Just him, alone. It was a good deal. He knew a lot about wilderness survival.

He just hadn't bargained on electronic contraptions tumbling from the sky.

If only he hadn't left his camp across the bay. It was solid and dry, tons of fish. A blue plastic barrel had washed up on his beach after that earthquake three days ago, and he'd used it as a giant bobber, fixing trotlines to it and letting it drift in the currents where trout gathered.

His arms felt heavy, as if weighed down with lead, but he also had the odd sensation that gravity had become a spent force. The ocean had swallowed him up, and he thought perhaps he was drowning. Images of home flitted past his eyes: his parents laughing on their rambling front porch; hiking the trails behind the house with his best friend, Terrell; everyone grilling fresh-caught perch over a fire.

He swam and reached the floating Skym. Tendrils of

seaweed grazed his body, and tiredness spread through his limbs. He felt no desire to spend the last of his energy making it back to shore. Maybe he could float for a while, bob along on the waves like the dead Skym.

If he could just rest for a bit, not worry about anything . . .

His mother, in front of a campfire, picking the tiny bones from a perch. She made a face. It wasn't her favorite fish.

Work it out, River.

It was like when she'd wake him in the morning to mow the lawn.

Leave me alone. I'm tired.

Get over it. Swim.

She was right. He probably shouldn't die like this. It would piss her off.

He summoned a last reserve of strength, grabbed the Skym, clipped it to his belt, then struck for shore in the distance.

How had he gotten so far out? He swam, arms aching, and when he finally touched ground, he couldn't take a single step. All that struggle in the water had been for nothing; it'd be just as easy to die here as in the ocean. He was wet and cold, had no fire or dry clothes. Too late to do anything about it now.

He dropped onto the sand, and his last thought was that the tide would pull him back out again and his bones would become coral.

When he opened his eyes, he found he wasn't dead, so there was that. The sun was too bright, and birds circled overhead. They dove in and out of his line of sight, swooping for fish. The sound of crashing water was distinct from the rushing noise in his head. So the ocean was on his right. The Skym was grounded to his left, green light gleaming and pointed directly at him.

His Skym was recovered and charged. He somehow was still alive. And he was, it seemed, naked. Which wouldn't have been a big deal, except for the Skym staring at him.

His next thought was that something was on fire, *he* was on fire. Smoke cloaked his lungs, and he gasped himself upright. He shivered as a Mylar blanket slipped from his chest. A fire roared in a pit beside him. His jacket, shirt, pants, and socks hung from a nearby branch like a string of dead fish. His boots hung upside down on two stakes pointed toward the fire. It looked comical, as though someone had been buried in the dirt with their feet sticking up.

He shivered again and pulled the blanket around his shoulders, then looked for a clue to what had happened, who had built the fire, who had saved his life.

He hadn't anticipated what a pain the Skym would be. The producers said he'd get kicked off the show if he couldn't keep it going, so he'd had to do that, even if it meant taking risks he knew he shouldn't.

The lady producer had asked, "How comfortable are you with operating the Skym?"

He'd shrugged like it was no big deal, he could handle it.

He remembered the way her eyes had narrowed and she'd jotted a note in her clipboard.

She'd been right to doubt him. The Skym made everything harder in the wild. Lugging the batteries, making sure they stayed charged, the low-grade buzz as it followed him like a giant bug. And now he'd almost died rescuing the thing, and it was all on display for . . . how many people watching? Each one strapped into an overpriced visor, mouth hanging open in a trance? River couldn't remember the number he'd been told. It'd been in the millions.

Everything else he could deal with, even the lousy weather. That was the easy part of the whole thing: surviving.

It was the show, apparently, that was going to kill him.

He wasn't dead yet, though, for whatever reason. River checked his clothes, hanging from the branch, damp but warm from the fire. He put them on and crouched close to the flames until he felt like he was being cooked, his skin tightening and tingling with heat.

He retrieved the canteen from his pack and discovered that the dried trout he'd been carrying was missing. Only the neatly wrapped leaves he'd stored it in remained. Now that he didn't have any food, a pang of hunger clenched his stomach.

Worse than the cold and hunger, he felt lost and confused. His fingers, still stiff, fumbled with the screw-top lid of the canteen until he cursed and threw it into the trees. Even before it hit the ground, he forced himself to take a breath. If he were sitting at home watching himself on the live stream, he'd know that an outburst like that was the first indication of a contestant who wouldn't last. Not if he couldn't keep his cool, get his bearings.

A voice behind him said, "Guess you're awake."

Out of instinct, River reached to his side for his knife. Of course it wasn't there, and he immediately felt foolish. What was he going to do with a knife, stab another contestant? He needed to settle down.

The guy was more than a head shorter than River and wore a hoodie that he'd probably filled out better when the show started and he'd weighed a few more pounds. His lank, straw-colored hair fell over his ears, and his pale green eyes darted in every direction. He held two cups, and handed one to River, then poured steaming water from his canteen into each.

"Thanks," River said, sitting on a log. The water burned his throat, but he took two more sips before stopping to blow on the surface.

"I ate your fish. Sorry about that."

"It's okay."

"I figured it was payment for saving your waterlogged self, but to be honest, I was just hungry."

"I can get more."

"Oh yeah? So you're, like, one of the real survivalists? A mountain man or whatever?"

"Not so far."

The clouds over the mountain now blocked the sun, and the air chilled. It was late afternoon. He'd been out for longer than he realized.

"Right. Well, I totally saved you, didn't I? I remembered what they said about water, about hypothermia and all that. I fished you out, whipped your clothes off. Sorry about that, too, but it's what the book said, so I did it. It is what the book says, right?"

River nodded.

The boy gave a lopsided grin and winked. "I like your tattoo. There some kind of special meaning to it?"

River had gotten the star compass on his left shoulder blade last year, the first anniversary of when his parents died. It was based on the Mariner card deck he and Terrell used to pack when they camped. It reminded him of when things were different. When he'd had friends—a best friend, even—and had actually liked spending time with them. That wasn't the case now. He'd been lousy about answering texts or showing up. He hadn't talked to Terrell in ages, let alone gone on one of their monthly backpacking trips. He felt bad about it, but he wasn't good company nowadays. He was too in his head, too lost. The image of the compass was meant to remind him to find his way back again, no matter where he was.

It was wishful thinking.

River didn't tell the boy all that, however. He'd already shared enough with him, not to mention the rest of the world. The guy seemed unconcerned with River's silence and kept on chattering.

"What's your name, anyway? I saved your life—I should at least know your name."

River shifted position on the log. "River."

"River." The boy sat on a large rock near the fire. "Like 'cry me a river'?"

"Just River."

"Your parents hippies or something?"

"No." Even through the fog still clouding his mind, he

could tell that the guy's jittery eagerness meant he was waiting for something from him, so he finally asked, "What's your
name?"

"Are you kidding?" The boy rubbed a hand on his cheek,
his eyebrows jumping high enough to raise his hairline. River
had asked the wrong question. "I mean, I guess I look kind of
ragged from being out here so long, but seriously, you don't
recognize me?"

"Sorry." River used a stick to push another log into the
dying fire.

"ThreeDz?"

"Three-D? That's your name?"

"No, man, my name's Trip."

"Trip? Like falling down?"

"I prefer 'What a long strange Trip it's been.' Or 'Trip the
light fantastic.' Ever hear that one?" He studied River's face,
which remained politely unruffled, for a reaction. "But yeah,
like falling down, too. Come on, are you serious? Internet-
famous computer whiz kid? I was on the *Today* show. You've
never heard of ThreeDz? The ThreeDz app? I created that."

River shrugged. "I don't know what you're talking about."

"You're something else, River. I mean, you go for a morning dip in icy water and nearly kill yourself, and now you tell
me you don't know about ThreeDz?"

"So, what is it?" River asked, trying to keep irritation from
his voice.

River had never given much thought to whatever the latest

tech gadget or app might be, and he certainly didn't care what happened on the *Today* show. His parents had built their home on the edge of 1,500 square wilderness miles. He could bring a walkie-talkie into the woods for weeks at a time. What did he need a smartphone for? He didn't need to check e-mail in front of a campfire. What it meant, however, was that sometimes it felt like everyone was speaking a language he'd never wanted to learn. The language Trip was speaking now when he lifted his arms high and spread them wide.

"ThreeDz, man! It made all this possible. The live stream, the Skyms—that's ThreeDz tech."

"So why's it called Three-D?"

"Three*Dz*, Three*Dz*. It's a three-D camera stream. That camera you almost died for this morning? You made the right call. It's worth more than your sorry ass."

"You invented the Skyms?" River said, impressed. They were small and flat, like a frying pan about eight inches around, with five separate, detachable camera lenses and a tiny screen in their center. He could tell they embodied a complex system, the way they tracked the contestants, how the lens zoomed in and focused on minute detail and slight movements as if propelled by instinct. When in the air, they split apart into five minicameras, capturing every angle of the environment to transmit a 3-D image, then joined together again. A week into the show, River realized he'd started imagining the Skym was some kind of intelligent alien creature. He'd had to remind himself that while it was a smart machine, it was mindless.

Skyms had movement trackers, recognition data, motion sensors, and facial-expression readers, but they weren't alive. They couldn't think.

"Nah, I didn't invent the Skyms," Trip said. "But I did design the app that streams the three-D VR content. Without me, those things are useless."

"It's pretty useless to me. You should have invented a battery that lasts longer." River regretted the comment when Trip grimaced, as if his feelings were hurt. "Sorry."

"No, it's cool. You're not a tech guy, I get it." He held his own cup up to River, toasting him in the air. "I'll still share dinner with you. Nothing fancy, just snails from the rocks." He nodded to where water lapped the shore. Pebbles rustled as waves rolled them out again, and the ocean rippled with foam and strips of seaweed. River welcomed the offer. Having something in his stomach, even the little pile of snails, would take some of the chill away.

Trip gestured to his temporary shelter. "My real camp is over the ridge. I didn't mean to be gone this long, but I didn't want to ditch you, you know? You're the first person I've seen in weeks. Anyway, this is all I put together for tonight. Not bad, though, considering."

River surveyed the ramshackle lean-to. It was wobbly, and if it rained tonight it wouldn't offer any cover.

River inhaled the cool, salty air. They hadn't been told where the show was filming, but the landscape reminded him of the Pacific Northwest, where he'd grown up.

What Trip had said earlier wasn't exactly true: he hadn't

saved River's life. If any of them got into real trouble, they'd be rescued. The show wouldn't let anyone die. But getting doused in freezing water, with no fire or dry clothes, River would have had to tap out, and the deal with Jim wouldn't fly after only a few weeks as a contestant. At least Trip had saved him from that.

River looked out at the bay, wondering if he'd caught any fish on the line of his blue barrel. He'd never make it back to his own camp before dark, however. He could afford to stick with Trip for a while. They weren't a team—River didn't want a team. He'd camped for days at a time by himself, and he'd never missed the sound of someone else's voice, had never wanted company badly enough to trade the security of having only himself to worry about. But after listening to the other boy yammer for the past hour, he realized he could use a break from his own thoughts.

He dug in his pack for a length of rope, pulled on his boots, and set to work reinforcing the roof of the shelter while Trip kept up a steady chatter about apps and celebrities and tweets and what seemed like a million other things River didn't care about.

He'd stay with Trip until tomorrow at most, get the guy safely back to his own camp, and then he'd head out on his own again. No harm done.

■ ■ ■

They started hiking early the next day. The sun brightened and grew warmer as they walked, but once they entered the trees, only patches of light filtered through the forest. Late morning, they found a path that River identified as a game trail, which made him cautious. He had no desire to confront whatever wild animals lived in the area. He followed the trail anyway. The hike would be easier, they'd get to Trip's camp faster, and then he'd be on his own again.

In the trees, it was a different world from the ecosystem of the shore, where River had been spending most of his days. He'd trek into the woods to forage, but otherwise the ocean provided everything he needed. The forest made him think of his home and of wandering for hours through his own little plot of wilderness—except his home was much less mountainous, and also quieter. Here he was accompanied by Lawrence Johnson III, otherwise known as Trip, founder of the ThreeDz app, millionaire whiz kid who occasionally halted their hike to narrate to the Skyms. He talked about hunger; he talked about being sick of hiking; he talked about the three cars he owned back home, the yacht he'd bought his mom, and the flying lessons he'd been taking for the past few months.

At times the narration was about River himself, and Trip made him sound like some kind of modern-day Grizzly Adams, only without the beard, and those times were particularly irritating.

Although Trip didn't seem like someone who could survive by himself in the wilderness, he was at ease wielding his machete when they whacked through a tangly stretch of the trail. He was skinny, but wiry, confident in his body.

The hike was uphill, and they stopped for a water break

in a flat, sunny spot, sitting on a fallen tree free of moss. River felt the warmth of the sun absorbed by the tree's smooth bark. His fully assembled Skym hovered overhead. Trip's had broken apart, like segments of an orange, so five minicameras swarmed above them.

"Look at that," Trip said, pointing to them.

"What?" River asked.

"They know we're together, so your camera is getting a straight-ahead shot, and mine is getting the three-D shot."

River took in the way the cameras surrounded him and Trip. "How do they do that?"

"They're smart. Without anyone telling them, they talk to each other, figure out how to get the best content for the show."

River nodded without really understanding. He was more comfortable with real, solid things. He trusted his hands to solve problems, and he didn't like dealing with the misty abstractions of high tech. Sometimes he felt like he'd grown up in a different century.

"Impressive," he said.

Trip let out a yelp when a spider the size of an acorn landed on his shoulder. He jumped from the log and slapped it away. River looked at him blankly until Trip shrugged.

"I hate spiders. Most bugs, really. God, why are there so many here?"

"There's nothing wrong with spiders. They eat mosquitoes."

Trip shuddered dramatically. "They're tiny monsters. Too many legs."

River shook his head. "They have eight. That's how many

they're supposed to have." He couldn't understand Trip. Why come on a show like this if you jumped at everything that moved?

River foraged for mushrooms and edible greens as they hiked, without finding anything really substantial. He still felt the effects of his near drowning the day before. Everything remained a little askew, like he'd not gotten enough sleep.

Once they reached the top of the ridge, River took in the view. It revealed the wider area in a way that had remained hidden when down in the bay. He oriented himself and surveyed the south, which disclosed another bay beyond his own. Another mountain, higher than the one they were on, rose to the east, and to the north the land curled into the ocean. Nearby, just below them along the shore, what looked like an immense swarm of bees drifted up into the sky. He focused, shielding his eyes from the sun. It wasn't bees. It was smoke, and a lot of it. Too much for a campfire.

"Trip." River pointed down the side of the ridge.

Trip's eyes widened. "Damn. That's my camp."

"Well." River gauged the rising plume. "It's on fire."

CHAPTER 02

HITCHENS: So, Cameron, why do you want to be on *Cut Off*?

CAMERON: I go by Cam.

HITCHENS: Okay, Cam. Why do you want to be on *Cut Off*?

CAMERON: The money. What other reason is there?

HITCHENS: Not everybody is doing it for the money. For some it's
    the challenge, or to find time alone, some space. A few want to be
    famous.

CAMERON: . . .

HITCHENS: What do you need the money for?

CAMERON: What does anyone need money for?

HITCHENS: Is it because of your mother?

CAMERON: Like I told that other guy, I'm not talking about my mother with you.

HITCHENS: Why not?

CAMERON: That's none of your business. *She's* none of your business.

HITCHENS: Cameron, when you signed on to participate in this process, you knew —

CAMERON: I go by Cam.

HITCHENS: Right. When you signed up, you knew we would ask you questions.

CAMERON: I signed up for a game show, not therapy. Thanks, though.

HITCHENS: This is more than a game. You can't win or lose in the usual ways. It's about who you are as a person.

CAMERON: Oh, come on. None of this is new — we've seen it a million times. Whether it's singing or surviving or, I don't know, dating. Whoever's still standing at the end wins. Don't pretend your show is any different.

HITCHENS: We think it's quite different.

CAMERON: Okay.

HITCHENS: On your intake form, you sound very confident in your ability to win. How do you plan to do that?

CAMERON: Elimination. Make the other contestants tap out.

HITCHENS: This isn't the Hunger Games, Camer — I mean Cam. What if you need help from another contestant and have to seek them out? What if you need someone?

CAMERON: I don't need anyone.

HITCHENS: Do you feel that way because your mother was never there for you?

CAMERON: . . .

HITCHENS: It's a simple question.

CAMERON: She was there for me.

HITCHENS: Really? Because it says here that she has two drug convictions. That three years ago you were living with her in a car. And now, well. It's hard to say she's there for you, given where she is. Are you trying to tell me that's good parenting? Do you think it might be why you have trust issues?

CAMERON: . . .

HITCHENS: And what about Ben? Are you worried about him?

CAMERON: . . .

HITCHENS: Cameron?

CAMERON: You totally cheat on your wife, don't you?

HITCHENS: Excuse me?

CAMERON: With that assistant, I'm guessing. The one who brought you the coffee.

HITCHENS: Don't be ridiculous. I'm not –

CAMERON: It's embarrassing how obvious it is, Greg. Aren't there rules about things like that? Sleeping with someone who works for you? I mean, you could probably get fired, right?

HITCHENS: You can't . . . you don't know what you're talking about.

CAMERON: You just seem like that kind of guy. Your face is turning red, so I must not be completely off base. What, you don't like anyone making assumptions about your life?

HITCHENS: You think it's that easy to figure people out?

CAMERON: It's not hard. Think your boss would like to know how—

EVALUATION:

Ms. Jaimes is hostile, aggressive, and clearly has emotional issues. In short, she does not play well with others. She would be a danger to herself and to those around her.

Recommendation: Hard pass.

—G. Hitchens

The campsite Cam was scouting had been set up by the computer guy, the famous one named Trip. Reaching it required a steep hike from the base of the mountain, and she'd left later than planned, only arriving by mid-afternoon, when the sun was already sinking in the sky. Whatever lean-to she could build in the short time before dark would be barely adequate, but it'd be worth it if she could get rid of Trip. There was little chance he'd last longer than her, considering what she remembered from the gossip sites and news stories about him. He was the kind of guy whose disheveled hair took an hour to get perfect. Wilderness wouldn't suit him. That he was even on the show could only mean one of two things: He wanted to use it as a platform to market his app, which he hardly needed to do because it had been the hottest thing on the internet for months. Or he wanted to be not just a famous tech kid but a legit TV celebrity, and his agent couldn't get him on a reality show where all he had to do was learn to cook or shack up with a bunch of other celebrity wannabes.

It had been easy to find Trip's campsite. She'd moved her own twice to avoid being discovered, and it was a puzzle why none of the others seemed to care if they were found. The producers had suggested the possibility of working together, but Cam didn't see the point. Cooperation would only prolong the show, and while Cam figured she could last at least until spring, even plant a garden before then, she'd rather not be out here for a whole year.

Trip's camp was a disaster, with clothes strewn around the shelter where they'd get soaked if it rained, and cooking pots left out next to a haphazard fire pit. He hadn't even washed them. They were encrusted with bits of seaweed, and the place smelled of sweat and ashes. Looking around, she figured he'd been gone for over a day. With some luck, he wouldn't be back before sundown, and then she could stay at least overnight. Better yet, maybe he'd already tapped out.

She explored the camp, considering what she could do to make him quit. He was no survival expert, that was clear. A book of matches was soaked from the rain. Why bring a book of matches out here anyway, when a flint was more practical? She didn't need to push Trip to leave the game, she could simply rely on his own incompetence.

She checked the shelter, although without much hope. It was simple, just a large blue tarp draped over a point of slanted logs. It was dark inside, especially compared to the sunny outdoors. The shadows cleared as her eyes adjusted to the dim light, and her gaze fell on a crumpled wrapper with red lettering. She squinted, trying to comprehend what she was seeing, realizing it had been weeks since she'd seen anything so bright. Living in the woods, she'd grown used to the soft greens, grays, and browns, with sometimes a vivid blossom tucked into a tree root. The writing on the wrapper was the color of supermarkets and TV ads, with the garish cheerfulness of kids' lunchboxes. The lettering said OATMEAL CREME PIES. Cam was so distracted by the color, so confused by how out of place it was, that it took her several moments to examine the rest of the place.

"What the . . ." she murmured, dimly aware that one of her Skym's minicams had ducked inside with her. It focused on her face, with her mouth dropping open, like a parody of someone too stunned to finish a sentence.

The place was stocked.

A box of oatmeal pies sat to her left, the picture on it showing the familiar crinkled cookies held together by white icing. Cam grabbed the box. There was only a single package left. She squeezed it, denting the cookies so the filling oozed out the sides. She stuffed it into her pocket while scanning the shelter, realizing that the empty box of cookies was just the beginning.

Trip's shelter was littered with discarded food wrappers and plastic forks. There was another unopened box of oatmeal pies like the squashed one in her pocket, a bag of candy bars, and six bottles of a blue sports drink.

Had he been allowed to bring snacks?

None of it made sense.

A low hum sounded from over the ridge—a Skym. It overlapped with the sound of the remaining four cameras of her own Skym hovering outside, waiting for her and the fifth cam to emerge from the tent.

Someone was coming.

As the noise of the Skym grew louder, Cam's instinct was to stuff her pockets before running to hide. But her own Skym was still out there, visible to anyone heading into the camp. She needed it to follow her into the trees and hide before she was discovered.

Spinning around with a muttered curse, she left the tent. Her Skym swooped behind as she dove to crouch under the ferns. The sound of footsteps came from the rocks on the other side of the camp. A layer of spongy leaves cushioned her feet in the dirt.

She'd assumed that Trip had returned, but she was wrong. The fanlike ferns rippled into themselves, leaving enough space for a view of a girl approaching, her Skym drifting several feet in front of her. Cam had seen her before while scouting.

She looked rough—her clothes faded with dirt, stains mottling the fabric, soot across smooth, dark-skinned cheeks. Cam supposed she didn't look any better herself. She hadn't worried much about what she looked like on the camera footage. The producers would do what they wanted with it in any case. For the first week she'd scrubbed her face with sand and water, done what she could, but after a while it seemed like wasted effort. It was actually pretty funny. She used to put on makeup and topknot her hair just to go to the convenience store on the corner. Now she was on display for millions of people and she couldn't even be bothered to wipe dirt off her nose.

The girl searched the site much as Cam had just done, and Cam tensed, thinking about the treasure trove she was about to find. Cam cursed again under her breath.

The girl picked up the ruined matches Cam had discarded, inspected them for a moment, and then tossed them into the fire pit.

The girl's posture was strong and confident. She wore a nose ring, and a blue bandana covered most of her black, pink-streaked hair. Her mouth turned down in concentration and her lips flattened into a straight line as she poked around the camp.

Cam abandoned her crouch and sat in the dirt. The ferns tickled her neck and she picked at the leaves until she had cleared a space. She brushed a spider from the cuff of her socks. It looked like she'd be there a while.

The girl continued her search. She scraped a fingernail over the discarded cooking pot, flicking off dried green bits before tossing it aside, and then she headed toward the shelter.

Cam shifted position, anxious at the prospect of hiding while the competition stole what she thought of as hers. She consoled herself with the knowledge that at least if the girl took the stuff, Trip was out of luck, and then most likely out of the game. He wouldn't last long without his comforts. He hadn't even smuggled energy bars, but candy, which was the stupidest thing she could think of. She had no idea how he'd snuck them in. Their luggage had been searched, along with their clothes and supplies. Maybe he'd bribed someone. He was certainly rich enough.

A noise came from deep in the trees, and Cam searched the brush for movement. There was nothing, only some spiderwebs. The longer she stared, however, the more the woods seemed to move, the branches tangling into knots. A chill scurried down her spine that had nothing to do with the wintery air. Sometimes it seemed the emptiness at her back had a presence, like hands moments away from brushing her skin before she turned around and they vanished into the vines. This place didn't feel quite right. If she listened hard, past the rustling leaves and twittering birds, she heard a sound like the woods whispering to her, voices just out of reach — but the whispers were never loud enough to make out the words.

She'd swear sometimes it sounded like her name called through the darkness: *Cam, Cam, Cam . . .*

She shoved the feeling aside. It was only her own spooked mind, of course. She'd grown up in the city and wasn't used to the wilderness.

Cam reached in her pocket and touched the oatmeal-pie wrapper, her fingertips running across the smooth plastic. She should save it until she really needed energy from the calories. In the past three weeks, it was the hunger that had surprised her the most. It's not like she thought craft services would show up with ham sandwiches out here. She'd been prepared. In the two weeks of survival training before the show officially started, she'd gone on treks and missed a meal now and then, been resigned to the freeze-dried ziti, feeling like she'd just as soon eat it cold as cook it over the fire. The stuff was mushy and flavorless, worse than any high-school cafeteria, but out in the woods, after a twenty-mile hike, with her stomach grumbling, it'd been a four-star meal. Now that she was on her own, Cam figured she'd be fine. Sure, sometimes she was weak, mostly in the mornings, when she'd lie on her bed of logs feeling like her limbs had somehow turned to bricks.

She'd experienced plenty of hunger in her life before the show, and she knew that real hunger was pain. It was feeling like your stomach had teeth and was eating itself from the inside out. She'd thought her experience would help her in the wilderness. What she hadn't expected was for that familiar feeling to bring back the same old fear she'd had when she was a kid, when she didn't know where the next meal would come from or how anything would ever change for the better. The surprise was the way it now set an aching fear at the base of her skull, yanking her back until she again was that scared little kid she'd thought she'd left behind when she stepped on the shore to set up camp.

She pulled the cookie out from her pocket and squeezed it. It was warm and gave easily with the pressure, soft and inviting, a slight slip where the cream glued the cookies together. Bandana Girl was out of sight for the moment. As she thought about the way the cream would melt on her tongue, the muscles of her cheek contracted painfully and her mouth watered. She tore open the package, ignoring the crinkling of the cellophane, unconcerned that it could be heard from the camp. Cam wanted to savor the taste, make the cookie last as long as possible, but instead she shoved it in whole and almost moaned as she bit into it, the icing squishing out the sides. The sweetness was so overwhelming it hurt her teeth, but she didn't care. She closed her eyes as the sugar rushed through her veins.

Her eyes snapped open when Bandana emerged from the shelter holding a small colorful bag that Cam hadn't seen earlier. She had something in her mouth, and grinned as it snapped when she bit it in half. Even from this distance, hidden behind leaves, Cam recognized the candy.

Gummy worms.

For the first time, Cam found herself contemplating that an alliance might not be the worst thing. Even while still tasting the sugar of the oatmeal pie, she wanted candy. It was as if an urge she'd managed to suppress for three weeks had been set loose by the taste of something sweet, and now it was on a rampage, a devouring monster.

Cam's gaze stayed on the girl as she moved about the camp, then slipped back into the tent after a few moments. Cam could already feel the way the gummy would resist her teeth like soft rubber, the way the flavor would fill her mouth like fruit punch.

Her first indication that something was wrong was the smell. There was the odor of damp earth and salt water that always lingered in the air, and the usual campfire smell, which she was used to. This smell was no campfire, however.

Cam searched the area, looking for smoke, and then she saw the thin tendril rising from the top of the shelter. Even as her gaze landed on it, it grew larger and wider. The whole shelter was ablaze.

Without thinking, Cam scrambled from the ferns and ran for the tent. The girl turned and gaped at her. Cam ignored her and threw back the flap of the tarp. A blast of smoke hit her face. The acrid tang of burning wood filled her nose and stabbed into her lungs, but she dove in anyway.

"What are you doing?" the girl said behind her.

The tarp wasn't burning. It held in the smoke, creating a black blanket around her. The wood of the poles smoldered white with surface ash.

This was a bad idea. Nothing here could be saved, and the shelter was seconds away from becoming an inferno. As she backed out, coughing, her arm brushed something and she pulled away with a cry to find a fragment of melting tarp sticking to her skin.

Once outside, clasping her burned arm, she breathed in fresh air, but the shelter poured out smoke and she couldn't get far enough from it. She moved sideways and bumped into the girl, who caught her before she fell, overcome with a sudden overwhelming dizziness.

The girl blurred in front of Cam. What was that look on her face? It seemed more irritation than concern.

Cam heard her own voice, as if from far away, say, "You set the fire. Why would you . . ." Before she could finish, the world dimmed. She was on the ground, and the girl hovered over her, brow creased, lips pressed closed. Then the face disappeared into a narrowing black aperture, until it blinked out like someone had flipped a switch.

CHAPTER 03

Trip's camp didn't trouble River—he could always build a new one—but the fire could climb the mountain and take out the whole forest. The producers might be creating a fake reality for the sake of their show, but this fire was real.

River and Trip descended the hill to a ridge just above the camp. The smoke was thick and distorted River's sense of the scene. He crouched down and tried to determine where the fire had originated. The wind, which had been blowing inland, suddenly shifted, and the view cleared.

Two girls emerged from a ragged blue-tarp shelter, the source of the fire. One of them stumbled and collapsed.

There was a chemical tang in River's mouth from the mantle of smoke, and his eyes stung. He closed them, and when he opened them again, Trip was bounding down the hill. River followed.

Reaching the flaming shelter, River went to the first girl, the one who'd collapsed. She had dark hair cut to her chin and loose-fitting clothes. He knelt next to her.

"Are you okay?"

She blinked at him with eyes as dark as wet earth, the pale skin of her brow puckered in confusion. He wanted to say something calming, because she was scared, not just confused.

Terrified, in fact, like if he couldn't find the right words she might shatter. He touched her shoulder and thought suddenly of his mother's bud vases, how the sun shone through them, revealing the delicate glass.

"Something's wrong." Her words seemed tangible, as dense as the smoke-laden air.

"There's a fire, it's still going. You're safe, though."

"No." Her gaze searched the sky. "Not the fire."

"You took in a lot of smoke."

The air burned his lungs. He turned to Trip to ask for his water only to find him running toward the burning shelter. "Trip! What the hell?"

"Just need a second, man," he called over his shoulder.

"That thing's going to collapse!" River yelled, but Trip was either ignoring him or couldn't hear him over the crackling flames. River jumped to his feet and chased after.

Before Trip reached the smoldering tent, the wind shifted inland, and smoke engulfed River's body as the structure became a towering bonfire, glowing blue and white above him. In the forest, the flames licked the understory of trees, searching for fuel. The shelter teetered precariously. Trip lifted aside the plastic flap, then jerked his hand away with a hiss. He ducked as if he thought he could still get inside.

"Trip!" River yelled. "Stop!"

He was probably trying to retrieve a special item, a memento or a family photo. But if he went inside that shelter, it would collapse around him.

The sweat on River's body dried like a layer of skin peeling off, hot air rolling over him in a wave. The ground itself was charged with heat.

"Come on!" River grasped Trip and pulled him away from the flames.

"No." Trip resisted. "I just need a second."

"Don't have one."

River dragged the boy away from the fire. It was easy enough — his body was light — but Trip fought him awkwardly, and once free of the searing air, River pushed him away with a bit more force than necessary. Trip didn't seem to have a problem risking River's life along with his own. He'd acted rashly, and out here that kind of thing would get him killed. They stood outside while the tent swelled in a burst of orange and yellow. They fell back together as the structure crumpled into a pile of burning refuse. The other girl, the one in the bandana, tugged River's arm, guiding him to clear air.

Trip wavered on his feet, but he still stared at his burning shelter, running his hands through ashy hair. He flashed one of his giddy grins. "I hope we got that on camera. That's good TV."

River was ready to say something withering. Trip didn't seem to understand that, even though this was only a TV show, there was real risk in the wilderness. Then River saw the panic that colored the edges of Trip's smile, and it was clear the boy was shaky, hanging on by a thread.

River wondered if the producers would show up to put out the flames. There was a lot of dead wood in the forest, fuel for a conflagration. They could only hope that the winds shifted or that it rained. Some of these trees were a hundred years old, and they'd be destroyed in less than a day. And why? Because a bunch of kids were playing at wilderness adventure.

The girl on the ground was sitting up now, and she didn't seem confused or scared anymore.

"What were you thinking?" She included both River and Trip in her question.

"Don't look at me," River said. "I was rescuing him."

The girl with the blue bandana blinked at River. "You ran right toward the fire. Are you okay?"

River nodded, rubbing his neck.

This girl was small, only coming up to his shoulder, and she had a silver nose ring and color-streaked hair. She gazed up at him with eyes so wide, you'd think he'd saved a basket of puppies.

"I didn't know what to do. It was terrifying," she said.

"Do you have water?" he asked.

"Of course." The girl handed him a canteen. "I'm Liza Rojas, by the way. And that's . . ." She indicated the other girl, who now had her back turned and her arms resting on her knees. Liza then addressed her directly. "Yeah, who are you?"

"Cameron." The girl looked over her shoulder and frowned at Liza. "My name is Cam."

Liza crossed her arms. She said to Trip, "What were you doing, trying to run in there like that?"

"You saw the food he had." Cam turned to Trip. "Candy and meat sticks, right? This guy was trying to save you"—she flapped her hand at River—"and you were trying to save gummy worms."

Liza shook her head. "That's cheating."

"Just a few snacks," Trip said. "It was nothing, really."

"And you," Cam said to Liza. "You burned it all down. What the hell?"

Trip's head jerked to Liza. "You what?"

Liza's mouth turned down, but otherwise her face showed no concern at the accusation. "I don't know what you're talking about."

Cam said nothing. She looked Liza up and down, seemed to be taking stock of the girl and filing information away for later, brown eyes sharp and assessing. River shifted his own judgment of Cam. She no longer reminded him of delicate glass, and he felt ridiculous for having had the thought. Everything from those few seconds, in fact—when he'd first seen her and her eyes had drifted over him like smoke, those brief words they'd exchanged—it was all fading like a dream.

It figured that Trip would smuggle in candy.

The four Skyms spun in the sky above them. They zipped around one another like birds, as if excited by the drama playing out for their audience behind the lens.

River coughed as Liza handed him the canteen. He took a tentative sip of brackish water.

Steady and controlled, Cam said, "So what I understand, Trip, is that you cheated and you're going to tap out now, right?" Cam met everyone's eyes in turn. "You all heard that?

Trip's going to tap out." There was no doubt or hesitation in her voice.

"No way. I'm not going anywhere."

Cam's expression was veiled as she considered Trip.

The sun set, and although the twilight was suffused with smoky ash, the sky glowed gold in the distance. The wind shifted and swirled, and behind the mountain, to the north, thunder rumbled. The fire was out of control now, but hopefully would be doused by the coming storm. The air chilled— or else River's body was responding to the shift in temperature after being in the blaze.

"Let's talk about this after we make camp," River said.

"He's right," said Liza. "It's getting late. We need to work together for now, help each other. I mean, that's the spirit of the show, right?"

Cam laughed dismissively. "What show do you think you're on?"

"A storm's coming," River said. "Unless you want to spend the night cold and wet, we should get started."

"Aye, aye, captain." Cam offered a sarcastic salute, the sleeve of her loose-fitting shirt falling to her shoulder. Her baggy clothes draped her body, making her look younger than she was. "But this conversation's not over."

As it was, they were only halfway through building the shelter when rain poured down, dousing what remained of the fire and thoroughly soaking them. River had worried about preparing a shelter big enough to fit the four of them, and what they ended up with was worse than he'd feared. They huddled, dripping, around a feeble campfire, made all the more pathetic after the blazing inferno earlier, while bugs crawled over their feet. It was freezing, and Liza leaned heavily into River's arm. Normally he'd find such closeness awkward, but right then he was perfectly happy for another body to stave off the chill. He folded his arms, his muscles tight with the effort not to shake.

Cam sat farther away, clutching her drawn-up legs. Her lips had turned blue and she looked miserable. River thought about offering his jacket, even though it was stiff with dampness and smelled like fish. Something told him she'd decline the offer. She was closed off, purposefully not clustered with the three of them, and distracted, as if she was still troubled about Trip. She seemed to be all about the game, and wouldn't like giving the impression she wasn't as tough as the rest of them. If she didn't warm up soon, he'd give her the jacket whether she wanted it or not. The wilderness was no place for pride—or games, for that matter, reality show or not.

Their packs were stacked in the back of the lean-to, and the Skyms circled as always. Even with the rain and their numb fingers, they'd switched out the batteries so their conversation could be streamed, but none of them wanted to talk. Cam's faraway look broke, and she rubbed her bare arms vigorously, her eyes on Trip. He felt the weight of her stare. He reached into his pack and came out with a handful of conciliatory meat sticks and passed them around. They peeled back the plastic with trembling hands.

Once the food was eaten, they went back to shivering silently, the brief moment of comfort gone too quickly.

Trip shuddered and brushed frantically at his shoulder. "Ugh. This shelter sucks," he said. "God, I hate spiders."

Cam nodded to Trip's pack. "So what else you got in there, Trip?" She reached past Liza and snatched the bag.

"Hey!" he said.

She lifted out a package of juice boxes, which she tossed to River.

"That's theft," Trip said. "I was going to share them anyway."

"Really?" Cam said, searching deeper. "Were you going to share this, too?" She pulled a phone from the bag, holding it up for everyone to see.

Trip dropped his head in his hands as the reflection of the fire danced red on its black screen.

CHAPTER 04

AMARI: Do you ever have trouble getting along with people? In school or social situations?

CAMERON: What happened to Greg?

AMARI: He's been reassigned.

CAMERON: That's too bad. We were just starting to get along.

AMARI: He recommended you be cut from the process, you know. He refused to continue interviews with you.

CAMERON: Really? I didn't figure him to be so sensitive.

AMARI: Yes you did. You knew exactly what you were doing. You wanted the upper hand.

CAMERON: It didn't work. Like you said, he almost got me kicked out of the interviews.

AMARI: You're still here, though, aren't you?

CAMERON: Yeah. Why is that?

AMARI: You know why.

CAMERON: I think you're giving me more credit than I deserve. I don't know how you people run things or make decisions.

AMARI: Greg was just doing his job. He was trying to trigger you, to see how you handle conflict and difficult social interaction.

CAMERON: I guess it worked, then.

AMARI: After that stunt you pulled with Greg, and then with Markus yesterday –

CAMERON: You mean the camera guy?

AMARI: You said he had mobsters after him.

CAMERON: Yeah, that was stupid. I don't know anything about mobsters. But he looks like he gambles a lot, so I figured –

AMARI: But why call him out like that?

CAMERON: He's a creep. Have you seen the way he looks at you?

AMARI: The point is, I was the only one left willing to talk to you.

CAMERON: I guess TV people have lots of dark secrets they don't want exposed, huh?

AMARI: Everybody does, including you. I think because of your past, you have a lot of defense mechanisms in place to make sure nobody figures that out.

CAMERON: How many times do I have to say it? I'm not talking about my mom. That's my life – it's not part of your show.

AMARI: That's fine, you don't have to talk about her. I've already told Gregory and everyone else I want you on *Cut Off*, and what I say goes. Congratulations, you made the cut. But Cameron, you need to understand. Your life *is* the show.

Cam clutched the phone, the chill leaving her body. She held it out to Trip accusingly.

"Gummy worms, meat sticks, and now a phone?" she said. "Seriously?"

Every contestant had the beacons: boxy GPS devices with a button that enabled connection to the producers. It had been made clear that it should be pressed only if you were ready to go home or had suffered a critical injury. This, what Trip had, was a cellphone. A connection to the outside world. Smuggling in candy was bad enough, but a phone crossed the line.

Trip lunged for the device in Cam's outstretched hand, but River halted him. "Easy, Trip." His voice held a clear warning. Then he turned to Cam. "You too. Let's all calm down."

"I'm pretty calm, thanks."

"Give it back," Trip said. "That's mine, man."

"Give me your code."

Trip laughed. "No way, princess."

"Fine." Cam dangled it over the campfire with two fingers. "Guess it burns."

"No, no! Jesus. One-two-one-two. Happy?"

Cam rolled her eyes. "*That's* your code? Some tech genius you are."

"This is an invasion of privacy. There's important stuff on there—like, intellectual property."

"Whatever." Cam slipped it in her pocket. "It's dead anyway."

"Hey," Liza said. "Why do you get to keep it?"

"Why not me?"

Liza glanced around nervously. "Let River hold it. I trust him."

Trip piped in eagerly. "Yeah, River. River can hold it."

"Nope." Cam patted her pocket. "He showed up with Trip,

they're partners. I'm the only one here I trust." She shrugged. "Sorry, but that's the way it is."

"I'm not partners with anyone," River muttered.

Liza opened her mouth to object, then River stepped in again, his hands outspread and placating. It was the second time he'd tried to settle everyone down. Cam made a mental note next to his name: *peacekeeper*. It wasn't much. She'd been taking mental notes on everyone. Liza was dodgy, but only around Cam, which Cam was trying to figure out. The girl had avoided Cam, had barely said two words to her, and it wasn't because of this sweet-girl shyness act she put on. And Trip—Trip was easy. His desire for attention made him put everything out there. He was smart. He was dangerous, if only because he was the kind of guy people gravitated to. Even after being revealed as a cheat, he was still kind of likeable, and Liza and River were ready to defend him. It put her at a disadvantage in arguing that he should have to tap out. She'd need to be careful how hard she pushed.

River was something else. Cam examined him by the campfire. He'd sat back down on the log and remained still, as if he was used to it, unlike the others, who didn't know how to get comfortable without at least a camping chair. Also, he was attractive. Annoyingly so, and he clearly gave no thought to it, like he had no idea girls would fall all over him. When she'd been hazy because of the fire, she hadn't been so out of it to avoid the ridiculous thought: *God, I look terrible*. It irritated her as well that she'd become aware that she must smell bad. It had been easy not to worry about it when she'd been alone, and even around the others she didn't care. They didn't smell great either. But somehow River smelled like wood smoke and salt. His hair, unruly and obviously longer than he was accustomed to, fell across his forehead and shadowed his eyes, which passed quickly over everyone around the fire. Washing in ocean water had defined those curls better than any product could advertise. Cam ran her fingers through her own short hair, stiffened by dirt and ash, wondering if she should have kept it longer. A ponytail wouldn't be sticking out at these odd angles. She dropped her hand, disgusted at her own vanity. She wasn't here to model for the cameras, and certainly not for some pretty boy. She'd come thinking of it as a job, no different from when she'd worked last summer frying funnel cakes at the county fair. At least then she'd been able to shower off the smell of sugar and grease at the end of each day.

River was protective of Trip, that was obvious, while still concerned about being fair. Certainly the game affected how all of them interacted. Cam saw in herself how aspects of her personality were amplified by the cameras and the competition. They were probably secretive, ruthless, conniving, or distrustful in ways they wouldn't be in real life. River seemed unlike the rest of them, however, as if he was indifferent to the game. That didn't make her trust him any more than she did the others, because he was still holding a lot back, but she got the feeling he thought he was somehow above it all. In an abstract sense, maybe that made him admirable, but it also meant it'd be easier for her to get him out of the game. He had no defenses. Why play if not to win?

"It's late," River said. "We're cold, we're tired. We should sleep and talk about this in the morning."

Cam pointed at Trip. "I'm not going to sleep until he taps out."

Trip barked out a laugh. "That's not happening, sweetheart."

Cam glared. "Call me *sweetheart* again."

"Oh, come on!" Trip said, throwing his hands in the air.

Cam didn't really care what he called her, but Liza's lips had pursed when he'd said *princess* before, and Cam figured she could use that.

River ran a hand across his cheek. "I don't think he needs to tap out."

"Why not?" Liza said. "I don't know about you, but I've been starving. He's been out here with secret gummy worms. It's not fair."

River scuffed his boots in the dirt. "I mean, yeah. It doesn't seem fair . . ."

Of course River would have a finely tuned sense of fairness. Cam lowered her voice as if she were speaking only to him. "And what if he wins the whole thing? That wouldn't be right."

"I don't know . . ."

"C'mon, buddy, don't be like that," Trip said, and suddenly all eyes landed on River, looking to him as if he were the final arbiter of rules.

"Hey," Liza said. "We shouldn't put this all on River."

River sagged gratefully. "Like I said, let's sleep. We'll figure out what to do in the morning."

Cam couldn't see any benefit in arguing further. By morning, Trip would have shared his juice boxes and what remained of his food, been his friendly self, and they'd all be over it. River and Liza already acted like Cam was some kind of mean girl, bullying Trip into tapping out, and since she couldn't afford to be cast like that, she let it go.

It was too cold to sleep, however, so instead of lying down they ended up crowding as close to the fire as they could. They were soaked and shivering, suspicion hovering over them like a fog, but still they sat close for warmth.

Liza sighed heavily. "I'll never be able to sleep. It's freezing. And God, I'm bored."

Trip fidgeted, his feet tapping a steady rhythm in the dirt.

Cam scowled at him. "Do you mind?"

Trip tapped faster, giving her a look that said, *Deal with it.*

Liza sighed again. "It's cold."

"No shit," Cam said.

"You know," Trip started, jabbing a finger at Cam. "Maybe if you—"

"Anyone play cards?" River said, interrupting Trip. He pulled a deck from a waterproof plastic bag in his pack, and began shuffling.

Cam rolled her eyes. "What, like Go Fish?" She'd been lonely all these days in the woods, but somehow, now that she was surrounded by people, she was determined to act like a jerk. She knew why, of course. If she was friendly, they might think she was weak. Whatever happened, no way she would let them think they could beat her.

"Sure," River said, undisturbed by her sarcasm. The cards bridged in his hands and flipped together again. "Or rummy, or poker."

"We don't have anything to bet," Liza said.

River fanned the deck and held it out to Cam. "Pick one."

"You're serious?"

He waited placidly for her to choose.

She drew a card. The four of hearts.

He took her card and reshuffled it into the deck.

"You remember what it was?"

She nodded.

With one hand, he split the top of the deck away from the bottom, rotated it, and then slid the two halves together again. He coaxed a card from the center with a crooked finger.

"This your card?"

It was the ten of spades. Cam shook her head, and Trip tittered.

River eyed the deck, acting perplexed. "Huh." He pulled another card, the queen of diamonds. "Is this it?"

Cam shook her head, not sure whether to be unimpressed or wait for the trick that was obviously coming. Still holding the queen of diamonds up to them, he flicked the back with his finger, and with a snap the queen turned into her card, the four of hearts.

Trip jumped to his feet. "Show me how you did that!"

Liza's mouth dropped open.

"That's my card," Cam said, pleased despite herself.

They spent the next hour with River showing them tricks. It was only later, as they lay down to sleep, that Cam realized what he'd done. They'd been bored, irritable, and ready to start fighting again. River had distracted them, redirecting their thoughts just like he'd shuffled that deck of cards. He wasn't as incapable of duplicity as she'd originally thought. And he'd been friendly, brought them all together, and somehow done it without seeming weak. The realization brought back all her irritation. He'd managed to pull off what she never could.

Trip and River slept back to back, and Liza slipped in next to River, her head resting on his outstretched arm. Cam found herself imagining how it might feel to lay her head against his chest. It was a diverting distraction from the pocket of cold air she slept in three feet away, but her distance from them made it easier to slip outside before daylight.

First she grounded all the Skyms. What she needed to do required privacy. They were allowed to disable their Skyms for things like bathing or going to the bathroom. The producers wouldn't like that she was doing it for this, but the machines could still record inside the shelter even if they couldn't follow her outside. She felt her way in the dark to a rock a short distance away. The lingering wetness of the earlier rain made the chill in the air worse.

Cam perched on the rock, ignoring the dampness and cold seeping through her cargo pants, and took out the phone. The case was brown and waterproof, clearly meant to blend in with the surroundings, except in one corner Trip had placed a tiny sticker of Spider-Man. It peeled at the edges, worn by the harsh conditions outside.

She pressed the power button and waited while the screen booted up. A breeze lifted from the water and rustled the leaves. She tilted her head at the sound, muttering branches rubbing against one another, leaves fluttering in the dark. The more she listened, the more it sounded like voices, that *whisper-whisper-whisper* again, like the trees telling hushed secrets to one another.

Cam, Cam, Cam, and now sometimes she heard, *Where are you?*

After being alone for so long, she was probably losing it.

The phone lit up gray and then brightened to white as the home screen flashed into view. She smiled. This little bit of civilization let her push away the superstitious unease of being in the woods.

She'd been able to tell by Trip's desperation to have the phone that it wasn't actually dead, just powered down. She checked for a signal, but there was nothing. No bars, not even the empty signal of the bars. She checked the browser, but the spinning icon didn't stop churning. She went back to the home screen and was searching through the open apps when Trip emerged from the shelter.

"Spider-Man?" Cam said, indicating the sticker. "I thought you hated spiders."

He gave her a withering look. "That's Spider-Man. He's not an actual spider. Also, that's *my* phone. It's private."

Cam didn't look up. She flipped through Trip's apps and e-mails. "I can see why."

"Give it back." He'd cast aside all traces of his earlier good nature.

"Not likely. Who's Ethan?"

"None of your business."

"Really? Does the show know about him?"

"Of course. They know about your exes, don't they? If you think you can blackmail me, you're way off. It's not like I'm in the closet. I came out to my parents when I was fourteen. Not that it went well, but that was three years ago. Nobody cares."

"I mean, do the producers know this Ethan guy is threatening to sue you?"

Trip said nothing, only stood there for a long moment before saying, "He won't go through with it."

"Was ThreeDz really his idea?"

"He gave me some feedback on it, but it was always my idea. He's bitter, that's all. He wants money. He's trying to make people think I couldn't have done it myself. But I'm good at that stuff. Better than him, that's for sure."

"I can tell he's bitter. Did you really turn down ten million dollars for it?"

"Yes."

"I guess you have all the money you need, then, huh? No need to stick around here."

"I turned it down *because* I wanted to be here. I offered *Cut Off* the app for letting me on the show after I failed the

59

psych eval." Cam's eyebrows went up. Trip shrugged. "What can I say? I wanted to bring my plane pills."

"Plane pills?"

"That's what my mom calls them. She gets the same medication because she's afraid of flying, but I take them for panic attacks. I started having them a few years ago. Anyway, the app is what made the show such a big deal. I didn't want to sell it. I wanted to showcase it."

"And get famous while doing it?"

Trip gave a halfhearted grin. "Sure. Isn't that what everyone wants?"

"No," Cam said. "Some people could use ten million dollars." She looked back at the phone. "Ethan is making a lot of claims. If those claims come out on the show, you're done for. True or not, there are people who'll believe him." Cam quirked her mouth at him. "You don't come off well in these e-mails."

"It doesn't have to be public. I'll give you the phone—you can have it."

Cam reached behind her for the beacon she'd slipped from the pile in the shelter. She tossed it to Trip.

"I don't want the phone. I want you to press that button."

"That's blackmail."

Cam shrugged. "It's just a show."

"It's not just a show. This is my life."

"Your life *is* the show, Trip."

Trip looked down at the boxy device in his hand and shook his head. Cam was surprised to feel a twinge of guilt when his face dropped in resignation. It muddied her victory.

"You know I don't want the money," he said. "I was just . . . I wanted to rub it in their faces. The assholes in my school, the ones who gave me a hard time, and then I'm on the *Today* show one morning and they pretend we've been best friends forever. Screw them, right?"

"Right, screw them." Cam didn't have time to feel bad for ruining Trip's game. Guilt wasn't going to help her mom, or Benji. That's what was important. Trip's life was his own problem. "Go on. Press it."

Trip's thumb circled the red button a few times until finally he thrust down and brought the beacon to his ear.

They waited. They both unconsciously glanced up at the shimmering stars, as if the words they expected to hear would descend from above.

They waited some more.

Nothing happened. There was no voice on the other end. There was no sound but the twittering of insects. Just when Cam was about to say *press it again*, a blast of static erupted from the speaker. Trip snatched the device from his ear and then put his hand over it as if he were in pain.

"What the hell?" Trip cried just as Cam said, "Damn, what'd you do?"

"Nothing!" After a long moment, he handed the beacon back to her. He used both hands, like he feared injuring a fragile creature. His mouth twisted into a grimace. "I did nothing." A thread of panic skeined through his voice. For a second Cam thought he was overreacting, it was just a dumb device. But the beacon was their only connection to the outside world.

What if Trip had been calling because he was hurt or sick? What if he'd needed to be rescued? It wasn't a game. If the GPS beacons didn't work, that was life and death.

Cam pressed the red button again. Nothing. There was a switch on the side. She tried turning it off, then on again. She pressed the button. Static once more shattered the night. Trip stared at her, immobile as an effigy. Her thumb cramping, Cam pushed the button repeatedly every second or two. A minute ticked by, and soon even the flare of static fell away. A silence louder than the electric hum of the insects in the trees rose up in the confining forest. Cam stared at the lifeless thing in her hand until the silence closed in and the trees came alive, their voices whispering far above her head. Without meaning to, she strained to make them out. Then, just over her shoulder, she heard the words:

They're already dead.

The voice was clear and cold in the darkness, but there was no one behind her, only her spooked mind playing tricks.

Trip took the beacon back. "Why aren't they answering?"

Cam shook her head. She had no idea. She clutched her arms as dread settled over her like a shroud of chilly fog gusting in on the early-morning air.

CHAPTER 05

PROSPECTIVE CONTESTANT: RIVER ADAN

THIRD-ROUND INTERVIEW (EXCERPTS)

INTERVIEW CONDUCTED BY EXECUTIVE PRODUCER DARLENE
   AMARI

AMARI: Would you be open to starting a relationship on the show?

RIVER: What?

AMARI: A friendship, or a romantic relationship?

RIVER: I thought the point was to live on your own, in the wild.

AMARI: That's one part, certainly. But there's more to it than that. The contestants have the freedom to make choices, decide their best path to success. I know your experience and instinct may lead you not to form relationships, I just asked if you were open to it. If it happened, would you actively avoid it, or see what comes of it?

RIVER: It'd make everything harder.

AMARI: Not necessarily. Some things would be easier.

RIVER: I can't think of what those things would be.

AMARI: Won't you get lonely out there? Every day, only your own thoughts to keep you company, no phone or television or anyone to talk to?

RIVER: I'm used to it.

AMARI: Has it been difficult, being alone so much?

RIVER: Other people complicate things.

AMARI: And you don't like complication.

RIVER: Is that a question?

AMARI: No, I guess it isn't. But people are messy, aren't they?

RIVER: Usually.

AMARI: What's the hardest part of that for you?

RIVER: I don't know. I suppose when –

AMARI: Would you mind phrasing your answer to include the question? For the cameras?

RIVER: What? Oh, right. Well, a hard part about trying to survive in the wilderness with other people, I guess, is that they don't handle stress well, and then they end up arguing. People get caught up in their anger. That's when they make dumb decisions, decisions that are dangerous for themselves and the people around them.

AMARI: And you want people to be safe.

RIVER: Of course. Who wouldn't want that?

River dreamed about being warm. Last night, once they'd settled in to sleep, he'd ended up with Trip on his left and Liza on his right, and there was nothing really to say about that except at least it was warm. They slept wearing the same grungy clothes they'd spent the day in, and no one smelled especially great, so if the viewing audience thought it might lead to an interesting situation, they'd be disappointed. Except that at some point before daylight, while half asleep, he imagined the jumble of limbs around him had something to do with Cam, and there were considerably fewer clothes involved. Even though it was still dark out, he untangled from Liza and Trip's oblivious cuddle before he embarrassed himself. Outside, he took in lungfuls of cold air, let it prickle his skin and clear his mind.

Swells on the water glinted in the moonlight, and the night smelled of the briny mist that had settled above the silver-capped waves. It was still too dark for anyone to be awake, but movement against the far trees led his eyes to Cam sitting on a rock several yards away. She didn't turn, or give any indication that she'd heard him over the crash of the breakers.

River knelt to poke at the dying fire, taking a moment to consider her from a distance before she noticed him. She held her knee, and her back curved forward, shoulders hunched as she absently plucked the hem of her pant leg. She wasn't wearing a jacket, and even in the dark he could see her spine rippling the fabric of her shirt. She must be freezing. She gazed out at the water, her mind someplace far away.

Her features were hazy in the dim light. In her profile, however, he saw what he'd focused on the day before: short dark hair, straight shoulders, a chin turned up in a way that suggested both contemplation and defiance.

He should talk to her, but he didn't want to give up this moment of seeing her unguarded, before the veil that kept her screened from the others fell over her again.

Then he remembered his Skym, and sure enough, there it was, the tiny ocular light trained on him from inside the shelter. For some reason it hadn't followed him outside, but that didn't stop it from recording. It watched him watching her, and beyond it was an enormous audience watching him watching her. He cupped his hands behind his neck, relearning what apparently he had to learn over and over again.

The cameras changed everything. A quiet moment, something private and intimate, was rendered something else entirely through that stupid lens. His dream had melted away now, but no audience could see that, at least; no camera could record it. His dreams, and what he thought when he looked at her, belonged to him. But being caught watching her was another story.

"Damn," he muttered. He didn't want to talk to her now. Not after the Skym had cast him as a creep, a stalker sneaking out at night to spy on a girl. He'd turned back, crawled into the opening of the shelter, and fallen asleep again.

He woke in gray morning light to voices arguing outside. It was a relief to wake up alone, but when he groaned and dragged a palm across his face, the camera clicked on, watching, as always. Once outside, he busied himself with the fire, keeping half an eye on the other three, who were wrapped in an intense conversation. He couldn't hear what they said until Liza shouted, "That's not possible!"

Still, River waited. Nobody had tended the fire recently, and if he didn't get it going again now, they'd have no boiled water for their canteens. Plus, he needed time to gather his thoughts and decide what to do today. Then Trip hurled his GPS beacon at a tree. It splintered, bits of plastic strewing the ground.

"Oh, brilliant," Cam said. "That really helps."

River stood with a sigh, brushing his hands as the day took shape in his mind. Part of him had known they'd pull him back into their drama, whatever his own inclination. He wasn't sure what he'd planned, whether to stay or go off on his own, but the decision had become complicated, and complication was exactly what he wanted to avoid.

He made his way over to the group, but before he reached them, Cam tossed him his own GPS. She must have raided his things to get it.

"Press the button," she said.

He gave a wry smile. She thought she could get rid of him simply by asking? He'd thought she was more strategic than that kind of barefaced move. He tossed the beacon back to her. "Nice try."

"Seriously," Trip said. "We all pressed ours. Yours is the only one left."

"What are you talking about?"

"No one's coming," Cam said. "No one's answering. It's like we've been forgotten, abandoned here."

"We haven't been abandoned!" Liza said, her voice scattering a cluster of birds. "They wouldn't do that to us."

Sweat stood out on Trip's forehead. "How do you explain it, then? I should be eating pancakes in a hotel right now, but nobody showed up! What if I was injured? Or dying?"

Liza turned on him. "They know you're okay, don't they?" She waved her hand at the Skyms. "They can *see* you."

"Everyone calm down," River said. He took his beacon

back from Cam and turned it over in his hands. He didn't understand computers, but he was familiar enough with walkie-talkies and two-way radios. River clicked the device apart to reveal a green circuit board with a mass of tiny transistors. Everything looked clean and connected. He disengaged the battery, turned it in his hand, snapped it back in place, then slid the case closed again.

"You're sure?" River asked.

"Look." Cam held up her own device and pressed the button. When River took it from her, their fingers touched briefly, and even in this odd situation he was aware of his nerves tingling where their skin met, as the remnants of his dream sped back to him. He opened her GPS. It was the same inside as his.

Were the producers really not showing up?

"Maybe it's part of the show," Cam said, "and this is what they meant when they called it a 'social experiment.'"

That was a thought.

River had understood the show to be about survival, plain and simple. Who could last the longest, who knew how to work with the land, seek out resources, stay alive.

Growing up, River had spent most of his time outside. He didn't watch much TV. Terrell's family had a television that took up an entire wall of their living room, and the lights and colors overwhelmed River. It was loud and fast and too bright. Terrell's mom liked to watch *Let's Make a Deal*, with its jangly music and frenzied contestants. *Cut Off* certainly had a more sophisticated veneer, but in the end it was just another game show, and they were meant to hop around like wind-up toys, a camera always pointed at them. Maybe he was the only one who didn't understand what was happening.

Yesterday, while Trip had been rambling, one of the things he kept talking about was "good TV."

"You think they'd change the rules without telling us?" Trip said.

"Sure," Cam said. "They can see us on the feeds everyday. They know we're not starving to death or at the bottom of a cliff with a broken leg."

"But . . ." River raked a hand through his hair. "Is that even legal?"

"I don't know," Cam said. "I mean, did any of you read your contract? Did it say anything about this?"

Trip shook his head. "I was just happy they took me."

"I read it," Liza said. "We signed away pretty much every contingency where we're injured or sick. The producers aren't responsible in that case. Once we sign, they can do what they want. I just wish they'd let me—I mean us—know."

Trip let out a shaky breath, as if relieved to have the issue settled. "That's it, then. Of course, it's TV. They can do anything they want if it makes the show better. They'll rescue us in an emergency. They have to, right?" He glanced at River, who could only shrug. Trip knew the rules of this world better than he did.

Cam's forehead wrinkled. "But how are you supposed to win if it's not about tapping out?"

"If they only pick us up when we're dying, that means the show is about *literal* survival." River said. "That's . . . I don't know what that is."

"It's sick," Cam said. "They would have told us."

Liza motioned to the GPS still in River's hand. "Yours is the only one left."

River took a breath and gazed out toward the ocean. Waves crashed, the residue of last night's storm. Morning tinted the sky as the sun rose behind the mountain.

It could be a trick—he knew that. Something Trip and the others had plotted among themselves while he slept, a maneuver to bump him from the game. But Trip's hands hadn't stopped shaking, and the remnants of his GPS littered the ground, evidence that he truly was freaking out. And Cam's eyes, looking to him, shimmered with fear and expectation. He had that feeling again from yesterday, of wanting to help. No, *needing* to help. He cleared his throat, hoping his libido wasn't determining his decisions. *Something's wrong,* she'd said yesterday, with that same look in her eyes.

He pressed the button.

At first the radio squealed like a fox caught in a trap, but the noise immediately resolved into static. River held it to his ear, and the static cut in and out and then stopped altogether. He pressed the button again, but there was nothing. "Hello," he said, and again, "Hello. Anybody there? Come in."

Nothing.

The silence through the handset was eerie. Not precisely

empty, but hinting at an electric presence on the other end of the line.

Blood drained from Cam's face until she turned sickly pale. She reached for a nearby tree. River held out his hand, thinking she might faint, but just as the tips of his fingers brushed her sleeve, the earth gave a violent shudder.

CHAPTER 06

PROSPECTIVE CONTESTANT: CAMERON LOUISE JAIMES

PSYCHOLOGICAL EVALUATION (EXCERPT)

INTERVIEW CONDUCTED BY DR. SATYANA KAPOOR

KAPOOR: So, Cam, it's my job to make sure everyone will be safe, and that the contestants cast are able to handle the stress of the show.

CAMERON: Yeah, but not really.

KAPOOR: What do you mean?

CAMERON: You have a strange job. You're supposed to evaluate us to see if we're mentally fit, but we can't be too mentally fit, can we? That'd be boring.

KAPOOR: You think that would be boring?

CAMERON: I think an audience wants to see the contestants lose it. They want meltdowns. They want fights and conflict. Conflict is fun.

KAPOOR: Why do you think people enjoy watching conflict?

CAMERON: I don't know. Watching others fight makes them feel better about their own messed-up lives?

KAPOOR: Does it make you feel that way?

CAMERON: I get enough conflict in my real life. I don't need to see it acted out on TV.

KAPOOR: Are you talking about your mother?

CAMERON: . . .

KAPOOR: Cameron, I know you're not comfortable talking about her, but in my experience these kinds of things come out when you become a public personality. You should think about whether you're prepared for that. Like you said, the show wants to portray conflict, right?

CAMERON: If I don't talk about it, will I be rejected from the show?

KAPOOR: That's not how my evaluation works. I don't make any final decisions. I do believe it might help if you talk about what happened, however.

CAMERON: It's not a great story. You probably know most of it already. It was on the local news. It's just one day my mom had enough. She busted Brad's gun out of the lockbox and shot him. He was sleeping in his recliner.

KAPOOR: Were you home when it happened?

CAMERON: I was at my friend Madison's house. I came home and he was covered in blood. It was all over his yellow polo shirt. He'd been golfing earlier. He always wore that stupid shirt when he golfed. My mom was doing CPR. She kept saying she didn't mean it. Like, over and over. As if that mattered.

KAPOOR: It doesn't matter whether she meant to shoot him?

CAMERON: She should have meant it. If it was up to me, I'd have shot him ages ago. If it was up to me, my mom wouldn't have given him the time of day and we'd never have moved in with him. Though I guess if it wasn't Brad, it'd have been some other loser. Mom never picks good ones.

KAPOOR: You seem angry at your mom.

CAMERON: I'm not. Except that Brad's healed up and perfectly fine now, and my family has fallen apart. And the thing is, she didn't even

73

shoot him during a fight when she could have claimed self-defense. They would have these huge, dish-smashing, blow-out fights. But no. She found out he was sleeping with a waitress at the golf club. That's why she snapped. She didn't shoot him because of the yelling, or the hitting, or because he was a huge asshole. You'd think she'd be happy for him to run off with a waitress. Instead she's sitting in prison crying about how it's not fair the court said they're not allowed to see each other. Why would she want to see him again?

KAPOOR: Women in domestic-violence situations are often trapped by cycles of abuse. It's not always easy to understand from the outside.

CAMERON: All I know is, because of her choices, Benji and I spent six months going back and forth from a courthouse to a foster home, and now she's in a prison three hours away, and Benji's living with an aunt I hardly know. That's why I have to be on the show. You better pass me, because I'm going to win this thing. I'll take the money, turn eighteen, and get custody of Benji. You're going to pass me, right?

KAPOOR: Is that the only reason you told me your story? You thought it'd help your chances of getting on the show?

CAMERON: I figure I struck the appropriate level of screwed up that a reality show requires. Yeah?

KAPOOR: You might consider seeing someone regularly once you return home.

When River's GPS was silent, Cam realized how much she'd been counting on their last device working. Trip's had failed, then hers, then Liza's, and the whole time they'd been arguing outside, in the back of her mind she'd been thinking, *There's still River's.* She was sure that competent, calm River would for some reason have the only working GPS. And now here they were, stuck, him right along with the rest of them. She hadn't realized how hard she'd been clinging to that last bit of hope, and now that it was gone, her chest felt crushed in a vise.

A covey of birds wheeled up, a black cloud rolling feverishly across the sunrise. Her hand found the tree, and she wondered if she imagined the trembling of the trunk and the shuddering branches. Or perhaps she was doing it somehow, her vibrating body shaking everything around her, with no control over the damage being done. Touch something and it falls apart. That had to be the worst superpower. The thought made her giggle, and even she could hear the hysteria in the sound. She was losing it.

She felt a shove from behind, but no one had shoved her. There was no one there, and that was when she figured out it was the earth jolting under her feet in a hard push, a pause, and then a shaking—like one of those funhouse platforms that jiggled and twisted until your knees buckled.

Another earthquake.

No, not again.

When had the last one been? Just a few days ago? It had begun when she was hiking. She'd tripped on a trail that ran along a sheer drop of fifty feet and almost fallen over the edge. The rush of panic and adrenaline had kept her frozen on that cliff, imagining the plummet she'd barely avoided, seeing herself hurtling through the air and slamming onto the rocks below. Even now the thought made her palms itch. She'd taken two steps from the edge, and that was when the earthquake had started. She'd watched as rocks tumbled down the face of the bluff.

Just like I would have.

That night was the closest she'd come to tapping out, crouched in her shelter, unable to stop picturing what might have happened. Sleepless and alone in the dark, she imagined that the shaking earth had set loose a legion of monsters slouching through the desolate woods, calling her name over and over.

Cam hugged the tree, eyes squeezed shut.

River's hands landed on either side of her, his body sheltering her from falling branches.

"Don't move," he said. "It's safest to stay put."

The knobby bark scraped Cam's cheek. "I know."

She was from California, after all. That stuff about doorways was nonsense. Get down, avoid buildings and overpasses — easy enough in the middle of nowhere — and stay put.

A rumble worked its way from the ground up through the trunk. The only other sound was River's breath and the rustle of leaves, as if they were agitated by a furious wind.

"It's just like the last one," she said.

She felt River's nod, a quick tip of his head brushing her hair. He stood close, and she let his nearness distract her, breathing in his smell of minty pine and ocean. It wasn't fair that he smelled good, out here of all places, where they were all filthy and unkempt.

The earthquake went on and on. The tree shook, and leaves tumbled at her feet.

"You want me to distract you?" River said.

"I'm fine."

"You seem kind of freaked out."

"I'm not," Cam said, even though it was obvious she was. "Why, you want to do more card tricks for me?"

"Would it help?"

"No," she said, then after a moment, "How'd you change that card in your hand?"

He smirked. "Magic."

She rolled her eyes. "I bet you're a big hit with the seven-to-ten-year-old crowd."

River seemed like he was about to respond with an equally wry comment when his head jerked up. "Liza! Get down!" he called.

Liza was running, stumbling like a drunk, her Skym speeding along behind. Where did she think she was going? She should lie flat.

"Damn it," River muttered into Cam's neck. And then, "You all right?"

"Sure," she said, surprised at the steadiness of her voice, because she didn't feel very all right. River's efforts at distraction had actually been working, but then a rush of cool air replaced the warmth of his body. He went to Liza, who'd fallen and was clutching her leg.

Of course she'd fallen. *That's why you don't run, Liza!*

Cam mentally shushed herself for sounding like a schoolteacher.

Cam's fingers were raw from digging her nails into the wood. Her heart pounded against her rib cage as if it were a seesawing pendulum.

I hate earthquakes.

With River gone, her earlier dread came rushing back. What if the producers never answered? What if they never got home?

What if we're stuck and the world keeps shaking apart?

Cam tried thinking of River near her at the tree, but it wouldn't work. The pounding was in her ears now, and the oxygen seemed to be pulsing, like it was alive and closing her in.

Her camera broke into its separate pieces and circled. She didn't want to be seen like this, like she was looking for attention, like she was helpless, a burden out here, they couldn't see her like this, and—

What if we're stuck?

Trip was next to her, leaning on the same tree for balance. He held something in front of her, inviting her to take it. A white pill, pinched between his finger and thumb. One of his plane pills.

"Here," he said.

Cam worried she'd drop it because she was jittering as badly as the ground. Before she could take the pill from him, however, River knocked Trip's hand away.

"What are you doing?"

"They're for anxiety, panic attacks. It'll help."

River cast him a scornful look. "I'm sorry, I missed the part where you have a medical degree." He knelt next to Cam, his hand resting on her shoulder. "Look at me." She looked up, held his eyes, but he blurred before her. She blinked, trying to clear her vision. "Breathe with me, okay?"

"I'm familiar with how to breathe," Cam said, but in an awkward, breathless rhythm that belied the words themselves.

"Thought a reminder might be useful." River took a deep breath, acting it out for her, then exhaled. He waited for her to follow along.

He breathed with her until her chest stopped aching and the flaring, bright energy faded.

Then, as suddenly as it had started, the shaking stopped.

"Better?" River asked.

"I'd have survived."

"Well, thanks for humoring me, then."

"The pill would've worked," Trip said.

River looked up at him, "You're not a doctor. You can't just hand out prescription drugs. It's dangerous."

Trip shrugged. "So are panic attacks and earthquakes in the middle of nowhere."

River shook his head, and Cam wanted to tell them both to shut the hell up.

"Stop talking about me as if I'm not here," she said. "How's Liza?"

"She'll be fine," River said. "She cut her leg."

He helped Cam to her feet, but she dropped his hand as soon as she was up, pretending her legs weren't made of jelly.

Liza sat next to the fire. She flinched as River rolled up her pant leg to reveal a long, shallow scrape, and she whimpered dramatically at the sight of blood.

River ripped strips of cloth from a shirt he pulled from his pack. Cam stood by, feeling useless, Trip next to her, hands in his pockets, looking as helpless and edgy as she felt.

"I was in my shelter when the last one hit," Trip said. "I guess I didn't build it so great, because it came down on top of me."

"You're still alive," Cam said. "That's good."

"Yup. The logs were too thin to crush me. Something to be said for incompetence."

"Are you okay?" she asked.

"Who, me? Sure. I can handle a little earthquake."

As if sensing how untethered she felt, Trip draped an arm around her shoulder.

Liza rested on her sleeping bag. The scrape wasn't serious, but River muttered to Trip, "We don't know when they're coming to get us. It can't get infected."

"So you still think they'll come?" Trip said.

"Of course. They didn't abandon us out here. They're going to show up."

Cam tucked her beacon in the bottom of her pack. It might not be working, but she didn't want to lose it. "The first earthquake may have knocked out the communication system."

"Possibly," River said, rubbing his face. Cam had seen him do it enough times to know that the gesture signaled skepticism.

"But if that were the case, they'd be looking for us. There'd be helicopters, search parties."

Liza opened her eyes at that. "The first earthquake was a few days ago. There were helicopters before that. They'd come in and then head out again."

"I saw them almost every day," Trip said. "They were definitely from the show—they had the logo on the side."

Liza nodded. "They were probably picking up tapped-out contestants and bringing them to base camp."

Cam had seen the helicopters as well. Every time they flew overhead, she felt a combination of smug superiority that she'd outlasted another contestant, and envy that whoever was in there would get to eat a decent meal and sleep in a real bed that night.

"Guys," Cam said, worry creeping into her stomach. "Has anyone seen a helicopter since the day of that earthquake?"

Everyone thought about it, and in that moment, from the looks on their faces, the same conclusion became clear to the others: a new consideration by which they'd evaluate their fate. No, there'd been no helicopters since then, and not a single bit of evidence that anyone was still out here.

"It means nothing," Liza snapped, adjusting the bandage River had secured, her movements brusque. "It's only been a few days. It makes sense that most tap-outs would happen in the beginning, and then they'd slow down."

Liza rose from her sleeping bag and limped to her pack with a touch of drama. It was a trivial scrape, after all.

"In any case, helicopters were headed in the same direction," Cam said. "I say we go that way and try to find their base camp."

"It might be better to stay put," River said. "We're healthy, we still have energy. We'll exhaust ourselves hiking through this." He waved at the dense foliage surrounding the clearing. "And we have no idea where we're going. This area's huge. We could hike forever and walk right past base camp. If we stay, we can prepare. Build a solid shelter, gather food, set traps and fishing lines. Even if they abandoned us, which I seriously don't believe they did, they're not going to abandon their million-dollar cameras. Someone will show up soon enough."

As they spoke, the Skyms cycled above them in a mechanical arabesque, capturing their conversation for the audience that was out there somewhere.

"River might be right," Cam said, eyeing Liza as she loaded her pack, recovering quickly from her fainting, damsel-in-distress routine. "We don't know where base camp is. A compass direction isn't enough to go on."

"I know where it is." Liza lifted her pack to her shoulders. "A day's hike north." She stood, waiting impatiently for them to join her.

"How do you know where it is?" Cam asked.

Liza propped her hands on her hips. "I've seen it before, okay?"

Trip shook his head. "And you're only telling us that now?"

"I don't see how it matters." She turned to River. "You're

the resident survivalist. We're better off with a roof over our heads, aren't we?"

"We are," River agreed, and that seemed to settle it.

River and Trip started collecting the rest of their things.

Cam held her tongue.

How could Liza be sure where base camp was, and how far? Her certainty seemed odd, but Cam didn't argue. She didn't have a better idea, and Trip and River had swung their packs onto their shoulders and were already following Liza's decisive stride. Cam trotted to catch up before the trees swallowed them completely.

CHAPTER 07

PROSPECTIVE CONTESTANT: RIVER ADAN

PSYCHOLOGICAL EVALUATION (EXCERPT)

INTERVIEW CONDUCTED BY DR. SATYANA KAPOOR

KAPOOR: Do you mind telling me about your parents' death?

RIVER: What about it?

KAPOOR: Well, how do you think it has affected you?

RIVER: I don't know. How hasn't it? I'm not the same person I was before it happened.

KAPOOR: How did you find out?

RIVER: It was sunny, a nice day. I'd been hiking. When I got back, the cops were on the front porch. I don't remember what I was thinking when I saw them. Sometimes I remember having an immediate sense that something terrible had happened. Like a premonition, you know? Why else would cops show up, right? It's never for good news. I remembered thinking, *Turn around.* I wanted to go back into the woods. I wish I had. It would have been nice to have another hour of not knowing. Hell, another five minutes.

That sense of foreboding might be my imagination, of course. I probably wasn't thinking anything when I walked up the steps. I probably thought my normal life would never change, that it'd keep being normal forever. It was like there was a line, a before and after. Before was normal, and after is whatever's left when that goes away.

Anyway, the cops told me my parents were dead. Some guy ran a light. I moved in with my Uncle Jim.

KAPOOR: How has that been?

RIVER: It's what it is. It's fine.

KAPOOR: You said before that he wanted you to try out for the show because he thinks you've isolated yourself.

RIVER: That's what he said. He wants me to be more involved in the world. It's hard, though. I've felt pretty out of it since it happened.

KAPOOR: You're grieving. That's normal.

RIVER: I don't know what normal means anymore.

KAPOOR: Do you think your uncle is right? That being on the show might help?

RIVER: If the goal is to feel normal, I don't know how a reality show is going to accomplish that.

KAPOOR: You're here, though. Something about it must appeal to you, something beyond the deal you made with your uncle.

RIVER: I don't mind the idea of taking off. Camping by myself, indefinitely.

KAPOOR: What is it that you like so much about camping?

RIVER: That feeling that the world is still out there, still doing its thing, but to me it doesn't exist. I don't have to worry about it.

KAPOOR: That sounds like more isolation.

RIVER: I guess. But I used to go camping all the time, before. It helps me feel normal, you know? Like getting those five minutes back.

While they walked, the Skyms lifted into the air as precisely as a military squadron. There was something organic about the way they communicated with one another. For them, traveling in the wild was easy, floating over tangled underbrush and fallen limbs, gullies, and cliffs.

On the ground, it was a different story.

The hike was treacherous and exhausting. River took the lead, his machete a constant pendulum, hacking at tall grass and vines, clearing a path for the others. Now and then he'd call out a warning—*log*, *rock*, *vine*, even *snake* a few times—hoping to keep anyone from twisting an ankle, getting bitten, or falling face first into a branch rising from the dirt like a spear. They concentrated on placing one foot in front of the other, every step like navigating a minefield, requiring the energy of trudging through giant snowdrifts. It was risky, pushing themselves this way, expending so many calories, chancing injury, exhaustion, and dehydration, but there was one benefit. The distraction of the hike meant that the others, so close to panic earlier, no longer focused on the unresponsive beacons.

River had seen it before, hiking remote trails and camping with various groups. The biggest danger in the wild was giving in to fear and losing hope. Plenty of times he'd seen people hungry, freezing, and sick go on for days beyond endurance simply because they were buoyant and optimistic. Maybe it sounded like a catch phrase on a poster of a kitten, but a positive attitude was the most valuable resource out here.

By the time they stopped to rest, they'd been hiking for five hours with only a single break. River's shoulders burned, and his body radiated a heat that, with a clinical composure, he identified as the first stages of dehydration. They'd reached a wide bay edged by boggy shoreline, well removed from thudding waves.

Trip, Liza, and Cam collapsed in the clearing as if they were incapable of taking another step. River walked farther into the trees. He foraged edibles, tucking them away in his pack, moving slowly, head down, letting his pulse slow. He found a spot to rest in a patch of pine needles dried in the sun. Light peered through spiderwebs stretched between branches, the mist on the strands glinting like teardrops. The prospect of a few minutes of solitude pulled at him. All day their clamor —tromping feet, arguments and complaints—had built a wall around him, closing him off from the trilling birds, the buzzing insects, and his own quiet thoughts.

River sat down and idly shuffled his deck of cards while his mind wandered. The air smelled of wet dirt and green woods. The unsparing heat of the day dissipated into cool afternoon, and a breeze coming off the bay dried his sweat-drenched hair and sent a chill across his skin. He could almost pretend he was back home, in the woods behind his house.

Footsteps approached, and he looked up to find Liza holding out a canteen. The water tasted metallic and gritty, and he had to catch his breath when he finally pulled it away from his lips. He had to be more careful. Dehydration came on suddenly. By the time you felt thirsty, it was already too late.

"I wanted to thank you for taking care of my leg," Liza said. She plopped down next to him and lifted her pant leg to peel back the bandage, letting out a hiss of breath when she touched her fingers to the scrape. It seemed to be healing well enough. It was only a few inches long, a minor abrasion.

"Sure," he said, handing the canteen back to her and picking up the cards again. "Keep it clean. You want to avoid infection."

She covered the cut. "Have you always been so chill about everything, River?"

He split the deck, lifted the ace of hearts, then slipped it back in again. "I don't know what you mean."

"Just that not a lot scares you."

River shrugged, unsure why she would say that. "Not more than anyone else, I guess."

"I mean, you saved Trip from running into that fire, the earthquake didn't freak you out, and you sure don't seem scared about being out here all alone. Ever since my mom died, I feel like everything's a little scarier, you know?"

"Your mom died?"

"Five years ago. Not a lot of people know what it's like, to lose a parent when you're young. It's scary."

"Yeah. But out here isn't scary. It's nice. Quiet."

She gave him a crooked smile. "We're too loud for you, aren't we?"

He shrugged again. She was trying to get at something, but he couldn't figure out what.

"You don't even seem that worried about the GPS beacons, that we can't get ahold of anyone."

"Worrying doesn't do any good."

"So what does scare you?"

"That sounds like one of our confessional questions."

The producers had dropped River at the beach with a list of questions, and they'd asked him to use them as a jumping-off point when he talked to the cameras. *What's the worst thing about being in the wild? What qualities do you possess that will help you succeed on* Cut Off? *Who is the most important person in your life?* River had tried to talk about those things (*Remember, please, to include the wording of the question in your answer,* the woman handing him the list had said), but he wasn't any good at talking to the cameras. It was like trying to bare your soul to a vacuum cleaner.

She laughed. "Confessionals are the worst, right? But I think people might want to learn more about you. Like what makes you tick, you know?"

River's gaze rose to the two Skyms bobbing above their heads. Was she trying to get him to perform for the audience? He didn't know why she would care. Whatever the case, he didn't feel like an interview right now. He put away the cards, stood, and stretched out the stiffness in his back. Liza stood with him and her hand landed on his arm.

"It's just . . ." She bit her lip and gazed up at him. "It's scary out here, and we're alone. You really saved me in that earthquake. It's nice to have a friend."

Her hand rose up to his face. She slid her palm along his jaw.

River cleared his throat. He tried to move her hand away, but she twined her fingers through his.

"I'm glad you feel like I'm a friend, because I am." He tipped his head to her. "We're friends. Okay?"

"I see." She hadn't yet let go of his hand. "It's Cam, isn't it? You like her?"

River untangled his fingers from hers. "I don't *like* anybody, Liza. At least, not the way you mean. Honestly, that's the last thing I'm thinking about."

Whether it was true or not, he didn't have to talk to Liza about it, on camera no less, and he certainly didn't have to act on a few random feelings.

He hadn't meant to sound harsh, and even as he spoke, it occurred to him that he might be the one who didn't get it. He had no idea how he was expected to behave on a reality show, just like he was a failure at the confessionals. Did people really act like this? The shows and movies about high school always seemed fake as hell—everyone acting like they were thirty years old and in the middle of a soap opera. Like Liza was acting now.

Or was that exactly it? The cameras. They made their own reality, a sort of feedback loop. Liza saw how kids acted on TV, and when a camera was pointed at her, she was drawn into a performance, and everyone watching nodded along without considering how staged it all was. In any case, he wanted nothing to do with it. He'd signed up for a few months of wilderness survival, and only because his uncle had strong-armed him into it. Anything else the show wanted wasn't his problem.

"I feel like we've all bonded," Liza said. "Like we've been together longer than we actually have. It must be the stress of the situation."

"We should get back to the others."

Liza smiled like they shared a secret. "You'll still be my bunkmate, won't you? I didn't scare you away?"

"No, it's fine." He answered curtly, bristling at her confidence that she had him all figured out.

When they returned to the clearing, Trip was dozing, head propped against a log, and Cam was gone. River scanned the beach to find her about a quarter mile down, carrying her shoes, bare feet in the water.

"I'll be right back," he said, leaving Liza behind. He didn't dislike her or anything. She was just more than he was willing to handle right then.

When River reached the shoreline, he took off his shoes and waded out to Cam. He'd been meaning to talk to her since the earthquake, but hiking the woods didn't offer many opportunities for conversation, especially with the others listening in. They stood together silently for several moments while River fumbled for something to say other than *Are you okay?*

Cam spoke first. "I don't like earthquakes."

He didn't respond, because of course she didn't, nobody did, and it felt like she had more to say. "I was in an earthquake. At home, in Salinas. I was twelve. My mom and I, my little brother, we lost our apartment. We lost everything. We moved in with Brad, my mom's boyfriend. Everything kind of went downhill after that."

"I'm sorry," River said.

"We'd just moved to California, and I didn't know it was possible for the whole world to shake. When something like that happens, nothing feels safe. Do you know that feeling, that no place is safe?" River didn't answer, but she continued as if he'd said yes. "I wanted you to know that you were right. I was freaked out."

She spoke with determination, like she wanted to get all the words out before she changed her mind.

"You don't have to explain."

"I know. But with the beacons not working, we're not really competing anymore. If we have to work together, we need to trust each other."

She fell silent, her eyes cast down to the ripples made by her feet in the water. River pulled up his sleeve and showed her his forearm where a crooked, faded scar lined his skin. "See this?"

She nodded, coming out of her thoughts to listen.

"I was out walking my mom's dog, a little poodle named Sugar. I was seven or eight years old, and this black mastiff —it was huge—goes after Sugar. I tried to fight it, you know? Get it off her, but it turned on me instead. I kicked at it until the owner finally showed up and pulled it off. The whole thing scared the hell out of me." He dropped his sleeve, rubbing his arm where the scar was. "Ever since, I get nervous around dogs. Especially big ones."

River realized he'd answered Liza's question after all, and the camera hovering behind his left shoulder had eaten it up. His first real confessional: *What are you afraid of?*

He should have told Cam the truth, that ever since, whenever a strange dog ran up to him on a trail, he couldn't make his feet move until it passed, that he held his breath waiting for it to attack. He could have told her how the owner of the mastiff had grabbed River's shirt, gotten right up in his face. *Touch my dog again and I'll kill you, you little shit.* The man's breath had smelled of beer and cigarettes.

"Was Sugar okay?" Cam asked.

"She had stitches in her belly. But yeah, she was okay."

"So dogs are your earthquake?"

"Something like that," he said. "Cam, you were about to take that pill. Did you know Trip had them?"

"He told me."

"I'm surprised they let him on the show with those things."

She tipped her head at him. "You think they shouldn't have?"

"It's dangerous out here. The worst thing you can do is let fear take over, or worse, panic."

"I guess the pills help with that."

"Trying to survive in the wilderness under the influence of drugs is hardly a solution. That'll get you killed."

Cam shook her head. "Haven't you ever felt like you were, I don't know, barely hanging on? Like you needed help?"

"Sure, who hasn't? But I take care of it. I get out of my head, get fresh air, go camping or something."

Cam laughed, but without any humor. "That's a charmed life you've led, River."

River stiffened. "Don't assume you know what my life's been like."

That was two back-to-back conversations in which someone thought they had him figured out. Her dismissive smile faded, although she continued to hold his gaze. "Then don't assume Trip's either. Or mine, for that matter. We've all lasted as long as you. Nobody here is weak. Needing help doesn't make you weak."

"No, but he shouldn't be sharing his pills. They're not candy."

Cam looked up the beach to where Trip was pulling himself off the ground as if weights were strung on his limbs, and Liza watched the two of them.

"What do you think about her?"

River took a second to catch up with the change in topic. "Liza? I don't know. She seems . . . confident."

River didn't miss the scowl that passed over Cam's face. What had she expected him to say? No question Liza was confident. She was also observant, attractive, and occasionally confusing. Not unlike Cam, actually. Maybe they were too much alike, and so were destined to clash. Trip would say that shows like *Cut Off* selected contestants who promised conflict, the more personal and scathing the better. Once it occurred to him, River felt sure he had it figured it out. Psych 101 for TV. Listening to Trip's ramblings had proven useful after all. As long as he regarded the show through Trip's eyes, River thought he could navigate the alien landscape of reality television.

"I don't trust her," Cam said.

"What do you mean?"

"Did you notice her leg?"

"The scrape?"

"Not the scrape. Listen, I don't know about you, but I haven't had access to a razor for most of a month. They were on the *not-allowed* list."

"Huh." River considered this. "You're saying she should have hair on her legs and she doesn't?"

Cam replied with the embellished patience of someone speaking to a toddler. "Yes, River. That's what I'm saying."

"Did she—I don't know—wax before coming?"

Cam rolled her eyes. "You've never had a girlfriend?"

"Sure—sure I have," he stammered, unprepared for the question. "I mean, there've been people who—"

A grin spread across Cam's face. It was the first smile he'd seen from her that didn't seem calculated or guarded: a true, beaming grin. Except she was laughing at him, and warmth spread across his cheeks. And just like that, the footing River thought he'd gained crumbled away, like a little earthquake only he could feel. He knew nothing about how you were supposed to interact on reality shows, and he had no idea how to navigate this particular group of people. And now Cam, and presumably the entire viewing audience, assumed he knew nothing about girls, too.

Perfect.

"Fine, I haven't taken much opportunity to study the leg-hair practices of American girls, okay? I'm not all that concerned about it, honestly."

Cam's grin widened into a full-on laugh as she bent double over her knees. She stumbled backwards and landed on the wet sand. "Shit," she said as water seeped into her pants. She tried to get up, but she was laughing too hard to rise gracefully, and that made her laugh more. She reached out to him. "Come on, help."

Her hand was damp and gritty with sand, cool and firm. Once she was standing, she didn't let go right away, only looked at him with that giddy smile reaching all the way to her eyes. He reminded himself that she was laughing at him, but her giddiness caused a rush through his chest that was impossible to ignore. Everything was a mess, but he wanted that smile to stay.

"Seriously, though, I don't get it," he said when she dropped his hand to brush off her damp pants. "Trip had contraband. So Liza smuggled in a razor, that's all."

"She's also been flirting with you from the moment she laid eyes on you."

Now it was his turn to smile. Liza had been flirting with him, and not just in the clearing a few minutes ago, and apparently Cam was paying attention. Liza's fingers had fluttered along his arm last night in the shelter, and he hadn't been sure if he was supposed to think she was asleep or not. He'd rolled toward Trip as if he was asleep, though. It wasn't that Liza wasn't pretty, or smart, but she made him feel like she was following a script and he didn't know his part. Not to mention the fact that they were living outside, with other people, cameras pointed at them day and night.

He couldn't help wondering what he'd do if one night Cam ran her fingers along his arm. If she ever stopped sleeping three feet away.

"You don't like that she's flirting with me?"

"Don't look so pleased with yourself. She's doing it to manipulate you."

"It won't work, if that's what you're worried about."

"That's fine, but it doesn't answer the question of why she's doing it. Other than to have you on her side."

"She's probably doing it to make the show more interesting." That was what Trip would say. River raised his eyebrows at her. "Especially if it upsets you."

Cam's eyes rolled. "Nobody's upset. I only wanted to let you know something's up with her." She sobered as she spoke, as if reminded of their predicament after forgetting it for a moment. "Be careful. That's all I'm saying."

"We're going to be okay, you know," River said, sounding more confident than he felt. "We'll find people, we'll get help. And maybe it's like Trip says. It's part of the show, and all about drumming up drama. That we're scared is great for the producers."

Cam studied him. "You really think that's true?"

Her question was so direct, it caught him off-guard.

"Of course," he said quickly.

True or not, they were all scared. They needed something to keep them going, one foot in front of the other. Cam considered his answer, eyeing him like she could see through him and read his mind. She knew he was lying. But sometimes truth wasn't the only thing that mattered. Like the card tricks. They were just tricks, but they were meant to calm everyone down, and it worked. Even if Cam didn't believe everything would be okay, hearing his words had to help. If they were in as much danger as River feared, they had time before they had to admit it as a group, and that time could be spent getting a handle on the situation and, like she said, learning to trust one another.

Cam swept an arc through the water with her toe, and the ripples drifted out, widening into the open bay.

Liza called down the beach to them, "It's dark soon. We're not going to make the trailer tonight."

River gauged the height of the sun. The surface of the water reflected mirror white against the distant hills. The bushwhacking was slow going with a group. River could move faster by himself. If Liza was right, it'd be another night of a thrown-together shelter and a sputtering fire, but more importantly another night of fear, of not knowing what would happen next. Another night of not even knowing how scared they should be.

"We'll camp here, then," he called back. The more time they had to make themselves comfortable, the better.

Cam had pulled the GPS beacon from her pocket. She held the button down, a forlorn smile on her lips.

"Doesn't hurt to check now and then, you know?" she said.

"Doesn't hurt." Then, sensing she needed a distraction, he said, "Come on. Help me collect firewood."

■ ■ ■

That night, River awoke to a cold space on his left side. Liza was on his right, curled into him, and Cam had taken her usual spot a few feet away. He turned to his cold side, toward her.

As his eyes drifted closed to the hush of Cam's soft breath, a distant scream made him bolt upright. He was on his feet and outside, machete in hand, before he had time to comprehend either the sound or that Trip wasn't in the shelter. He stared into the night, looking for movement, listening for another sound, anything. The sliver of moon in the clouds dropped a half glow that lit the clearing in a chalky gray.

The scream came again, fainter now but terrified. It wasn't an animal. River had heard foxes scream at night, warding off predators from their cubs, and they sounded like murder, but this was human. It was Trip. And Trip was running, his scream growing fainter with each repetition. River's fingers curled around the machete's handle. Hearing the scream again, he ran toward it, but a dozen feet into the trees, blackness fell like a shroud. He could see nothing. River stood transfixed, trying to figure out what to do, his heart pounding and every muscle rigid.

Trip's scream came to a stop. It didn't trail away like a fire truck's engine fading into the distance. It stopped like an axe had chopped the very vibrations from the air. And he knew, with a thought as black as the starless forest.

That sudden stop was worse, much worse, than the scream itself.

CHAPTER 08

"GET TO KNOW THE CONTESTANTS"

LOCATION: TRIP JOHNSON'S HOMETOWN

ON-CAMERA INTERVIEW: LAWRENCE JOHNSON JR. (FATHER)

Why are you asking me why he's on your show? Don't *you* know? I have no idea why the hell that kid does anything. He's always running around, making a fool of himself, showboating. He knows I don't approve of his lifestyle, but he never asked me, did he? You asked if I was proud of his accomplishments, all the money he's made, the attention. I'd be a hell of a lot prouder if he wasn't preening all the time, taking selfies and posting on social media–*for his followers,* he says. It was his mother that made him that way, not me. Coddling him, telling him he's special, and now he wants everybody's attention and approval, doesn't he? It's like he needs it, and can never get enough. Of course, he doesn't care about *my* approval. I tried to make a man out of him. I had him running sprints when he was eight years old, and he loved it. I timed him, and he didn't get to eat until he beat his last time. I had him like a soldier by his twelfth birthday. So I tried, not that it mattered. Do I care if he wins? No. The people who watch these shows, they don't have anything better to do with their time, I guess. He can try to make everyone think he's the best thing since, I don't know, one of these singers the kids like, or a celebrity, but he'll never convince me he's anything but a degenerate who has no idea what it means to work every day for what you have, provide for a family, to be strong. He wants to disappear into the wilderness? Fine.

The woods were dark. The beams from their flashlights didn't so much illuminate the blackness as create a small circle that feebly pushed back the shadows. Running around like this was dangerous, and they didn't have much to go on. To Cam, the scream had seemed to come from the whole forest, from the sky, from all around them, but River said it'd come from the north, the direction of the trailer they'd been hiking to.

"We should split up," Liza said. "We'll never find him like this."

River's face was tight, and with a voice hoarse from calling out to Trip, he said, "No. It's safer this way."

They yelled Trip's name, and the sounds seemed muffled, as if the trees were swallowing their voices just like the blackness consumed the beams from the flashlights.

Cam strained to peer through the night, searching for Trip, or for the lit eye of his Skym. The more she tried, the more the inky-black shadows shifted and the darkness became a living thing pressing in on her. "Are you sure the scream came from this direction?"

"Yes," River said, then stopped, crouching with his head in his hands. "No. I don't know." They'd been searching for an hour, and the strain in River's voice made Cam stop walking.

"We'll find him," she said.

Up ahead, Liza called Trip's name again and again.

River straightened, rubbing the back of his neck. "It's not even light out, we can't *see* anything. I don't understand. Why would he leave the shelter? Why run?"

There was a red flash in the distance, high in the air. Cam's heart jolted, thinking it was *them*, the producers. The producers had come back. They were rescued. Then River said, "Trip's Skym," and hurried toward the flash. And of course he was right, she could see it now, hovering above the beach at the bottom of a six-foot drop, the camera pointed at Trip's body sprawled in the sand. His face was turned away.

River reached the edge of the cliff and slid down, his boots kicking up flakes of rock that spilled in a small avalanche before him. He knelt beside Trip, pressing two fingers to his neck. He called up to Cam and Liza waiting on the cliff, "There's a pulse."

A noise like a cry came from Cam, and she pressed a hand to her mouth to hold it in. She hadn't taken a breath in those few moments while they'd waited for River to say something. The prospect of finding Trip dead had encroached on her thoughts like an animal pacing the forest, repeating in her mind, *He's dead. He's dead. He's dead.*

"Do you need help carrying him up?" Liza asked.

River's hands moved over Trip's limbs, checking for breaks or injuries. "I can manage." River lifted Trip in a fireman's carry and Cam winced. He shouldn't be moved, but it couldn't be helped. The tide was coming in, and they were alone.

River climbed, his feet slipping on shale, and Liza and

Cam grasped Trip's arms to get him over the edge. Trip was heavy, his body dead weight, but he moaned when they pulled him up, and Cam figured that was a good sign. Liza bundled her jacket under his head. Blood covered his face. Cam found a knot on his forehead, just under the hairline, where the skin was broken.

Trip moaned again, and River said, "Hey, man. How do you feel?"

Trip's head rocked to the side.

Cam stepped back. River and Liza took charge, and they seemed to know what to do. She'd only get in the way. In the one day of training provided by the show, the instructor had taught her to deal with dehydration, a cut, a broken bone: emergency care, stop-gap methods to keep someone stable until real help arrived. But real help wasn't coming.

What had Trip been doing out here? Why was he running and screaming?

Trip woke more fully and looked around. "What happened?"

"You fell," River said. "Can you tell me where you're hurt?"

Trip made an incoherent sound, his hand weakly pushing River away. "My head hurts."

"That's probably because of the rock you bashed it into," Liza said. "Nice work."

Ask him what he was doing, Cam wanted to say, but she bit her tongue. He'd been running from something. She could still hear his scream.

"What happened?" River asked.

"I don't know." Trip winced, not just with pain, but with not having an adequate answer. "What'd you guys see?"

"Nothing. I woke up and you were gone. We heard you yelling."

"That's it?"

"That's it."

Trip shook his head. "You didn't see anyone?"

"A person?" Liza said. "No. You did?"

Trip nodded, but his brow furrowed, like he couldn't quite remember. "I . . . you guys were asleep and you wouldn't wake up. I was shaking you. You don't remember that?"

River blinked, puzzled. "I would've woken up."

Liza shook her head. Cam had the same response. She had woken up to River saying something was wrong, Trip was lost. She wouldn't have slept through yelling and shaking like Trip described.

"You seemed drugged. All of you. There was someone outside, yelling, telling us to get out, go away. The voice came closer and closer. And then . . . I had this overwhelming feeling. He was right outside the shelter, and he was going to kill me. I mean, I was sure of it. I've never been so sure of anything. He wanted me dead. So I ran. It was like a nightmare. I left you guys and ran. He was chasing me, and after that . . ."

"After that, you were unconscious." River waited a moment, then added, "Is it possible you were dreaming? A concussion can mess with your memory."

"There was someone out there." Trip gazed at each of them, confused and still scared. "I'm not making it up."

"There's a lot going on right now," Cam said. "We're on edge, all of us."

"Was it an animal? A wild boar or something?" River asked.

"No, it was a person, an angry person. Scared the crap out of me."

"And nobody else heard anything, and you couldn't wake us up." River wasn't asking a question.

Trip shrugged helplessly. "It was real. It was *really* real."

Cam cupped her elbows against the cooling air.

Liza brushed her hands, suddenly authoritative. "Let's get to the trailer. There's probably a medical kit there, phones, computers. We'll find help."

"Trip's in no shape for a hike," Cam said. "He probably has a concussion. He can barely stand."

"Well, he better get a move on, because staying out here isn't an option."

"Are you suggesting we leave him here?"

Liza turned on her. "Did I say that? We don't have a choice. If we stay here, we die."

"Both of you, stop," River said. "It'll be light in an hour. We'll go then. That'll give Trip a chance to get his bearings. I'll stay with him while you guys grab the rest of our stuff back at camp. How far is the trailer, Liza?"

"About two miles."

They couldn't hike on the beach without getting trapped against the rocks by high tide. Two miles wasn't far, but through this brush it would take them half the day. They'd barely slept, and Trip was in bad shape, and not just from falling. He was nervous and on edge. Cam bit down the feeling that rose inside her, that everything was swirling into a black hole and nothing could stop it. She shivered in the graying night.

■ ■ ■

Cam and Liza trudged back to the camp in tense silence. There wasn't a lot to collect once they arrived. They'd abandoned most of their non-essential belongings the day before to make hiking easier and in anticipation of reaching the trailer. They still carried their GPS beacons, however, and the Skyms continued to swirl around them. They'd discussed abandoning the Skyms, but they transported themselves, so they weren't a burden to carry. They could have gotten rid of the battery packs, but no one did. The Skyms were the only thing left that gave them a sense of connection to the outside world. Even though rescue hadn't arrived, someone was still out there, and nobody would forget about them as long as the cameras continued streaming on everyone's devices back home.

"How do you know where the trailer is?" Cam asked. "I've been out here as long as you, and I've never seen a trailer."

"I told you, I saw the helicopters."

"But you said you've seen it before.

"We're on an island, in case you didn't know. It's not that big."

Cam hadn't, in fact, known it was an island. How did Liza? "When did you see a trailer? You ran into it, that easy?"

"Does it matter? We'll get there, we'll find help. There'll be people there, or we can call someone."

"If someone's there, why is no one here now?" Cam asked. "Trip could have died, and no one came. His Skym was broadcasting, they knew he was down there, bleeding and hurt. If the producers were still around, they'd be here."

"They lost track of us, that's all. The GPS is down. It's up to us to find them."

"They don't need GPS. They have helicopters, search parties. Where are they?"

Liza spun on Cam. "What the hell, Cam? I'm not hearing any of your brilliant solutions."

"Liza, what year were you born?"

"Oh my God. What's that got to do with anything? What is your problem?"

"It's a simple question."

Liza opened her mouth to answer, but it took a beat too long, and they both knew it was too late. Cam had her answer.

"No way you're a teenager. Why are you lying? Did you have to so you'd be cast on the show?"

"Oh, for God's sake."

"Plus you're a completely different person around River than with me or Trip. You've been putting on an act this whole time. Why?"

Liza smirked. "Maybe it's because I like River."

"If you want a tip, by the way, you're acting way younger

than you should. The way you flirt, pretending you're helpless. You're supposed to be seventeen, not twelve. It's like something out of a bad teen rom-com. That might fool a forty-year-old producer, and apparently River, but not someone who's actually spent time in a high school recently."

Too quickly, Liza said, "Fine, I lied about my age. What's it matter now? We're all equally screwed."

"I guess it doesn't matter," Cam said.

For Cam, it was simply another piece of information. Anyway, Liza was still lying, just not about her age anymore. Either that, or the show knew she had lied and was willing to let her think she got away with it. Cam wasn't surprised that Liza thought she could pass for seventeen. She was small, shorter than average, slightly baby-faced, with heart-shaped lips and big eyes. But the producers had birth certificates, high school records, internet histories. Cam was expected to buy that Liza had forged documents, changed her identity, all to get on a reality show where everyone would know who she was anyway? It made no sense. Still, it was intriguing that, however unlikely Liza's story was, she preferred it to the truth.

"Come on," Cam said. "They're waiting for us. But listen, I don't know what's going on with you, or if you know what's happening out here, but if Trip isn't able to get to the trailer, we're staying with him. Me and River. You're on your own if you want to leave him behind."

"No one's leaving anyone behind." Liza slung her pack to her shoulders. "Don't be so dramatic, Cam. I didn't—" Liza stopped suddenly. "What the hell is that?"

Cam followed her gaze to a spot on the ground. She stooped to get a better look. "It's a footprint."

It was large, a full-grown man's, and the outline of each toe sank into the dirt. Was it Trip's or River's? Whoever it was hadn't been wearing shoes.

Liza studied the print too. "Trip had his boots on, and we all sleep with socks. It's too cold not to. That's not one of ours." She pointed. "Look, there's more. And here's the prints from Trip's boots. They're all mixed together."

"Someone was out here. Trip wasn't dreaming."

"That's what it looks like."

"Do you think it was another contestant, stuck out here like we are?"

"Could be." Liza scanned the ground, following the footprints to the edge of the trees.

The prints depressed the earth among the ferns. They were side by side, as if someone had stood there, facing the shelter, waiting. They'd been hoping to find evidence they weren't alone. Now that they had it, a chill slithered down Cam's back. She felt the woods watching again, the trees whispering words she couldn't decipher no matter how hard she tried.

CHAPTER 09

Fog rolled in off the water, diffusing the morning light in an overcast glare.

While Cam and Liza collected the gear at their camp from last night, River stayed with Trip as he gradually recovered. He sat propped against a tree, his head bandaged, most of the blood washed from his face. Head injuries bled a lot, making them appear scarier than they really were. River hoped that was the case here. It was a good sign that Trip's color had returned.

"You feeling better?" River asked.

Trip nodded, but seemed distracted. "You don't believe me about the man last night."

"It's not that I don't believe you. It's just hard to work it out. It doesn't make sense. Your Skym followed you out. Can we see what it recorded?"

Trip shook his head. "They're not designed to hold memory. They stream out as they're recording, and they have only the most recent fifteen minutes, overwriting that the whole time. So, basically, we can watch this conversation. Nothing from last night."

"I see." River sat back on his heels. "Listen, let's leave aside whatever happened last night. Let's get out of here. Can you hike?"

"If it means I can sleep indoors tonight, yeah, I can manage."

■ ■ ■

When Liza and Cam returned, the four of them headed out, leaving behind the briny air near the shore where the inlet pinched down. Their walk was quieter than yesterday's, when they'd been chattering and complaining about fatigue. Now they were each in their own heads. River made a walking stick for Trip from a branch, and he leaned on it heavily. Sweat soaked the bandage on his head, but he was moving faster than River had expected. His thin-lipped determination kept him going, especially after the girls came back saying they'd seen unaccountable footprints in the camp. It stood to reason there were other contestants out here. River was surprised they hadn't run into anyone before now. Whoever it was wanted to avoid others. That was what River had been trying to do before he ran into Trip. He felt guilty for not having believed Trip when he said he'd heard someone, but the story sounded outlandish.

They'd found a faint trail, so River didn't have to fight the brush. Liza took the lead, while Cam held position at the rear, behind River.

After they'd walked half the day and stopped several times for Trip to rest, a white structure appeared through the trees.

"The trailer," Liza said.

Despite their exhaustion, in silent agreement they picked up speed.

The clearing was quiet and lifeless, and the building sat incongruously amid the trees, its mud-splattered aluminum panels pasted with a decal of the *Cut Off* logo. Liza tried the door handle. It was locked.

She banged on the trailer. "Hey! Anyone here?"

"Why is it locked?" Trip asked. His pale face contrasted alarmingly with the blood on his bandage.

River went around the trailer. He clutched the windowsill to pull himself up and peer inside.

"Looks like no one's home."

Cam bashed the door handle with a rock until it broke off.

"Flimsy construction," Trip said.

Liza shook her head, annoyed. "We might have wanted to lock it for ourselves, you know. At least be able to close the latch."

Cam tossed the rock away. "Let's find a phone that works and get the hell off this island."

River followed after everyone. The trailer smelled old, like the air had been trapped inside for days. There was also a metallic, sweet smell, like rot.

Once through the door, River found his way blocked by the others, who stood frozen in place. He pushed between Cam and Trip. The windows of the trailer were small and curtained, and it took a minute for his eyes to adjust from the daylight outside, but when they did, he understood the smell.

The scene was grisly, like something out of a horror movie.

In the beam of Cam's flashlight was a computer against one wall, and a trail of blood that led to the door. A bloody handprint smeared the glass. On the other wall was a couch with a large, dark stain on the cushions. It looked black in the dim light, but once the flashlight landed on it, River saw the red.

More blood.

"Whoever left that much blood should be dead," he said, then immediately regretted it when the others turned to him with alarmed eyes. "Or it's animal blood."

"Then how come the door was locked from the inside?" Cam said. "And where'd the handprint come from? Shouldn't there be a body?"

Nobody had answers.

Cam sat at the desk. She checked the phone before shoving it aside as useless, and then tried booting up the computer, careful to avoid the smudges of blood.

Liza peered over Cam's shoulder. "The trailer runs on a generator. The antenna booster probably drained it, although even a light left on would do that. If nobody's been keeping it going, I mean."

"How long does it take for the generator to die?" Cam asked.

"One that size? Five, six days," River said.

Trip blinked. "So no one has been here for five or six days?"

"Or longer," Liza said. "We don't know when it died."

A Skym lay on the floor next to the couch, just like theirs.

River picked it up and inspected it. "It's dead. Can we get it charged?"

Trip took it from him. "We can use one of our batteries. It'll have saved the last fifteen minutes before it died. The minute it's charged, though, it'll start overwriting with new footage."

"So if we watch it . . ." River said.

"We can only watch it once."

"Someone left it here to run down. It'll probably just be an empty room."

"They're motion-sensor cameras. We should see something."

"If you can bring up the footage, do it now," Liza said. "I don't like this."

Cam sat in the desk chair going through the contents of the drawers, but the rest of them remained standing. While Trip fiddled with the Skym and the battery pack, River searched the trailer for anything they could use. He found a first-aid kit, some bottled water, a couple bags of chips. There was a sense of emptiness about the place, as if it'd been a long time since anyone had been there. He tried not to think about what that might mean.

"Got it," Trip said. "Hurry. The minute it's up and running, it'll start streaming again."

They huddled around Trip as the Skym whirred to life. The screen was tiny, only a square two inches, but a black-and-white image flickered across it, and they pressed close together to see.

The first image was confusing, fast-moving and blurry,

then it resolved into a guy, long-haired and square-jawed. He sat at the desk where Cam had just been. He was sobbing. A computer screen in front of him was lit up, images moving across it, although it was impossible to see what they were. After a few minutes, the guy wiped his face and moved from the chair to the couch. He clutched his bloody side, looked into the distance for a long time, and then closed his eyes. He fell motionless, and eventually his hand slackened and fell to the floor. The Skym hovered in place. It was so still, River detected the rise and fall of the guy's chest. He said nothing when it fell and didn't rise again. They stood in silence, watching the footage until the end, waiting for something more, but there was nothing. Liza let out a cry when the image flickered and went black. River couldn't be sure, but he thought for a second that the last image was of the couch, but empty, just like it was now. It was probably a glitch from the recording looping back, like Trip had said it did.

"What was that?" Trip asked.

"We should leave," Cam said.

"Somebody came and got him, right?" Trip looked to River as if he had an answer. "There's no bloody guy on the couch anymore. They picked him up, took him to get help. Right?"

"The door was locked from the inside," Liza reminded him.

For the first time, River struggled for an argument that would keep them calm. At the point the recording had ended, the guy on the couch was dead. River rubbed his neck, considering the implications. Any chance that the lack of response from producers was somehow part of the show had vanished.

115

Someone, probably a contestant, had died not three feet from where he was standing. He'd died alone.

Cam's gaze landed on him. "We should go."

Liza sat heavily in the chair. "If we can power up the generator, get the computer working . . ."

"How?" Trip said. "It's gas-powered, and we don't have any."

"What could have happened, though?" Liza said. "How could they abandon us?"

"It could still be part of the show," Trip said. "They're scaring us. They wanted us to see that footage, they poured blood on the couch to make it look real. It's a setup."

River looked at Trip. He knew he'd shatter his hopes, but he wanted to do it as gently as he could. "You got hurt last night, Trip, and no one came. You could have died, and no one came. Someone *did* die here, and no one helped him. No one came."

Trip rubbed his bandage and then flinched as if he'd forgotten it was there. "Everyone got sick? Like, mass food poisoning, or an epidemic. Infrastructure has fallen apart, no one's available to rescue a bunch of kids on a reality show."

"The earthquake," Liza said. "Communication's down, GPS is down. They're out there, looking for us. They must be."

"Listen!" Cam yelled, her voice filling the small space of the trailer. "Whatever is going on, I don't like it here. We should leave—now."

"Where are we supposed to go?" Trip said.

Liza blew out a breath, her cheeks puffing out. "There's a

boat down the hill from here. We can take it to Cedar Springs. It's a resort here on the island, the other side from where we are now. It's where the crew of the show stays."

The pieces of what Liza was saying came together slowly in River's mind. "How do you know that?"

"Because," Cam said, tossing him a binder from the desk, the *Cut Off* logo emblazoned on the front. "She's one of them."

CHAPTER 10

"A NEW ELEMENT"

ON-CAMERA INTERVIEW: ELIZABETH ROJAS

The plan is to go into the game as "Liza" and shake things up a bit. And aren't you guys lucky—you get to watch! The contestants have spent the past few weeks wet, frozen, and starved, but according to the online poll, you all want to make things even harder for the final four. You guys are brutal! We've collected the list of questions and requests from viewers, so all of you watching have had the opportunity to make a real impact on the game. I'll ask your questions when I get the chance, and I'll try to maneuver the contestants to certain actions that might be exciting to watch. My first task is to make sure Cam knows about Trip's contraband—that'll piss her off to no end, right?

I'm not excited about the outdoor elements myself, but stirring up a little interpersonal drama? That's right up my alley. So keep your requests coming! They'll be fed to me by the producers through an earpiece, so your thoughts can be communicated to the contestants live, streaming on the *Cut Off* app. How exciting is that? Stay tuned, and wish me luck!

Trip hurried to keep up with Liza as she paced ahead with exasperated purpose. "You know why they're not coming, don't you? You can get us out of here. You know what's going on."

"No, Trip, I don't. If I did, we'd be out of here already. I lost contact with the producers the day after I joined the game. I figured there was some explanation, so I decided to get on with it and do my job."

The path to the boat was narrow, so they walked single file. It seemed recently worn, probably by those walking back and forth from the trailer.

There was a boat, and a resort nearby. Cam clung to that information. It would all be okay; they were saved. Whatever Liza was saying now, she knew what was going on. She worked with the producers. Everything would be okay.

The black binder Cam had found in the desk was inches thick with information about *Cut Off*. The second page included a list of credits: producer, co-producer, photographer, production designer, editor, casting. Under a list of "show producers" was the name Elizabeth Rojas. It appeared multiple times in the binder, with an asterisk identifying the individual as Liza. Although none of this explained why Liza was in the wilderness with them, or why she insisted she was just as clueless as they were.

The binder also included a profile of each of the contestants, including Cam. She'd known they had a file on her, but it was disconcerting to see it assembled in one place.

Trip persisted. "Even if you can't contact the producers

right now, you know they're at this resort place. Like, you *know* they're there, right?"

"I still have no idea why the tap-out buttons won't work."

"But you've known this whole time how to get out. I started thinking we would starve to death. You could have said something."

River kept to the back of the group, hands in his pockets, his face measured and indecipherable. "Do you know who the person was at our camp last night?" he asked Liza.

"No."

"Was it a contestant?"

Liza shook her head, apologetic. "I don't know. The last contact I had with the producers, there were four contestants still in the game—you guys, and Brandon."

"Brandon?"

"The guy on the Skym recording in the trailer," she said.

"So now it's only us," River confirmed, and Cam noticed he didn't include Brandon as still in the game. River thought the guy was dead, and he was probably right.

"Hey," Trip said to Liza. "How old are you anyway?"

"Twenty-one."

River's head tilted up at that, but he said nothing.

Trip grinned. He was so certain they were saved, but Liza's brow was wrinkled: Trip's questions flustered her. Liza had changed since they'd seen the blood and the Skym footage. Her scared, helpless act had vanished, replaced by legitimate worry and a businesslike demeanor that for the first time let Cam see who Liza really was—someone used to being in control, but also someone seriously concerned. If Liza, a show producer, was worried, what did that mean?

River had turned quieter, or at least quieter than usual.

"Twenty-one." Trip said. "So . . . a real adult. I guess you're in charge, then."

"I'm not in charge," Liza said.

"Of course you are!" Cam said. "You're our only connection to the producers, you being one of them and all. You're responsible for what happens until we find help."

"Listen, in case you haven't noticed, I'm in the same predicament as you."

"Why, though?" River said, his voice even.

"Why what?"

"Why are you in the same predicament? What's the point of pretending to be our age, and a contestant?"

Liza sighed. "It's my job. This show is different from other reality shows. It's streaming constantly. We don't have editors and story artists, the audience is living through everything with us, in real time. My job is to pose as a contestant, with the target of bringing you guys together, interacting with you."

River took this in. "Right. So when you did that, what were you aiming to accomplish?"

Trip grinned. "Make drama. Good TV."

River squinted at him, then looked at Liza for confirmation.

"No," Liza said, slowing her pace to walk alongside River, talking only to him now. His eyebrows went up when she touched his arm. "More like propel the story forward. It's not only about good TV. I wasn't being fake or anything."

With a shrug, River said, "It's fine. Doesn't matter."

Cam couldn't tell what was going on between River and Liza, but she sensed a current beneath the surface of the conversation. Liza's hand fell from River's arm as he walked a ways ahead, and Cam realized that the whole day they'd been hiking, he'd slowed his pace to accommodate them. He walked at his own pace now. He probably could have finished their two-day hike in less than one.

Liza stood still for a moment as she watched him go.

"Have you been out here as long as us?" Trip asked. He acted like finding out about Liza was no more than good gossip, like he was home watching the show rather than trapped in the middle of it.

"No. I came in a couple weeks after you all."

"Wait," Trip said. "You said you lost contact with the producers the day after you got here, so they stopped responding to you *before* the first earthquake. Does that mean it wasn't the earthquake that caused whatever's happening?"

"I don't know," Liza said.

"So you've been here, what? A little over a week?" Cam said. "Must be nice. I haven't had a shower in almost a month."

"There'll be showers at Cedar Springs. And a heated mineral pool."

"And there'll be people, too, right?" Trip said.

Liza didn't answer immediately. "Probably," she said. "But I don't know. None of this was planned. I'm just as confused as you."

A thought occurred to Cam. "Why did you set fire to Trip's camp?"

"Wait, Cam was telling the truth? You destroyed my stuff?" Trip said.

Liza sighed. "I was under orders. We looked the other way at his smuggling because we thought it made for an amusing storyline, but it became clear that Trip was coasting. He had it too easy, and we needed more tension. So we eliminated his stash of supplies. Also, we knew you guys were within shouting distance of each other, and we wanted more interaction."

"Bet you're having regrets," Trip said. "I could go for a meat stick right now."

They found the boat, a twenty-foot console with a covered T-top, tied to a tree, partially grounded on a sandy shore. A key was in the ignition. River took off his boots and waded into the water. He stood at the bow, peering at the line of waves breaking against rocks.

"The tide's low, and getting lower. We'd have to drag it out, and it looks like we'll hit those rocks even if we get out there." He looked at his watch. "It's about ten hours to the next high tide."

"It'll be dark before we can leave," Liza said. "Guess we'll get there tomorrow."

"No," Trip said, all humor dropping from his face. "No way. I'm not sleeping outside again, not after last night. I'd rather go back to the bloody trailer."

River sat on a piece of driftwood to put his boots back on. "Don't freak out. It'll be fine."

"No, damn it!" Trip flung his pack to the ground. "That . . . that *man* is still out there, and there's something *wrong* with him. What if he comes back? What if *he's* what got Brandon so bloody?"

"If we leave now, we'll wreck the boat, and then we'll really be stuck. We're a day's hike from where we were last night. It's doubtful he followed us. You said he told us to get out. Well, that's what we've done."

Trip faced River, his foot tapping, his whole body twitching. "You can't know he didn't follow us." He dug through his pack and came out with a pill bottle. He tapped a white pill into his palm.

River paused in lacing his boots. "Is that a good idea right now?"

"Shut up, River."

"We'll be okay. Panicking isn't going to help."

Trip glared. "Don't patronize me. You have no idea what you're talking about." He kicked off his shoes and lifted his pack. "You guys can do what you want. I'm staying on the boat. Hope we don't get murdered in our sleep."

"I'll come with you," Liza said.

River watched them clamber into the boat and look for a place to settle in.

Cam shook her head at him. "Nice."

"What?"

"You can't tell someone not to freak out and expect it to work. It's not helpful."

"I told him it'll be okay, not to be afraid. It's panicking that's not helpful."

"Yeah, but it's not okay to brush off what he's feeling." When River started to argue, Cam held up a hand to stop him. "In any case, he knows you're lying. It *is* a big deal. We're scared, even if you're not, and telling us we shouldn't be is dishonest."

River started to speak again, then stopped, his gaze dropping to his hands. He rubbed absently at the dirt on his fingers until he looked up. "You're right—it was an asshole thing to say. Tell Trip and Liza to get some sleep. I'll stay up tonight and keep watch."

"Do you want someone to stay with you?"

"No. You guys sleep on the boat where it's more comfortable. I'll have a fire, and a bed once we get to the resort. I'll be fine."

As River gathered branches from the nearby trees, Cam bunched together twigs.

River dropped a bundle of sticks and started breaking them into smaller pieces. "I am, you know," he said.

"You're what?"

"Scared. You said I wasn't, but I am. Of course I am."

"Well, you hide it better than we do."

It was dark by the time the fire was blazing. Cam tossed him a snack bag of chips they'd taken from the trailer, then climbed into the boat to join Trip and Liza.

River sat alone, watching the flames flicker in the dark.

CHAPTER 11

River fed more sticks into the blaze, and the smell of pitch rose from the drifting smoke as pine needles curled and turned ashy white. It was black outside the circle of firelight, and stars filled the sky like sparkling dust. He folded his arms against the chill.

The woods had always been a refuge for him, a place to block out the noise, to settle the restless, gnawing energy that sometimes consumed him. He used to go with Terrell, but for the past two years, ever since his parents died, he'd preferred going alone. Two years ago his life had been torn apart and then pieced together again. Getting away from the world and everyone in it was the only thing that dulled the sense that the pieces didn't fit together anymore.

The tide gradually came in, and the boat shifted in the shallow water, but it'd be a few hours still before it was safe to launch. With nothing but the sound of water slapping the boat and the mindless buzz of the Skym to draw his attention, he regretted not asking Cam to keep him company.

River poked the fire, the pulsing embers making his eyes heavy. He checked his watch. Three o'clock. Hours left until daybreak. He sighed and folded his jacket collar tight around his neck.

An emphatic rustling of leaves came from the trees behind him.

It was nothing, some small nocturnal animal or a falling branch. He took a deliberate breath and let it out, then poked the embers again.

A spider perched on a knot of wood at the edge of the fire. River lowered his stick, inviting it to climb on. It darted, scuttling, onto the stick and then up toward his hand. He'd been intending to bring the creature into the leaves, get it away from the fire, but it moved with startling speed, about to scurry up his sleeve. He hurriedly tossed the stick into the brush.

He rubbed his arms and set his machete at close reach. The woods never made him this jumpy.

Another rustling sounded in the trees, and with it a coarse growl.

River swung away from the fire, squinting into the dark. He saw nothing. It must have been his imagination. He admonished himself for letting Trip's jitters overrun his own nerves.

Then, twenty feet away, a shadow moved. It was large. Too low-slung to be a bear, and a boar never growled like that.

The sound came again, and a jet-black dog prowled into the moonlight, its eyes locked on River, its snout muscled back in a snarl.

River knew the rules: move slowly, don't make eye contact, don't turn your back, stand side-on, put your hands in your pockets.

Everything in him shrieked, *Run*.

A strand of saliva dribbled from the dog's muzzle, and

the rumble in its chest left River frozen in place, the fire at his back, the boat yards away. He clutched the machete. The weapon should have made him feel safe, but it felt like nothing, like cheap metal dulled by a month in the brush. Fear filled his mouth. It tasted bitter, like rotten oranges.

He wanted to call to the others, but his voice died in his throat. If he yelled, the dog would attack. Raised scars slashed its muzzle, and its fur was mottled with mud and wads of dead leaves. It moved as if it had shown up just for him, as if it lived for only one thing, a single purpose—to tear him apart piece by piece.

He struggled with the command "Go home!" but the words came out like he was choking. And anyway, it was a futile thing to say. This dog had no home. It was feral and wild. His mind flashed back to a hiking trail behind his old house, his own screams as a child, white teeth and black fur red with blood—his blood. The memory paralyzed him, and he swore he saw triumph in the dog's eyes.

A voice whispered from the woods, *I'll kill you, you little shit*.

River spun around, searching for who had spoken. There was no one.

"River!" Trip's voice rang out from the boat. "Hold on, I'm coming!"

Trip climbed down, his feet sloshing through the water. He was at least a dozen yards from River.

That broke River's paralysis. "Trip—stay back!" he hissed as loud as he dared.

The dog ignored Trip. It focused on River, the only prey that mattered. It pawed forward several steps, slobbering and growling, its black eyes never leaving him. Stepping away, River tumbled over a tree root. The machete fell from his hand. He scrabbled backwards as the dog saw its opportunity and hurtled toward him, throwing up gobs of sand in its tracks.

From the boat, Liza screamed. River threw his arms over his head, recoiling from the fangs about to rip through him.

A loud crack broke the air, and then a brilliant light flashed red across his tightly closed eyelids.

"River, run to the boat!" Trip yelled.

Cam held a flare gun pointed at the dog's head. It hunched low against the threat.

As if breaking from a trance, River scrambled to his feet and ran.

The dog followed.

Trip leaped back in the boat as the flare dissipated and fell. The water came up to River's knees, slowing his pace like he was stuck in a dream, running endlessly and never moving forward. There was a furious splashing and a snarl behind him. The dog was in the water. It was gaining on him.

Trip grasped River's forearm. "Hurry—Jesus, hurry."

River leveraged his feet on the hull, and then a tug ripped at his pant leg, teeth clamping down. Trip pulled. Another flash split the air.

Cam leaned out of the boat with the flare aimed at the dog, her face collected and implacable, elbows braced on the transom. River had enough time to consider how close the flare had come to him, close enough to feel its heat. He fell over the deck's railing with Trip under him.

The dog barked furiously, its claws scrabbling the hull of the boat. Cam had grazed it with the second flare. It didn't care.

"Go!" Cam shouted, and the motor kicked into a roar as Liza powered them out.

The boat barely moved. It dragged over sand in the shallow water. The dog leaped. Its front paws hooked the railing and its back feet scrambled for purchase as it tried to pull itself onto the deck of the boat.

"Liza," Cam said, a warning in her voice. Her eyes remained locked on the dog, the flare gun empty but still pointed at its head.

Liza revved the engine, and a wrenching squeal racked the boat as fiberglass ground against rock, locking them in place for a long moment before it shot free. The black dog howled from the shoals.

"What the hell," Cam muttered, watching it plunge forward in the boat's wake. "You can't catch us by swimming, asshole!"

River pushed his back against the railing and closed his eyes. Cam slid next to him, dropping the flare gun from her hand and reaching for his.

The boat raced into the dark.

THE
RESORT

CHAPTER 12

CEDAR SPRINGS RESORT AND
ECO-LODGE PROMOTIONAL VIDEO

[AERIAL SHOT: ISLAND. DISSOLVE TO MAN IN CARDIGAN
WALKING ON BEACH. BACKGROUND MUSIC: FLUTE.]

Here we offer remote lodgings in an unspoiled, natural environment. Cedar Springs Resort is a responsible option for all your relaxation needs, with no sacrifices to your comfort or desire for luxury. We provide gourmet meals prepared by world-class chefs, using only sustainable, regionally sourced ingredients. Ecological balance and biodiversity conservation are words we live by here at the Springs, with eco-friendly toiletries, organic linens, renewable energy, and a pristine natural environment. Take advantage of the resources on the island with boating and fishing expeditions assisted by our skilled and knowledgeable guides, or a whale-watching tour on one of our three private amphibious aircraft. Or simply relax with a quiet evening by the fire and a glass of wine. Please, enjoy your stay. We hope it is as memorable and magical as the beauty surrounding us.

The resort was on the same island, but it took over an hour to navigate the shoreline. The boat's motor prohibited conversation, so Cam leaned back in the upholstered seat, more comfortable than anything she'd been in for weeks, and let the wind whip through her hair. Liza sped along around the coast, toward comfort and safety, phones and internet. Toward civilization. Whatever they found at Cedar Springs, they were leaving behind the wilderness—wild dogs, strangers lurking in the night, whispering trees, ramshackle shelters. Whatever happened, she'd sleep in a bed tonight and eat decent food.

She'd kill for chocolate ice cream.

River sat next to her. She rested against his arm, and he met the pressure of her leaning body with a slump, his muscles finally letting go of the tension they'd been under for hours. She huddled into his solid warmth, a shelter from the lashing air.

The resort revealed itself dead ahead as dawn outlined the treetops, jagged and pointed as teeth above the hills. The boat puttered closer, and River's brow furrowed, his gaze fixed on the main building with a ring of bungalows behind it. Log construction, three stories, a massive fieldstone chimney, a shaded pool on one side, colorful umbrellas, pinewood tables, and fire pits spaced around firs adjacent to a crescent-shaped beach. It looked like the type of place patronized by the discreet rich and privacy-hungry celebrities.

She had to raise her voice above the noise of the motor. "What's wrong?"

He tilted his chin to the shore. "I don't see anyone."

And of course that's what was missing. For all the opulence and size of the place, they should see people. Waiters preparing the tabled patio, staff arranging lounge chairs by the pool, early-morning joggers.

Liza pulled the boat up to a short dock and cut the motor. Silence descended like a weight, leaving only the slosh of water and the boat knocking against the pier. Silence should have been welcome after the endless clamor of the engine, but instead it felt forbidding, threatening. The silence itself was a presence.

Cam had never seen anything like Cedar Springs except in magazines. It was the kind of place she imagined would be touted as "rustic luxury" or something. At first glance it seemed an organic extension of the landscape, but that was an illusion. The site was stylized to evoke nonchalant elegance, studied unpretension. Cam could picture fashionable ladies reclining in the Adirondack chairs, and croquet players on the manicured lawn shadowed by fir-covered hills. Seen now, the place screamed emptiness, the silence like sleeping wasps in a nest.

Without speaking, they made their way to the main building. The doors opened to a lobby with a sweeping front desk, a stone fireplace, mahogany coffee tables, and leather chairs flanked by stained-glass lamps.

Cam jumped as Liza's voice rang through the lobby: "Hello, anybody here?" There was no answer. She went behind the counter, flicked light switches, then checked the phones. "They're dead," she said. "And the computers aren't coming on. The power's out. You guys stay put. I'm going to look around." She took off at a jog down the hallway.

Cam's gaze landed on a postcard and a drinking glass left on a coffee table near the fireplace. The glass held an inch of water—melted ice, probably, because an amber tint that looked like whiskey had settled on the bottom. She pushed the glass aside to find a water stain on the wood. It'd been there a while. The postcard showed a picture of the resort with an ad running aslant: AN ENVIRONMENTALLY FRIENDLY VACATION, WHERE THE ONLY FOOTPRINTS LEFT ARE THOSE IN THE SAND! She flipped it over.

Dear Edmund, it said.

It's been lovely here so far, except for the

That was it, as if the pen had been dropped mid-sentence, the thought cut short. A pen was on the floor, beneath the coffee table.

"Guys, look at this," Trip said. He stood at the double doors leading to the resort's restaurant. A placard on the wall proclaimed CEDAR SPRINGS GRILLE in looping script. Trip held a hand over his nose and mouth, and as Cam and River stepped closer, it was clear why. The stench of rotting food hung in the air of the dining room like a cloud. The room droned with black flies.

The tables were set for dinner, and everything was neatly in place but for a few chairs knocked sideways. Plates held meals green and gray with mold. The air-conditioning had shut down, and the place swelled with the congested atmosphere of a greenhouse. Yellow light boiled in the ceiling-tall picture windows, turning chicken breast, prime rib, and baked potatoes to rotting heaps. From a dessert cart, ice cream from cardboard cartons flooded the floor and resolved in a gummy puddle teeming with flies.

On the boat, Cam had been starving, the prospect of a good meal distracting her from the bewildering circumstance that brought them here. But at the sight of the dining room, her appetite vanished. And it wasn't only the mold and rot.

It seemed as if everyone sitting down to dinner had stood from their tables all at once and fled without looking back. They abandoned their food and fancy cocktails. They abandoned their purses and jackets and credit cards and phones. A baby's car seat sat forlorn at one table and a high chair at another, a pacifier and pink rattle beneath it. Everyone had left the resort, left the island.

What happened here? Where had everybody gone?

And Cam couldn't stop the thought before it was too late: *What will happen to us?*

CHAPTER 13

The first thing to do was get out of the dining room. Cam and Trip were stock-still, taking in every detail, each of them growing more ashen by the second. River didn't blame them.

He'd prepared himself for any number of possibilities, but given what they'd seen at the trailer, he hadn't held much hope that they'd find rescue at the resort. Something on the island had gone horribly wrong. The producers knew about it, and for some reason there was nothing they could do. The four of them simply weren't going to find a crowded, functioning resort only twenty miles away.

Liza was probably right. The earthquake had triggered some kind of disaster that required evacuation of the island. There hadn't been time to gather the contestants left in the game, and the show would sacrifice them to save everyone else.

Maybe an explosion was imminent, a boiler in the basement, or perhaps the island sat on a previously inactive volcano that was about to blow any minute. There was a terrorist attack, or an alien abduction. He'd even considered a scenario where the producers were engaged in some illegal activity, like maybe *Cut Off* was a front for a money-laundering operation, and those in charge had fled the country, abandoning their project before the police caught up with them.

Maybe everyone had been dragged away by rabid dogs.

His theories weren't great.

In any case, while he'd anticipated finding the resort empty, what he hadn't been prepared for was *this*. The *way* the resort was empty.

As if everyone had simply vanished.

He steered Cam and Trip from the stinking dining room and closed the doors behind them. They wouldn't go in there again. They'd find a back way to the kitchen. They needed to contact the outside world, get something to eat, and then rest. Even with the weirdness confronting them, better to be here than in the woods with savage dogs or stuck in the blood-drenched trailer. Once they recouped their energy, things would start to make more sense. They had to, because this? This didn't make sense.

Liza returned from searching the hotel. "This place was running on a solar-powered generator, but it's dead. The lights and computers are all out."

"Any phones working? They have landlines here?" Cam asked.

Liza shook her head. "No dial tone. Nothing."

Trip threw his hands in the air. "Well, that's great. That's just perfect. Now what?"

"Don't panic yet," Liza said. "I've got the generator charging. It's going to take some time is all."

"How the hell much time?" he shouted.

Liza lost her patience and shouted back, "How should I know? You're some kind of computer wizard. Why don't you figure out how to get us online?"

"We can't get online without power!"

Cam glanced back and forth between them. "The pamphlets about this place say it's off the grid. Can we even get online?"

"It's a business, there must be something," River said. "An old dial-up maybe."

"The show brought in their own hotspots," Liza said. "Don't ask a bunch of television execs to stay off social media."

Trip spoke through gritted teeth. "None of that will work without *power*."

As Cam, Trip, and Liza argued, their voices reverberated through the empty space, their emotions ramping up with each word. It would only get worse if they kept debating things they couldn't control.

"How big was the generator?" River asked.

"I don't know!" Liza turned on him. "Generator-size!"

River kept his voice level. It wouldn't help to start yelling too. "Like the size of a suitcase, or the size of a refrigerator?"

She backed off and thought about it. "More like a car?"

"Okay. It's daylight now. Depending on what kind of battery it's using, and that we only need to charge one laptop or cellphone, I'd give it some time. We'll keep an eye on it, but I bet it's ready by tonight."

"If we find a master key, we can search the rooms for one of the hotspots and a laptop. We'll split up, each take a floor—"

"No," River said, noting Liza's pinched face and Trip and Cam's twitchy energy. "Let's get settled first."

"No, we search now," Cam said. "I want to go home."

"Even if we find a hotspot—" The alarm on Trip's face made River correct himself. "*When* we find a hotspot, like Trip said, it won't work until we have electricity anyway, and that'll be a while. We haven't had a real meal in weeks. We have some time to kill. Instead of spending it worried and miserable, we'll feel better if we eat, get cleaned up. None of it's any good if we collapse."

All three of them still seemed ready for a fight, but then one by one they slumped, a disappointed acquiescence to the situation. They'd been hoping for rescue, for someone in charge and answers to all their questions. They'd have to wait.

Liza found a master key behind the front desk without much trouble. There were scores of guest rooms at the resort. They selected one on the second floor, with a couch, a dining table, and two queen beds. They could have each had their own room, but an unspoken agreement made them stick together and not lose sight of one another for more than a few minutes at a time. Also, closing themselves off from the expansive space of the hotel offered a sense of security.

The room looked down on something called the Springs, a circle of manufactured rocks, ferns, and wooden railings surrounding a natural spring with a waterfall cascading into it.

This was unlike any hotel River had ever stayed in. The resort brochure that Cam showed him promoted Cedar Springs as an eco-lodge, which apparently meant a certain rustic but luxurious décor: vaulted ceilings, polished wood, wrought-iron chandeliers, plush down pillows, marble showers, leather armchairs.

Once they had established a home base, they set the Skym batteries to recharge and headed to the kitchen. They needed food. The items in the refrigerator had gone bad, but the pantry was stocked. They loaded their arms with peanut butter, pickles, prepackaged chocolate cake, crackers, and boxes of muffins. River took a can of mixed nuts and some bottles of water. They were going to make themselves sick with sweets after eating only tiny helpings of fish, snails, and berries for weeks.

Cam broke into a bag of cookies, satisfaction and desperation at war on her face.

"We can't possibly eat all this," River said.

"Watch me," she replied, her mouth already full.

They brought as much as they could carry back to the room, spread the food across the dining table, and ate. It was messy and overwhelming. The food was salty and sweet and rich, and they didn't stop until they were full, and even then they nibbled at bites here and there, leaving behind a mess of wrappers and silverware, cups and half-eaten cookies.

It was late morning before River stumbled away from the table, exhaustion heavy in his limbs. He fell onto the closest bed, dirty clothes and all, dimly aware of the others lying down to sleep at the same time. Someone fell beside him, but he knew nothing after that except the crisp smell of hotel laundry.

■ ■ ■

River woke up bleary and with no idea how long he'd slept. The others were already up, and Liza was digging through two suitcases she'd dragged into the room.

"I couldn't sleep," she said. "Check it out, though. I found a hotspot."

River rubbed the sleep from his eyes. "That's great. Does it work?"

Trip shook his head. "No power. There's an indicator light on the generator. It's still red."

"It's going to work, though, right?" Cam said. "Once the generator's charged?"

"I think so," Trip said. "In the meantime, who wants a drink? I'm going to find the hotel bar."

Liza raised her eyebrows at him. "You got ID?"

"Maybe you didn't notice," Trip said, "but this place is empty. No one's checking any IDs."

"Until help shows up, as a representative of the show I'm responsible for you guys."

"I thought you weren't in charge," Cam said.

Trip took a bite of a cracker spread with peanut butter. "Your show ditched us in the middle of nowhere. I almost died, and River was nearly eaten. You're getting fussy about liability now?"

"There's still the Skyms. Do you really want footage of you breaking the law?"

Trip looked up, staring into the eye of the Skym buzzing above his head. "Come arrest us, please! We could use the ride home."

Liza rolled her eyes. "Fine. Just don't get wasted. And pick up a decent bourbon."

When Trip returned with bottles and a six-pack of sodas, he cracked open rum and cans of Coke and made drinks. Cam sniffed at hers, and Liza scowled at the glass, dumped its contents, and poured bourbon. River took a sip of his. The sweetness was almost shocking, but between the sugar and caffeine, he found himself drinking it down too fast. Trip poured another.

"I wish there was hot water," Cam said, pushing aside her glass and drinking Coke from the can. "I'd kill for a real shower."

"The Springs," Trip said, handing River a new drink. "Let's go."

They didn't have swimsuits, so they raided the gift shop for shorts and T-shirts, all colored eco green and boasting the resort's logo. At the Springs, steam rose from the surface of the water and ferns surrounded benches designed to look like fallen logs. The place smelled of minerals and moss.

River took off his T-shirt and went into the water, a welcome sting of heat on his skin. Cam slid past him, laughing and kicking water in his face. She'd taken off the shorts and swam now wearing just the T-shirt and her underwear. River found himself staring for too long before taking a deep breath and plunging under the water. The combination of the icy drink, the natural heat of the springs, and Cam's nearness left him feeling unsteady.

The water soaked into his muscles, loosening the tightness that had been there from the beginning, and sinking into the pool was like floating in space.

River leaned against the rocks, his head swimming pleasantly with the drinks Trip kept refilling. Trip had found an old battery-powered CD player in one of the rooms, and music poured from its speakers. Cam complained that the songs were ten years too old, but the three of them knew all the words. River smiled, not knowing them himself, but not minding their sing-along. He gazed into the sky as it turned dark and let the heat of the water filter into his bones.

Cam rested at the edge of the pool, leaning back on straight arms and lazily drifting her toes in the water. Steam rose from her hair and shoulders, and the wet shirt clung to her.

River hadn't eaten enough to make drinking a good idea, that much was clear, because his thoughts were wandering everywhere, and the only thing he wanted to do was swim across the pool and brush his fingers along her bare skin.

He was so busy staring at Cam, he didn't notice Liza swim up to him.

"We'll be okay now," she said, as if continuing a conversation.

"You think so?"

"We have plenty of food and water, we have beds. At least

we won't die from starvation or exposure. We can stay here for a while, until help arrives."

"Well, that's something, I guess." It didn't answer the question of what had happened on the island to make everyone disappear, but she was right. Shelter and food would make everything easier. They'd be on the internet soon, and then none of what had happened would matter anymore—the dog, the strange man, the bloody trailer.

"You must know where we are," River said. "I'm guessing somewhere in the Pacific Northwest?"

"It's basically Vancouver Island, but more precisely a small island just to the north of it."

That wasn't far from where River had grown up, outside Seattle. This island—the landscape, a taste in the air, the saturation of green—had felt familiar the whole time.

On the other side of the pool, Cam chucked a beach ball at Trip, then shrieked when he splashed her and grabbed her around the waist to pull her in. They played at some sort of wrestling game that resulted in half the rum pouring into the pool.

"It's okay!" Trip shouted. "We have the vodka!"

Liza smirked. "You're staring. You should swim over there, start something."

"Looking to stir up some drama, Ms. Producer? Does your show need a romance?"

"Seems like my job description has changed. Mostly I want to keep us alive until help arrives. Anyway, I'm sorry I couldn't tell you." He peered sideways at her. "Honest. They wanted me to focus on you because you were so bad at the confessionals. But that doesn't mean I was insincere. I really did want to get to know you."

"And those times in the shelter, when you were cozying up to me?"

"What can I say? It was cold." She winked at him. "You were nice to cuddle with."

"And what would you have done if I'd made a move on you?"

"You're in high school. That's too young for me. I was flirting for the cameras, not propositioning you."

Something occurred to him, and he turned to face her. "You've been lying about everything. In the woods the other day, you told me your mother died. She didn't, did she?"

She shrugged. "It was a way in."

"So you've read all our files and know everything about us?"

"Yup. Your psych profile, intelligence test, character analysis, interviews." She saw his expression and shrugged again. "That's how this works. You signed on for it."

"I don't think I signed on for exactly this."

"Well, that's true. Do you accept my apology, though? I could help you with Cam. She can be pretty closed off, but that's only because her mother's been in prison for the past year. She shot an abusive boyfriend, and Cam's worried about her little brother living with an aunt they barely know. She doesn't trust easily, especially men, because of her mom, you know, so you'll need to—"

"Christ, Liza, stop!" He ran wet hands over his face. "How can you not know that's not okay?"

She gave a dismissive wave of her hand. "Suit yourself. You should at least talk to her."

He shook his head, seeing her as a completely different person than the girl he met only a few days ago. "You're unbelievable, you know that?"

She moved close to him and touched his stomach, then walked two fingers up his chest. Her face settled into an expression he recognized from their talk in the woods, wide-eyed and young, but now he could see the façade draped on like a costume. "Do I scare you, River?"

He was lost for a response, and then he caught Cam watching them. Liza followed his gaze and laughed, dropping the act as casually as she'd put it on. "Oh, go on. Talk to her."

"I don't need your help."

"Sure you do. You haven't stuck around anywhere long enough to really date anyone, and you've ditched all your friends ever since—" He gave her a warning glance, and she held up her hands in surrender. "Fine," she said, swimming away. "I'm only saying, it doesn't hurt to put yourself out there a little."

She'd been about to say *since your parents were killed.* She wasn't wrong. He always ended up taking off, holing up in a tent alone in the woods. The only reason he'd agreed to sign on to the show was because he wanted to isolate himself even more, although he realized now how absurd that idea had been. Tossing your life up on camera was a lousy way to hide from the world. Instead of hiding, he'd laid himself bare. The notion gripped him with a wave of dizziness, and the drinks weren't helping.

He hauled himself from the pool and dried off. It had felt good for a while, pretending this was a high school house party, that someone's parents were out of town and they were raiding the liquor cabinet, but now he only wanted to be alone. It would be the first time in days he *could* be alone. Between the drinks and the music and Liza rattling on, he couldn't hear himself think. His head was spinning.

Then Cam was next to him, her hand resting on his arm.

"You okay?" she said.

Was he okay? He didn't know, but he was running away again, that much was obvious. Right then, however, in the midst of all that sensory overload, and given the strange events of the past few days, Cam's cool hand on his arm was the only thing that mattered.

He liked her, and not just because she was cute, or because when she laughed he couldn't help laughing with her. She was like a whisper of green air drifting into a stale room, a crack in a window that had been nailed shut for years. He imagined for a second how it would feel to let himself *really* like her, the way he hadn't let himself before, not with anyone. The thought was terrifying.

Get over yourself, Terrell would say, because he was being ridiculous. But no, that wasn't fair. That was his own voice in his head, not Terrell's. Terrell would tell him that, after the past few years, he deserved a minute of being happy, and for that to happen, he had to risk . . . what? Losing everything, all over again. That was the problem, wasn't it?

What if, though? What if he made a space for her? What if that window opened wider?

He didn't know where it would lead, but he knew right then that he didn't want to be alone anymore. He wanted to be with her, more than he'd ever wanted anything.

CHAPTER 14

Cam had been chatting with Trip and eyeing Liza running her hand over River's chest. Trip had asked her something, but she couldn't answer because she hadn't been paying attention. He turned to find what caught her eye.

Trip sighed. "What kind of jerk gets to be that pretty and not even care?" he said.

He used the right word, too—pretty, with circumspect blue eyes, black eyelashes, and tapering cheekbones. He wasn't big and muscled, but fit, even after the past few weeks of losing weight. The tattoo on his shoulder blade drew dark lines that followed the contour of bone and muscle.

He tossed his head back when his hair, black with water, fell across his forehead.

"Oh, come on," Trip said, rolling his eyes like it was all a bit much.

Cam shoved her elbow into Trip. "Hey. I can't compete with Liza *and* you."

"Liza's just having fun," Trip said. "Me, on the other hand —I'd be competition."

"You get on his nerves too much. Anyway, I think he mostly likes girls."

He winked. "Mostly. But what he *mostly* likes right now is you."

"It doesn't matter anyway, even if he is pretty." Her arms crossed over her stomach. "I'm not here to hook up with anyone. I'm sick of guys turning out to be garbage."

"He almost got himself mauled by a dog last night because he was keeping watch for us."

"He felt guilty for giving you a hard time about the pills."

"I don't even know if they're helping. At home I take them when I get that feeling something terrible is about to happen, but there's never anything causing it that I can point to. It just happens. Honestly, it would be nice to be able to say something specific is making me anxious, the way my mom has her fear of flying. But there's nothing dire, just that *feeling*. Sometimes it hits me hardest when everything is great, and I have no idea why. I swear, out here it's almost a relief to have a reason to be afraid. How messed up is that?"

Cam looked up into the trees. There was no moon, but the leaves and branches stretched against the sky, leaving the stars peering from behind them.

"Not messed up," she said. "Complicated."

A sough in the trees caused Cam to look up again. She let the rush of water fill her ears; if she listened right now, she'd hear the muttering voices. The words she'd heard the other night in the woods came back to her: *They're already dead.*

She didn't want to hear the voices right then. If she pretended they weren't there, she could pretend the four of them were safe for a minute and she wasn't losing her mind.

River climbed out of the pool and grabbed a towel. He dried his hair and combed a hand through the dark curls, his gaze clouded and distant. He looked lost.

Trip gave her a knowing smile and drifted away on his back, implicitly giving her permission to quit talking to him. She wrapped a towel around herself, then went to where River stood, hands on his hips and staring at the ground, lost in thought.

"You okay?"

His head came up as if he hadn't been aware she was next to him. His lip pulled against his teeth like he was about to ask a question, but he didn't, and she flushed at the way he stared at her with such intensity.

They stood together in silence. He took her hand from his shoulder and held it, drawing her close as her heart thudded against her ribs. Wordless, he turned her palm up and ran a finger down her wrist, his touch leaving a trail of heat along her skin. A gentle pressure kept her hand in place as his gaze dropped to her lips. She felt them part as if they weren't her own. He was going to kiss her, and God, she wasn't ready. She was wearing a sopping T-shirt, she hadn't gotten ahold of a razor, and she felt about as attractive as a wet cat, but he didn't seem to care. He blinked slowly, and his eyes lifted to meet hers. A smile spread across his mouth.

"You hungry?"

"S-sure," she stammered, which wasn't even true.

Oh no, she thought. She really was in trouble.

But she couldn't help it. She would have said yes to anything with him looking at her with eyes like that.

■ ■ ■

They all dressed in new clothes—shirts and hoodies branded with the Cedar Springs logo—then ate at a long, stainless steel table in the resort's industrial kitchen. Once they finished a dinner of canned meat and beans heated on the gas stove, Trip and Liza left to check on the generator again. River sat with Cam while she pushed the last bits of food around her plate.

Cam had stopped counting how many days it had been, but when she'd left for the wilderness, she'd known she probably wouldn't be back on time for Benji's birthday. He'd be turning ten. She ached, thinking about Benji. Would Aunt Pam have a party for him? Would he have presents? Whatever happened to her out here, at least Benji was safe. He might be streaming the show now.

Cam waved to the Skym over her head. "Hey, Benji. Happy birthday!"

River pushed his plate away. "Benji's your brother?"

"Yeah. His birthday's coming up. Or just happened. How many days have we been out here?"

"I lost track. Liza said you were out here because of Benji."

Cam glanced up at the Skym. How much did she want to say, with so many people out there listening, and with River sitting across from her, obviously wanting to know about her life back home? What she wanted the audience to know was completely different from what she wanted to say to River. And really, she had no desire to divulge her pitiful story to anyone.

She'd been telling herself this whole time that coming on the show was only about the money. Sure, with it she could take care of Benji, get custody when she turned eighteen. But if she was being honest, she'd also wanted to forget the train wreck of her life for a while. The last thing she wanted was to bring it here, to let the world know how screwed up everything was, to show River how screwed up she was. Why would he want anything to do with her family's mess?

Except . . .

There was a softness in River's eyes when he looked at her. She'd seen it there when they'd been by the pool. He made her feel like she was perfect, even when she knew she wasn't.

Maybe Trip was right. Maybe River really was different.

Of course, that's what her mom always said. She'd find some new guy and tell Cam, *This one's different, he really cares about me. It won't be like last time.*

But it was always like last time.

Cam would never be her mom. Not if she could help it.

"I'm out here for the money," she said to River. "What other reason is there?"

He considered her, like he knew she was dodging something, but the sordid details of her family were nobody's business.

He looked away from her, and then the lights suddenly blinked on. The generator was working. It was as if thinking about Benji had brought her a way to call him. With the power on, Trip could get the hotspot running. She could be talking to him in a matter of minutes.

"Let's get back to the room, find the others," River said, standing up.

The hallway outside the kitchen led to a corridor of guest rooms. Recessed lighting cast a benign glow on the taupe walls. Carpeting with floral decoration spread before them, and Cam followed it, lost in her thoughts.

Maybe her instincts about River were right, and she should have told him her story. She *wasn't* her mother, and perhaps that meant she could make her own decisions and they wouldn't be a disaster.

"River," she said, forming his name slowly as she wondered what, exactly, she was going to say. This might be her last chance. The power brought back their connection to civilization. They'd be rescued, the show would be over, they'd all go their separate ways. "I think—"

There was a man. He stood at the end of the long corridor, expressionless, his head low and his eyes raised up, fixed on them. He wore a jacket and tie, his pale hair neatly trimmed. His feet were bare. They were also coated with mud.

The man's eyes narrowed, as if he'd been expecting them. As if he'd been waiting for hours for them to stumble upon him. His mouth twisted into a grimacing smile.

"Hey," River said. "Are you with the show?"

The man stood motionless and silent, hands at his sides.

Vertigo swept over Cam.

Something's not right.

His expression turned dark, brooding and angry. But more than that, something was *wrong* with his face. It seemed to shift before her eyes, as if his features were melting and reforming. She blinked, but the harder she stared, the more shapeless his face became, until all she could see was a menacing blankness in his eyes, and she felt dizzy.

The voices in the trees had faded in the background since they'd arrived at the resort. The comfort of being inside, the food and sense of safety, had made it easy to tune them out. All at once those whispers came back so loud they may as well be screams.

"You alone?" River asked the man.

"River," she said. She grasped his arm, overwhelmed with a need to get away, to be outside. "It's louder here."

He frowned in confusion, his gaze still fixed on the stranger. "What?"

She tried again. "It's the man from the woods. He'll kill us."

For a second the face settled in place—glacial eyes, sharp nose, mouth a tight slash of red lips against yellowish skin— and she knew it was true. She didn't know how, or why, but she knew. He would kill them.

The man's chin dropped and his mouth fell open, a black hole crowding the center of his face. His tongue worked its way around words, but no sound came out. For several moments he stood, eyes glinting, mouth agape, tongue restless. A sound issued from his throat, a glottal, creaky noise that reverberated down the hallway.

Cam pulled at River's shirt. "Come on."

The noise from the man formed into words.

"Get out," he said, a rasping command.

"Who are you?" River said.

Cam pulled again, but River didn't budge, he wouldn't until it made sense.

It won't make sense. We need to go.

"Get out!" the man bellowed. "Get out of my house!"

The man took two jerky steps forward, dark eyes reflecting the glowing lights overhead.

Cam's hands and feet went numb.

"River!" she cried, really pulling now as the man took several rapid steps, coming straight at them down the hallway.

CHAPTER 15

What is happening?

The man shouldn't be a threat. With his well-fitted suit and trim hair, he looked like a guest at the resort—a businessman, someone who worked in finance and raked in money, bought fancy cars and smoked cigars. Why would a man like that attack them, with no apparent reason?

If he was sick, he might need help.

What if whatever had happened to everyone else was happening to this man, some illness, and now they would catch it?

Logic urged River to stand his ground. The man didn't carry a weapon, he was barefoot, and even though he was large, he moved with an awkward, erratic gait.

When the man came at them, however, a nameless dread surged through his chest. He turned and fled with Cam. The thump of bare feet on carpet followed behind, not fast but steady. River slammed the double doors of the kitchen shut and shoved a prep table in front, then grasped Cam's hand and kept moving. The man smashed through the doors, sending the table skittering across the kitchen floor. The double doors swung into the walls on either side as the man punched through.

"Get out of my house!" he thundered.

Up ahead, Trip and Liza emerged from the doors of the lobby, Trip carrying a laptop and Liza the hotspot device.

"Go!" Cam yelled, waving her hands to urge them away.

Startled understanding dawned on Liza's face, but Trip stood immobilized, eyes wide, knuckles white as his grip tightened on the computer.

Seeing Trip, the man slowed.

"You," he said, staring at him, his mouth slanting into a sneer. "You make me sick. Come here. I'll teach you a lesson."

Trip stood frozen, feet pinned to the floor. Cam and Liza ran ahead, and River grabbed Trip's arm, dragging him toward their room, which was at least another fifty feet away and up the stairs.

The man marched forward with machine-like determination.

River hadn't seen the man's face distinctly before. The light had been strange in the hallway, and he hadn't been able to discern his looks, but now he saw him clearly. He was older, probably in his fifties, with close-cropped iron-gray hair.

Anger curdled his features.

Liza fumbled with the lock.

"Open the door!" Cam's fingers twitched like she was ready to grab the key.

"I'm trying!"

Liza frantically jammed the keycard in and tried to force the door handle to turn. It wouldn't budge.

The man was only a few yards away, no longer in a hurry. He was focused solely on Trip.

"What's happening?" Trip whispered. "What is that?"

Cam snatched the key from Liza and tried it herself, her trembling hands moving deliberately.

The lock clicked.

The four of them fell into the room. Before they could close the door, the man reached around it, seizing Trip by his shirt and slamming his face into the edge of the door. Blood dripped from Trip's nose, speckling a pattern on his shirt. River pried the fist from Trip's clothes, but once the man's hold dropped from Trip, he clasped onto River. River strained away, his feet sliding along the carpet as the man's pressure against the door shoved him back.

"Help!"

Cam and Liza rushed to hold the door as well, but the man's arm blocked it from closing.

"Trip, help us!" Liza shouted.

Trip fell, dazed, on the edge of the bed. He shook his head as if denying what was happening right in front of him.

The man didn't seem to care that his arm was crushed in the door. River tried to force it through the opening. The material of the man's sleeve was smooth, with a high, silky sheen, the sort of suit a wealthy man would wear. Under that, however, his flesh slipped in and out of River's grasp as if the buttoned-down shirt and jacket were full of snakes rather than a man's arm. River gritted his teeth and, ignoring the twist of muscle and flesh encased in the fabric, shoved hard. With a violent tug he was pulled partway out the door. He came face-to-face with shallow gray eyes.

In a coarse whisper mingled with the stink of expensive cologne and whiskey, the man said, "I know what you do. You're disgusting."

River recoiled and shoved the man back. Clear of the door, he slammed it shut and secured the door guard. He dragged a chair to brace it under the lever and then backed away.

The lever rattled, frenzied, for a solid minute. There was a moment of silence, and then a fist pounded on the door.

Bang bang bang.

Liza and Cam pressed against the far wall. Trip, pasty, sweating, and still bleeding, kept his eyes fixed on the door. In short, rhythmic bursts—*bang bang bang*—the battering continued. Again it stopped for a moment, and again it resumed, making them all jump at the renewal of wordless fury.

"What is going on?" Liza kept her voice low, as if they could hide from the man by whispering.

"I don't know," River said.

"It's the guy from the woods," Cam said. "He had mud on his feet."

Liza bit her lip. "How did he get here? He couldn't have followed us, there's no other boat. He sure as hell didn't swim."

"He was yelling, 'Get out of my house,'" Cam said. "What's that supposed to mean? Does he live here?"

The banging stopped.

They held still for the space of a breath, waiting for it to begin again, but it didn't.

River drew the curtains across the window. The glider screeched and they started at the noise.

"Do you think he'll try to get in through the window?" Cam asked.

"We're on the second floor," River said.

When he checked the locks on the window, a small spider, about the size of a pinky nail, slipped through a crack in the nearby sliding doors that led to the balcony. River brushed it aside, but another appeared where it had been, and then another, until a line of them streamed from the crevice and clustered on the carpet. River stomped the pile, but then hundreds rushed in at once, streaming and scurrying over one another, their legs and bodies tangling.

"The hell . . ." River squashed as many as he could, but the numbers overwhelmed him, and he backed away while the others screamed behind him. Spiders swarmed his boots even as his soles grew slick with the white-green mess of crushed bodies.

Dead spiders splotched the carpet, joined by more darting over them. They moved from the floor and climbed the walls until black specks, ceaselessly crawling in every direction, overlaid the walls.

Trip rose from the bed and pressed himself against the far wall as if he could go through it, not fighting the invasion but simply trying to get away. River, Cam, and Liza used whatever they could find to fight off the inundation—magazines, the room-service menu, the flat bottom of a wastebasket. River threw back the curtains to the sliding doors to find spiders inches deep against the glass.

"We have to go," River said. "Now."

There were too many. They didn't bite, didn't attack, they simply took over. They infested the beds, the open suitcases, the white down comforters and fluffy pillows now carpeted with slithering legs. Spiders dripped over the sides of a water glass next to the bed. A pillowcase writhed and rippled like it was alive. The spiders descended from an overhead light on silk, like squadrons of insect parachuters.

Liza screeched as they fell in her hair. Cam swatted at them with a sweatshirt coiled around her hand.

River touched his neck at the first tickle and his fingers pinched a spider. The legs wriggled against his skin. He tossed its still-squirming body aside with an inarticulate noise, then brushed wildly at his shoulders and arms as spiders fell on his back and made their way down his shirt. They dropped through the vents.

"We can't leave. That guy's still out there," Liza said.

"Well, we can't stay here!" Cam yelled, sweeping her arm above her head to bat the spiders away as they dropped from above.

With no further discussion, they dashed for the door, but Trip still wasn't moving. River grabbed him and hauled him out. The man was gone, the hallway empty. They headed for the stairs, seeking higher ground, the whole while frantically wiping their hands down their arms, through their hair, under their clothes, a trail of spiders dropping behind them. There was no sign of the man, but with every turn of the stairway River was prepared to run into him. At this point, he was prepared to run into anything.

"Liza, you have the master key?"

"Yeah."

She also carried the laptop and hotspot, and River was relieved someone had thought of that. It was their only way out. What was wrong with this place?

They climbed to the third, highest floor, and tried the card at the first room they came to. River went to the window and looked down at the steps leading to the Springs. They were covered in spiders, a carpet of them. Lit from underwater, the pool and waterfall were speckled black. Rocks in the center of the pool had become a wriggling archipelago of spiders; they crawled over one another, floating from rock to rock. River pulled off his hoodie, scratching at his arms. He itched every-where, and he wanted nothing more than to remove every piece of clothing and shower in scalding water.

River wasn't bothered by spiders. He'd once read some-where that there were three million spiders on the planet for every human being, and that was fine. They kept to themselves and so did he. At least, they usually kept to themselves. He'd never heard of them swarming like army ants, clogging vents, or raining from the sky. A shiver ran down his back, thinking about the way the legs had scrabbled on his neck.

"They're on me!" Trip tugged at his clothes. He shed his blood-spattered shirt and threw it across the room. "They're all over me!"

Blood seeped from his nose, and the cut on his forehead had reopened.

River understood how Trip felt, but he wasn't about to strip naked in a panic. Trip was bleeding, and breathing too fast. In a minute he'd start hyperventilating. Judging by Cam's and Liza's expressions and nervous hands over their own clothes, plus his own unease, Trip's panic was becoming contagious.

"It's okay," River said. It was a hollow expression. Nothing was okay, but he didn't know what else to say. "We're okay, Trip. We're safe." They were in another suite, and River walked through the bedroom to the bathroom and found Trip a washcloth. Trip pressed it to his nose.

"Maybe we're safe for now," Cam grumbled. "Until the next crazy thing happens."

River glanced at her, a silent condemnation. She wasn't helping.

"That was real, right?" Trip asked. He dropped the bloody washcloth, dug his pill bottle from the pocket where he'd stuffed it, and swallowed one. "Please tell me I didn't just imagine that."

"It was real," Liza said.

"Who was that guy?" River looked to Liza, hoping she had some idea. She was the only one who'd been to the resort before.

The spiders were a freak of nature, but that guy had been ready to attack them. He must be employed by the show, and he'd lost his mind out here.

"I don't know." She seemed as confused as he felt.

"I know," Trip said.

He ran a hand over the back of his neck, his movements fitful and nervous, still searching for spiders. He fell silent again.

"Well?" Liza said.

"Only it doesn't make sense." Trip looked to River for help.

"That's okay," River said. "It doesn't have to make sense. But you need to tell us who that man is."

"He's my dad."

"Okay . . ." River drew out the word, his mind racing through a kaleidoscope of scenarios in seconds. Trip's dad had followed him out here in secret? And for some reason the man was a violent criminal out to murder Trip and his three friends?

"You don't get it, though. It's *not* my dad."

Cam sighed. "Make more sense, Trip."

"I used to have a nightmare about him. He kicked me out when I was fourteen. I mean, I went to live with my mom, it wasn't the end of the world, but it was still a bad scene. He yelled a lot, said I made him sick, that he didn't have a son anymore, all that stuff. I used to have nightmares about that day, all the time, and it was *just like this*. That man is my dad, but . . . I don't know." Trip's voice caught in his throat. "It's not him."

"You're right," Liza said. "None of that makes sense."

"It's hard to describe," Trip said. "Like, my dad's not really that tall, you know? He's only that tall in my memories of that day. Does that make sense?"

"No," River said.

"Wait a second," Cam said. "His face. I couldn't really see it until we ran into you."

River shook his head, remembering his own impression of the man's face, that it seemed to shift like melting wax, and had only coalesced when they'd found Trip. Surely that was simply a trick of the light, though. What Trip was saying was impossible.

"Trip, the man we saw—you're saying you made him up?" Liza said.

"That's exactly what I'm saying. It's like that guy stepped out of my head, straight out of my fourteen-year-old self's nightmares. And the . . ." He shuddered violently. "The spiders, too."

"What about the spiders?" River felt like he was struggling to keep up.

"I hate spiders. Remember? I told you back in the woods."

Cam's head jerked up. "The dog."

River leaned away, his mouth going dry. "No."

Cam nodded, pointing at him like an accusation. "River, when we talked on the shore, you told me you were afraid of dogs."

"And you told me you're afraid of earthquakes. So now you think you *trigger* earthquakes? You realize how ridiculous that sounds?"

Instead of recognizing her theory as nonsense, Cam's eyes widened as if the truth was only now dawning on her. "That's right. The earthquakes, too."

Trip had been sitting on the couch, his shoulders slumped, exhausted by terror and living nightmares. Now his gaze sharpened. "It's the VR. It must be."

A solution had presented itself—a solution that fit into his world of apps and programs and ThreeDz. River swallowed his irritation. In a strained, steady voice he said, "What are you talking about?"

"The virtual reality. We got those injections of ions, and now our brains are basically creating a simulation, making us experience our fears."

"I didn't *imagine* any of this," River said, feeling the first prickles of anger. "It's not in my head."

"But the thing is, you wouldn't even know. That's the point of true virtual reality: to make a simulated experience *feel* real. Without visors or something separating you from the experience, you wouldn't know the difference between what you think is there and what isn't."

"You're saying that's possible?" Liza said.

"Sure. We've somehow entered a virtual reality that's so sophisticated, we don't even know we're in it. Except . . ." He made an incoherent noise and dropped his head into his hands. "Except somehow we're sharing the *same* virtual reality. That can't be possible."

"We were injected with the same ions," Liza said. "What if the ions are running a program, giving us the same experience?"

River folded his arms, then realized he looked defensive and dropped them. "That man was real. The dog, the spiders, the earthquakes. We were all there. I know the difference between what's real and what's not."

"If this really is virtual reality," Liza said, ignoring River, "who's controlling it?"

"Maybe we are," Cam said. "These are our fears, they came from our minds. Both earthquakes happened when I was feeling scared. That can't be a coincidence."

"Great," Liza said. "If we're controlling it, then we can go ahead and *unthink* the scary things, and we're all set."

"I say we start with the spiders," Cam added.

"Cam," River said. "We've all felt scared and anxious this whole time. That doesn't prove anything."

Cam tilted her head. "Liza, you're a producer. Did you have the same injection we did that connected us to the VR?"

Liza blinked. "Sure, I was part of the show. We wanted the audience to be able to follow me on the Skyms too."

Cam worked through the problem. "Why haven't we seen anything that might be a fear of yours?"

"I don't know. I don't have any phobias, really." Liza thought for a moment. "Although I'm not too keen on drowning."

"Did something happen when you were a kid? You almost drown or something?" Trip asked.

"No. And I'm a pretty good swimmer. It just seems like a terrifying way to die. But all I have to do is stay out of the ocean and nothing can happen. Nothing like the nightmares you guys are cooking up."

A lone spider scurried across the floor. Cam crushed it with her shoe. "You couldn't be afraid of teddy bears, Trip?"

"You're all talking about this as if Trip's right," River said. "But there's no way that dog was a simulation. It almost mauled me, for God's sake."

Trip shook his head, calmer now that he had a technical problem to solve. Either that or his pill was working. "It can't be real, though. That's not how any of this works. It's *virtual* reality. It must be connected to our entire limbic system, all of our senses. That's what makes it feel so real."

Liza slipped the master key into her back pocket. "Whatever it is, I'm not hiding out in this room forever. That guy is still out there. I want to search the rooms some more. I guarantee a few of the guys on the crew had concealed carry. I'm going to get me a gun."

"We shouldn't split up," River said.

Cam sat next to Trip. The bleeding from his nose had stopped, but he looked like he was in pain. "I don't want to go out there. We're better off staying put and figuring out the internet. We'll get help."

"It'll take time for anyone to get to us, and I'll feel better if while we wait I have something to defend myself with." Liza said. "You guys stay. I'll go by myself."

"It's not safe out there," River said.

"I'll feel safer with a gun. Come if you want, but I'm going."

She looked determined and pissed off. If Liza thought there were weapons on the premises, he wasn't sure he wanted to pass up a chance to have one either. Anyway, the room they were in had only one exit and was beginning to feel like a trap.

"Fine, let's go, but make it quick." He shook out his hoodie for spiders and put it back on. He pointed to the laptop and hotspot on the bed. "See what you can do with those. And lock the door behind us. Back in ten."

CHAPTER 16

Once River and Liza left, Cam bolted the door and closed the blinds while Trip fiddled with the hotspot.

She wanted a shower. Her skin crawled as if there were spiders *under* her skin, and she kept running her palms over her arms, brushing away creatures that weren't really there. Trip took two more plane pills. He shuddered every now and then as if the memory of the spiders dipped into his consciousness every minute or two.

The Springs remained littered with black bodies, but they'd thinned some. The squirming mass had diminished, like it was mostly the dead that had been left behind, but it was hard to tell from the third floor.

Emerging from the shower, feeling almost human, wrapped in a fluffy white robe from the closet, Cam found Trip on the couch searching the laptop.

"Do we have internet?" she asked.

The thought sent a surge of hope through her. Up to that point, nothing had worked out: not the trailer, not the resort. The internet, though. That would provide answers, and everything would be okay. They'd find out what had happened, why they'd been abandoned, and someone would rescue them. Finally.

"About to," Trip said. "I've got the hotspot running."

Cam sat next to Trip and peered at the screen. He typed in commands she didn't recognize, and then a browser popped up.

"Got it!" He considered for a moment. "So, what do you think? Text the police?"

"Yes, but first hashtag the show, and tell the audience to call the police too. May as well get the attention of millions of people at once."

Trip grinned and then brought up the website. The glowing screen, the names and words that appeared, it was comforting. It meant the world was normal and right, and now they could communicate. She could contact Benji, who must be worried.

Trip signed into his account and started composing a post, starting with *Help!*

"Wait," Cam said, something nagging at her. "Go back to the home page for a second."

Cam scrutinized the text as he scrolled up. She took the computer from him and, typing furiously, checked three other sites, then the major news outlets. The more she searched, the sicker she felt. "Nothing's updating," she said, handing the laptop back.

Trip examined the same information. The screen became a blur as Trip jumped from site to site, scrolling further and further back.

"You're right," he said. "It's like no one is online."

"Like they're gone." Even as she spoke, she struggled to wrap her mind around what her words meant.

"No, they can't be gone. It's a glitch. What if the electrical grid collapsed? There'd be a disaster, and no way to post about it."

"Electricity failing *everywhere*? And don't forget about here. We have electricity."

"But . . . it's solar, generated at the resort."

"What should we do? Should we still post something?"

"We have to try."

Trip gnawed a fingernail, his other hand hovering over the keyboard, poised to type but at a loss for which direction to go. Finally his fingers settled on the keys.

> **Help. Trapped on #CutOff. In danger. Send help.**

He hit send, and they saw the message blink into view at the top of his feed. He posted the same message on every platform they could think of, and then they sent e-mails and texts. They tried video calls, first Trip's mom and Cam's Aunt Pam, before working their way down to Trip's drug-dealing cousin Kevin and Aubrey Mitchell, who Cam knew from the fifth-grade after-school program at the YWCA. Nobody answered.

So they waited.

Cam breathed out slowly, willing her shoulders to stop tightening, but it was as if her body was turning to hardened concrete, trapping air in her lungs and turning her muscles to stone.

We're going to die here.

She knew it with undeniable clarity.

Maybe we're already dead.

Her body shook. She tried to settle down, but nothing seemed to work.

"Cam," Trip said, alarm coloring his voice.

She really couldn't breathe. How was she supposed to breathe if her lungs were solid rock? The trembling wouldn't stop.

"I can't stop shaking," she said.

"It's not you, it's an earthquake," Trip said. "Hang on."

So the world was reeling under her. It was happening again.

Trip stood, using an end table to steady himself.

You're not supposed to move around during an earthquake, Trip, she thought, but she couldn't get the words out.

He trotted unsteadily to the bathroom and filled a glass with water, then found his bottle of pills. He held one out for Cam.

She shook her head.

"It's fine," he said. She looked at him through watery eyes and he nodded. "Go on."

He was so confident the drug would help, and honestly, she'd swallow daggers at this point if it would stop the shaking. A lamp tipped over and smashed on the floor. The building seemed to tilt sideways as if its beams were noodles, and then it righted itself again. It was like being in a ship on a stormy sea. She meant to tell Trip that, to show him she could make a little joke in the midst of all this madness, but instead a glass-framed picture crashed from the wall and she screamed.

The fear was something tangible, heavy as a boulder, and it

was growing inside her, feeding on itself, and once it grew big enough, it would crush her.

She took the pill from Trip and closed her eyes. They moved to the floor and huddled together, holding each other, until, after an eternity, the shaking stopped.

Trip puffed out a breath, his arms loosening around her, making her realize for the first time how tightly they'd been hugging.

"See?" he said. "It worked. Plane pills to the rescue."

"Maybe it would have stopped anyway, pills or not. I mean, earthquakes don't go on forever. You have to believe I started the earthquake to begin with if you think it stopped because of me. That's a lot of guesses."

"I can't think of anything else that makes sense, or explains what's been happening."

"What if it happens again?" Cam said. "If I can't stop panicking, an earthquake—my own custom-made earthquake— might go on for hours. Or forever. If that's how this works, I could destroy the world."

"We'll figure it out," Trip said. "It'll be okay."

There was a bang on the door and they both jumped.

"It's me," River said.

Trip peered through the peephole before opening the door.

River entered quickly and placed a handgun and some clothes on the coffee table.

"Where's Liza?" Cam asked.

"We found a couple of guns and she wanted to keep searching the luggage, but I had to check on you guys after that earthquake. Are you okay?" His warm hand settled on her arm, and concern filled his eyes. She offered a smile, hoping it didn't look as shaky as it felt.

Maybe Trip was right, that their own mental states were causing this nightmare, and that the pills in some way worked against it. The tightness in her chest had released, and breathing came a bit easier. But a sense of unease lingered, and she couldn't shake it. Nothing had changed, nothing was solved. They were still screwed, and Trip's plane pills wouldn't fix that.

"We're okay," Trip said. "But look, you need to see this." He showed River the websites and explained what they'd found. Which was an unnerving lot of nothing.

"It's a glitch, a bug," River said, his brow furrowed. "It's specific to this place. You don't actually believe there's no one out there?"

Trip shrugged. "Or it's a problem with our internet connection, I don't know. But I was thinking: if all this strangeness stems from us, and we're the ones causing the problem, I bet we can stop it. When that earthquake started, I gave Cam one of my pills. Then . . . no more earthquake."

River turned to her. "Cam, you took one of those things?"

"I thought it might help. I didn't—"

"You didn't what? Care that it might mess you up more?"

Cam inclined away from him, stung. "Mess me up *more?* What's that supposed to mean?"

"It's not like she's taking them to get high," Trip said. "It's a legitimate treatment."

"Cam, you're letting Trip rub off on you. Drugs won't fix

your problems. Come on, I thought you were smarter than that."

Trip reared back. "Excuse me?"

"I was scared." Cam chewed the inside of her cheek. "And you heard what Trip said. The earthquake stopped."

"I'm not deaf. But what I *heard* was a bunch of nonsense about you being able to control earthquakes. Really, you can't believe that."

"I don't control anything, and I have no idea what to believe. None of us understands what's happening."

"Maybe not, but I'm beginning to understand how screwed up you are if you're willing to believe Trip's bull. At least Liza has her shit together and gets things done without whining about it."

"Why are you acting like this?"

"Like what, a reasonable human being? Sorry, I don't happen to believe Trip has magic power to summon up his old man any more than I think you can call up earthquakes whenever you get jumpy." He knelt next to her, his face softening, apologetic. "Listen, I just want you to be strong."

"I am strong," she said, not feeling strong at all.

He tilted his head. "Come on, Cam. How can you be strong when you're so needy? It's not strength to depend on drugs to get by."

"I didn't say I couldn't get by."

He took her hand and searched her eyes as if he were looking for something and not finding it. "I need someone who knows what she wants. Someone strong and capable, not gullible and dependent. I mean, do you think you can pull it together?" He stroked her hand gently. "Do it for me. I like you, Cam. I like you a lot, but if this is who you are, it's never going to work. Promise me, okay? Promise you'll try to do better."

"I guess I can . . . I don't really—"

"Hey, man, you need to back off." Trip watched them from the other end of the bed, his brow creased.

"Stay out of it, Trip. This is between me and Cam."

"Cam, are you okay?" Trip asked.

No, she wasn't okay. She was confused. They were abandoned in the wilderness, holed up in a hotel full of dead spiders and rotten food. In the space of a few hours, they'd dealt with earthquakes, a homicidal phantom father, and spiders crawling under their clothes. How was she supposed to react?

But what if River was right? God, she'd been so scared of everything, she probably *was* pathetic. She needed to hold it together. How was she going to take care of Benji if she fell apart when things went sideways? She had to be strong for him, if for nobody else. Her mom had never managed it, always needing a guy like Brad around to pay the bills, fix her car, make her feel like she had any worth. Cam refused to be like that. She wasn't like that.

Was she?

Trip tapped River's shoulder. "Give her a minute."

River batted his hand away. "I said, stay out of it."

Cam jumped at the abrupt gesture, and Trip tried again. "I'm not kidding—lay off."

River spun around, nose to nose with Trip, and shoved him backwards. "How about *you* lay off."

"What are you doing?" Cam said, alarmed, but they ignored her.

"What the hell, man?" Trip said.

"Do we have a problem?"

"No problem. I just don't get why you're giving her such a hard time."

"Cam," River said, still facing Trip, throwing the words over his shoulder, "what do you think? Am I giving you a hard time?"

"Both of you, please, stop it."

River turned back to her, his expression unreadable, his gaze flickering over her face. "It's not enough I'm risking my life keeping us safe? It'd be a whole lot easier if I didn't have to worry about you, and now you can't even defend me?"

"Defend you to who? Trip?"

Before she knew what was happening, he grasped her upper arm and hauled her over to the window. He picked up the gun, showing it to her.

"Take a minute to appreciate what I've been doing to protect you." The barrel of the gun slanted toward her temple. She flinched away and he shook his head, bewildered. "What, now you're afraid of me? You think I'm going to shoot you? Don't be stupid."

His grip on her arm tightened, his fingers digging into her skin through the thick robe. The room was too bright, the one lamp still standing after the earthquake burning light throughout, but somehow darkness was closing in on her, creeping up on the periphery of her vision. Vaguely she heard Trip yelling, pulling River away from her. His hold on her arm released and she fell to the floor, but now Trip and River were really shoving each other, ready to throw punches. That rush of noise filled her head again. A crescendo of whispers, the voices in the trees. She wanted to cover her ears, block it out, hide from the clamor in her head. It drowned out what Trip was saying to her. She tried hard to concentrate on his voice, but her arm hurt and the noise had the booming rush of a waterfall. Trip was shouting, insistent, pleading for her attention as River shoved him into the wall.

"Stop it!" she screamed, not sure if she was yelling at Trip and River or at the endlessly muttering trees.

River punched Trip in the stomach and he doubled over. Cam hurried to him, helping him up while River raged behind her, hurling a volley of abuse. She was untrustworthy, wasn't loyal, she was stupid and selfish and worthless, she never sided with him, and *why*, for God's sake, *why* was she always scared of everything all the time, it was so *stupid*, just like her, *stupid stupid stupid*—

Trip looked her in the eyes, his palm cupping her face, hushing the earsplitting racket. "Cam, listen to me. It's not River. It's like that thing attacking us wasn't my dad. My real dad's back in Arizona, and he's not the greatest, but he wouldn't try to kill me. *That's not River.*"

What was Trip talking about? That was River—of course it was. Part of her had always known he was just like all the others. They were all the same in the end. They wanted to control you, tell you what to do, and they were never happy, always insecure, needing constant reassurance, and if they didn't get it, they'd blow up and blame you for everything. And when they got mad, well, that was it. It was never their fault, either, it was yours, always yours—

The door burst open, and Liza entered, and behind her River, and now there were two Rivers in the room, one of them wild, storming and cursing, the other wide-eyed, struggling to put together pieces of a puzzle that wouldn't fit. Then the wild River lunged for her, rage burning in his eyes, and while the pieces still weren't fitting together for him, that was enough to propel River—the real River—into motion. He seized the attacking boy by the back of the collar and hauled him away from her. For an insane moment the two Rivers grappled. The River with the gun was thrown against the wall, his face red with fury.

"He has a gun!" Liza shouted.

Trip held a pill in his palm. "Here, Cam. Take it."

This really was all her fault, though. She'd started it by taking the thing to begin with, it was her fault. She'd known River didn't want her to.

"Please. Chew it up, it'll work faster."

The pill bottle dropped to the floor with a clatter. The angry River's hand scooped it up, his face contorted in a sneer.

"How about I do you both a favor?" he said, heading for the bathroom. In one swift motion he uncapped the lid and tipped the bottle into the sink.

"No!" Trip yelled.

The other River tackled him, but it was too late. The pills were gone, disintegrating in pooled water. All that was left was the one in Cam's hand. She pinched it in her fingers.

She expected it to taste bitter, like an aspirin, but when she ground it between her teeth, it was flavorless and gritty. She clenched her eyes tight and pressed her palms to her ears, blocking out the uproar and the violence and the whole rest of the disordered world.

CHAPTER 17

River and Liza rode out the earthquake in a room on the second floor. When it stopped, they started making their way back to the room, worried about the others, but then Liza remembered that Jason, the survival-training expert, kept cans of pepper spray for when he worked in the wilderness.

"Good for bears and murderers," she said, pocketing the still-sealed spray.

They figured it'd be worth having, since they'd had no luck finding a gun.

They didn't hear the shouts until they stepped from the stairwell on the far end of the third floor. There was a crash, like a chair being thrown into a wall, followed by a scream.

"Cam," River said, launching into a run once Liza passed the key to him.

They entered to find chaos. Tables overturned, a picture shattered on the floor, lamps tipped over. River had expected to find Trip's dad causing the commotion, but he didn't see him. There was someone else, someone wearing the same outfit as River. The exact same outfit, in fact, right down to the brand-new blue hoodie with the Cedar Springs patch on the chest.

Whoever he was, he was on a rampage, calling both Trip and Cam names, hateful slurs that made River recoil.

The guy lunged for Cam, who'd made herself as small as possible on the floor, Trip hovering over her, speaking in her ear. River bounded forward and spun the guy around, and found himself looking into his own face.

Before he could process what he was seeing, the guy launched a wild swing. River ducked and then bulled into him, shoving him against the sliding glass door.

The guy looked exactly like him. He searched for some difference, some evidence it was only a resemblance, but the sole difference between them was that River hardly recognized his own face so twisted with fury. The tendons of the guy's neck corded under River's pressing hands, and a guttural yell directed at Cam roared from him.

"You bitch!"

That word, directed at Cam, in a voice that sounded just like his—it made him feel ill.

The guy thrust River away and punched, knocking his head back.

Liza yelled from behind. "He's got a gun!"

River grasped the guy's wrist as the gun veered toward his head, and they grappled in a tug-of-war for the weapon. The guy's eyes were so *angry*, seething with a gleeful rage that only wanted to hurt. His mouth twisted in a mocking, ugly laugh, but the sound that came out wasn't a laugh at all. It was a growl, like a feral dog.

River staggered back, clutching the arm that held the gun until he'd gained control, but his hand shook. Was he supposed to pull the trigger and shoot this person who looked exactly like him? He swallowed. Even given the danger, he didn't think he could do it.

As if the guy was reading his mind, a sneering grin appeared on his face. He caught River's wrist and forced it in an arc until it pressed against not River's temple, but his own, as if he was going to shoot himself. He settled his finger on the trigger, overlapping River's, and the pressure built as he squeezed, the smile unwavering.

River's eardrums rang with the echo of a gunshot at the same time as his fist flew toward the guy's face, but instead of hitting him, it smashed into the glass door. Cracks spread through it like a web.

The guy had vanished.

He'd simply disappeared. A second ago they'd been fighting, and now there was no gun, no guy, nothing to indicate he'd existed except a wrecked room, the oily, acrid smell of gunfire, and Liza pointing a canister of pepper spray straight at the vacant space where he'd been. It wouldn't have helped much. She'd neglected to unseal it.

Pain shot up River's arm. His knuckles were lacerated, a ribbon of red dripping down to his wrist. His blood smeared the broken glass. He clutched his hand under his arm and swallowed a groan.

"What . . . ?" he said, but couldn't say more. The whole thing had lasted less than a minute.

And his hand *hurt*. He bit back a curse.

Liza brought over a first-aid kit. "Let me look at that. Can you bend your fingers?" Her voice was muffled in his still-ringing ears. He made a fist, pulling the torn skin. Liza nodded. "Probably nothing broken." She opened antiseptic and bandages and gestured for him to sit down. Her shaky hands slipped on the foil wrappers, but she worked quickly, embodying a return to calmness that he didn't feel.

"Cam," Liza said, wiping away the blood. "Was that you?"

Cam nodded, but it was like she wasn't really there. She was too distraught, unable to look at him.

"What are you talking about?" he said.

"Trip's theory about our fears. She manifested that guy. She's afraid that's you," Liza said, as if it was obvious. As if that made any sense at all.

"Cam's not afraid of me."

"I meant she's afraid that *could* be you. It's what Trip was talking about. The things we're afraid of are coming true. She's afraid that, deep down, you're a raging asshole."

He brushed off the rest of Liza's bandaging. "What's going on, Cam? Did that guy really appear because of you? Because you're afraid of me?"

Cam shook her head miserably. "That wasn't about you. Not really."

"How was that not about me? He looked just like me."

River tried to absorb the knowledge that not only had some version of him shown up and attacked everyone, but that Cam was, at least in some sense, *afraid* of him, no matter what she said. Whatever had happened in her past meant she didn't trust him, and there was nothing he could do about it. If he brought it up, she would tell him she did trust him, and her attempts to convince him would only make him feel worse.

He surveyed the trashed room.

They were trapped in a creepy-ass funhouse, where people could appear and then vanish out of nowhere, where things were trying to kill them. He needed to think.

"Listen," he said. "We should take precautions. We'll keep the door locked, and we'll stick together from now on. That . . . thing, whatever or whoever it was, could return. Or Trip's fake dad."

Trip was on the floor with Cam, his arm around her.

River crouched beside her. "Why don't you get some rest? We'll sort it out, it'll be okay." His assurances were more hopeful than true.

"You always say that," Cam said with a dry smile. "Maybe *okay* doesn't mean what you think."

He smiled in return, but when he touched her arm, she flinched away. He drew back his hand and suddenly realized his head was pounding.

"Give me a minute. I need to . . ." What did he need to do? He needed to get away. Be alone, splash some cold water on his face, and try to work through this mess. "I'll be right back."

He headed to the bathroom, but Trip followed. He shut the door behind them and sat on the toilet-seat lid.

"I don't feel like talking, Trip."

"You're white as these towels."

River ran the tap as cold as it would go, then leaned over the sink, cupping the water in his palms.

Trip continued. "We can't help what we're afraid of, you know."

River rubbed his hands across his eyes, the image of that version of himself bringing a gun to his own temple flashing through his mind. "I know that. But I can't make it better. I can't fix this."

"You don't have to fix anything. You can't, anyway. That's not how people work, we don't fix them. If we care about someone, we just have to be there for them."

River raked wet hands into his hair, head bent low over the rushing water. "I can't think straight right now. I'm going to take a shower. It'll clear my head." He looked at Trip, who simply sat there. "I'd rather do it alone, if it's all the same to you."

"Okay. But listen, we got on the internet earlier, before you —I mean, before that other . . ." He sighed and tried again. "Before that guy showed up. There was nobody there. I don't know what it means, but I'm worried. Either we have no way to communicate with anyone, or there's no one there."

Enigmas kept popping up a whole lot faster than they were being resolved.

"How can there be no one there?" River said wearily.

Trip shrugged, at a loss.

"Are you okay?" River said. "That . . . thing. It was calling you names. You know I wouldn't use those words, with Cam or with you. You know that, right?"

"Come on, man. I didn't need to see that thing disappear to know it wasn't really you. I can usually tell what people are capable of, and I knew the minute stuff went sideways."

River's eyes stung. With everything going on, he hadn't realized how much he'd needed Trip's reassurance. If Trip and Cam thought he was capable of that . . .

God, how self-absorbed was he? They're the ones who were violently attacked, and he was the one losing it because maybe they thought, for just a minute, that *thing* really was him.

River cleared his throat, trying to keep it together. "It did disappear. You saw that too?"

"I saw. You didn't imagine it."

What were the rules to this place? If Cam and Trip could both make a real, physical person appear, what else could one of them conjure? What if it was something they weren't able to fight, like a virus or a nuclear bomb?

"I won't be long," River said. "Come get me if anything else happens."

Trip nodded and gave River a quick squeeze of his shoulder before leaving.

River left the gift-shop clothes in a pile on the floor and stepped into the shower. He made it hot enough to scald, then leaned his forehead against the tiles and let the piercing stream of water pummel his back. When he came out again, he stood in front of the mirror. It had steamed over, but he figured he didn't much want to see himself right now anyway. His reflection only made him think about seeing his face mirrored in the webbed shards of the shattered glass door.

He got dressed, the sullen throb still pulsing in his hand.

He didn't want to leave the bedroom and face any of them. Cam didn't trust him, and now that her fear had been play-acted in front of everyone, she wouldn't want anything to do with him. And why should she? He was hiding from them, too worried that if he actually had to deal with the world, he'd have to deal with everything else in an avalanche—what happened to his parents, for one. They were gone, and he'd been running ever since.

The thought mumbled through his head: *This is what you do.*

He ran away. He left. He left before anyone could leave him.

She was right not to trust him. Maybe he wouldn't hurt anyone, but she deserved better than him.

It was quiet behind the bedroom door.

They were most likely asleep on the couches. After what they'd been through, they needed the rest. He should at least talk to Cam, however. He clung to Trip's words, a counterpoint to his own damaged instinct that told him to run away. Like Trip said, the important thing was to simply be there.

He entered the sitting room, toweling his hair, and froze. The room was empty.

Their Skyms were there. With nothing to record, they'd settled on the carpet. How could the Skyms be there when they weren't? They wouldn't have left without telling him. And anyway, the Skyms would have followed them out.

He went into the hallway. The nearby rooms were empty as

well. He knocked on the doors, and then used the key to open every room on the third floor.

He went through the lounge, then headed to the Springs, the desiccated bodies of dead spiders crunching like peanut shells under his heels. He made it as far as the steps to the pool before live spiders started dropping from the trees to his shoulders. Looking up, he saw that the branches were tangled in drawn-out webs, and spiders dangled from strands of silk.

There was no way he'd find them outside by the spider-infested pool. So why had he come out here?

Because they weren't inside, that's why. He hadn't found them anywhere inside.

And now they weren't outside.

They wouldn't have ditched him, he knew that. They wouldn't have abandoned him.

How do you know? his mind said. Maybe they were angry, or disturbed by the River doppelgänger tearing their room apart. *It makes sense.*

He pushed the thought from his mind.

In any case, there was nowhere to go. They were on an island.

Something had happened to them.

Trip had said there'd been no one on the internet when they'd searched, that they hadn't found anyone in the outside world. He'd only been speculating, and his theory made no sense, but . . . if Trip was right and there was no one out there, and there was no one here either, that meant—

Stop it.

They *had* to be somewhere. Just like the whole world couldn't disappear overnight, neither could Cam and Trip and Liza disappear in the time it took to take a shower. They were roaming around and he'd missed them, that was all.

"Cam!" he called. "Trip! Liza!" Hearing the sharp, glassy edge of panic in his own voice was worse than the deathly silence.

His Skym bobbed overhead, its motor buzzing, its lens zooming in on his face. It had been following him the whole time. It lingered relentlessly, staring at him, empty and constant. Its light blinked yellow. Trip had been diligent about the cameras, dutifully carrying the batteries and keeping them charged, when River would have just as soon let them die. It should die. He should leave its light to turn red and let it die wherever it landed. He resolved to do just that, but then instead, on an impulse, he lifted it out of the air and hurled it against the wall, then stomped on it with the heel of his boot until the lens cracked and the blinking light went dark.

He was over the cameras, over the pretense that anyone was actually watching, and especially over the pervasive, intrusive sensation that everyone really *was* watching. Standing alone before the last door in the last hallway, he watched with tight eyes as the pieces of the Skym continued to whir and buzz on the floor, driven by its algorithmic imperative, even as it died, to get a good shot.

He was done with the cameras, and also done fighting the throbbing pain that coursed through his body and mind, threatening to tear him apart.

He'd been searching for hours and it was late. He felt brittle and thin, his hand unsteady as it slid the key in the door of yet another room. When the lock clicked, it was as if something inside him clicked as well. Though that wasn't right, it wasn't really a click, more like a snap, like something splintering apart, something pretty important, too, because once it broke he leaned his back hard against the hallway wall and slid down as if his knees had forgotten how to work.

His gaze followed the swirling lines that decorated the carpet. It was soothing, the way the lines grounded him in this spot, and there wasn't anything to be done about it but follow those lines over and over until he slipped into a comforting and utter blankness.

■ ■ ■

It was impossible to say how much time had passed. He was stiff and sore, the rough, industrial carpet prickling his face.

"River?"

Trip was saying his name. There was a question mark after, as if he wasn't quite sure River was exactly *with it*, which, honestly, he wasn't. Even given the state he was in, he could tell that much. He was in as many pieces as his shattered Skym.

A hand brushed sweaty hair from his brow.

"It's Trip and Liza. Come on, get up, buddy."

Someone pulled his arm, hoisted him upright. He leaned on his hand and hissed at the pressure. It was swollen and bruised. From what? Oh yeah. Trying to punch himself in the face and hitting a glass door instead. The sharp pain cut through the muddiness long enough for him to find Trip and Liza hunkered next to him.

"Hey," he said.

"Here." Trip held a glass of water. "I wanted to get you a shot of whiskey, but Liza the house mother said no."

River pushed the glass away and flexed his fist, stretching out the stiffness. He concentrated on the pain, letting it clear away the fog in his head.

"Where were you guys? You left. I looked everywhere, for hours. Couldn't find you."

"We weren't anywhere. But we lost a bunch of time," Trip said.

"Huh?"

"You were in the bathroom and the three of us were together," Liza said. "First Cam disappeared, and then Trip. They were there one second and then they were gone. And the next thing I knew it was six hours later, which I guess means I disappeared too."

None of this helped clear his mind.

"Disappeared? I don't get it. Where's Cam?"

The two of them glanced at each other over his head.

"Come on. Come back to the room. We're out of pills and we don't particularly want to lose time again, you know?"

River squeezed his eyes shut and struggled to think straight. So they thought that *he'd* done it, that he'd made them disappear. Cam started earthquakes, Trip made spiders and pissed-off dads, and River caused people to vanish into thin air. That made as much sense as anything.

"Where's Cam?" he asked again.

"She's not, um . . ." Trip looked to Liza again, unsure what to say. "She's not back yet."

For a few seconds River found himself staring at the lines of the carpet. The scabs on his knuckles were almost the same color as the paisley leaves weaving away from the swirling branches.

He shook himself out of it.

The three of them had disappeared, and Cam wasn't back yet. Only two of them had come back from . . . where? Nowhere. From nothing, from lack of existence. Cam didn't exist anymore.

Oh.

Trip pressed the glass into River's hand, and this time he took it. The liquid jumped as he held it, and the edge of the glass tapped his teeth so badly that Trip had to hold his wrist steady.

He really needed to eat something.

"Come on," Liza said. "Let's get back to the room. That's where she'll show up."

"How do you know she'll show up?" River said.

"We did."

"What if she doesn't? What if she's gone and she never—"

"Stop," Liza said firmly. "You're spiraling."

"I don't know what that means."

"It means your rational thoughts are distorted," Trip said. "You have a lousy thought, and it makes you feel lousy, so you have more and worse lousy thoughts until everything feels like a catastrophe that you'll never emerge from."

"How do you know all that?"

Trip laughed. "Are you kidding? That's my life."

They arrived at the room, and when they walked in to find it empty, River sagged against the wall. He rubbed his mouth with a rough hand.

"Hey," Trip said. "Show us a card trick."

"What?"

"A card trick," Trip repeated. "Something to get your mind off things."

"Cam is *missing*, Trip."

Liza dug the pack of cards from River's pack and shuffled. "When any of us freaks out, bad things seem to happen. The point is, maybe if you relax a little, she'll show up again, the same way we did. Get it?"

"I'm not in the mood for card tricks," River said.

"Poker, then," Trip said.

They opened a box of cookies and sat around the coffee table. They used toothpicks for betting. Liza dealt Texas hold'em for six rounds, and they talked about nothing, trivial things like the terrible dates they'd been on, and the time Liza was on the set of a cooking reality show and a celebrity smashed an outrageously expensive camera, or when Trip threw up five minutes before his *Today* show interview. They weren't particularly funny stories, but they told them in a way that made them funny, except that the tension hovering over the table wouldn't go away. River couldn't laugh with them, couldn't relax like they wanted him to, and they were trying so hard to make everything seem normal that it made him feel worse instead.

"What happened to your Skym?" Trip asked.

"I broke it."

Liza took a moment to summon up a response in an exaggeratedly calm tone. "River, do you know how much those cost?"

"Send me a bill," he said.

Trip huffed a laugh. "You'll be paying that off the rest of your natural life."

River didn't care about the cameras or the card game. He didn't know how they could pretend to care. "This isn't working," he said, unable to stand it any longer. "I'm tired. I'm going to lie down."

"Leave the door open, okay?" Trip said as River headed to the bedroom.

"Try not to worry about us," Liza added unhelpfully.

Try not to make us disappear again was what they both meant to say.

"Yeah," he said. "Good night."

He sat on the bed with barely the energy to kick off his boots, then sank into the pillows, eyes dropping shut. He fell asleep focusing on noise from the other room. Not on what they were saying, which probably involved how he'd essentially killed them both, if temporarily. And Cam, of course. They'd be talking about what he'd done to Cam, and whether that was temporary or not. He focused instead on the back-and-forth tones of conversation—Trip's light, tumbling inflection and Liza's no-nonsense steadiness—until the tightness in his chest unwound enough for him to drift off.

Not long after, a weight sank onto the bed and a cool hand lay flat on his chest. He placed his own hand over it.

"Cam," he murmured, even before opening his eyes.

"Trip and Liza told me what happened," she said. "I just wanted you to know that I'm here. It's not that easy to get rid of me." She pulled away with a tentative smile, as if she was going to leave.

She was right to get away from him. If she hadn't before, she had a real reason to be afraid of him now. They all had reason to worry. At least they could fight a man in a murderous rage. How do you counter an unconscious fear with the power to render you nonexistent?

"I'm sorry, River," she blurted, then continued in a ramble. "It was my fault. I made that . . . thing appear that looked like you, and it was awful, and then I wanted to disappear. That's what made all of this happen. I risked everyone. My mom's messed up and she clearly messed me up and I'll mess up some poor future kid, and that's just how it is. I wish it wasn't, but . . . there you go."

She stood to leave, but he held her wrist. "Stop."

She sat back down, her face a riot of guilt and confusion and also that wall he'd seen behind her eyes on that first day

—a protection, but something to hide behind as well. He hadn't just seen it on that day, he'd recognized it. He had his own walls, after all.

He sat up and leaned his back on the headboard, realizing he needed to say this as much as he needed her to hear it. "How about this? Neither of us apologizes for the things we can't control. Ever."

"You were right, though. I'm a mess. And it almost got everyone killed."

He exhaled slowly. "First of all, *I* never said that."

"Right, sor—I mean, right."

"Second, who the hell isn't messed up?"

"I know," she said, but he could tell she was just acquiescing. She didn't believe him. "Go back to sleep. I didn't want you to keep worrying, that's all."

He reached for her before she could leave. "Don't go. Sit with me for a bit."

She took a quick breath in and covered her mouth like she was about to cry, but she didn't. Instead she let him hold her hand. After a while, she pulled the blankets aside, and he shuffled over to make room for her, and after fumbling for a moment, all of a sudden they'd surrounded each other, a curved line forming where their bodies met, like the line of a lake meeting shore, her body starting where his stopped. The pressure of her arm draped across him and the weight of her leg over his own was so real, solid, and whole that he felt weak and strong at the same time when he buried his face into her neck and breathed in her soft scent, like the herbs and oranges of the hotel soap, but under that her own scent of honey and clean skin, and he stayed awake and still for a long time after she'd fallen asleep.

CHAPTER 18

Sometime in the night, Cam woke to find River awake but quiet. They were wrapped around each other, their bodies together. She slipped a hand under his shirt and ran her fingers along his back, touching the place where his tattoo was, imagining its lines. He shifted against her, and for a long while their lips were almost touching. They breathed the same air, and then the rhythm of his breathing changed and hers seemed to stop altogether. She was going to kiss him.

Her Skym, sensing their closeness and movement, whirred to life. It was well trained to catch this kind of thing.

"We have an audience," she said.

"Huh?"

She tipped her chin to the Skym.

River muttered, then rose from the bed and shepherded the camera to the closet, latching the door behind it.

He came back to her, and she combed her fingers through his dark hair, pulling him to her. His lips were on hers, and they kissed until she wanted more than kissing, until her body was fluttering like ribbons and she could barely catch her breath to say, "Let's slow down."

His lips brushed hers once more before he dropped onto his back, their fingers still twined together.

It was frustrating. She wanted more, but she wasn't prepared for what *more* meant.

What if the reason he wanted to touch her was because he was afraid if he stopped, she'd disappear again? Plus he was probably worried that she didn't trust him, given that she'd manifested an asshole version of him that had attacked her and Trip just a short time ago.

She did trust him. That wasn't the problem. The problem was that she didn't trust herself. When she'd believed it was River yelling terrible things at her, she'd been confused and upset, but not angry. If she'd been angry, she'd have yelled right back, told him to go to hell, all the things she'd wished a thousand times her mom would have done with Brad. Instead she'd done nothing, cowered in a corner hoping he'd stop, paralyzed that she'd done something to set him off. Cam knew it wasn't River she had to worry about. He would never do and say those terrible things.

It was herself.

She'd had boyfriends before, but her insecurities coming to life in front of everybody turned everything with River into a complicated muddle. If they went beyond kissing, wouldn't their fears and insecurities only grow stronger?

And then they would push each other away when it became too scary. Fear did that. She'd seen it before. It fed on itself, and sometimes what you're most afraid of is the very thing you force yourself to confront over and over, even when you already know you'll fail every time.

She knew all this, but still she wanted to melt back into his drifting hands and lips that traveled down her shoulder, making her shiver.

She smiled. "I'm not the first person you've kissed, am I?"

"No," he said.

"Am I the first person you've slept in the same bed with?"

"Maybe," he said with a lopsided grin.

"Really?" she said. "I'm the first?"

"You didn't ask about sleeping bags."

She curled next to him and his arms went around her. She meant to go to sleep like that, but then they were kissing again, and kissing for a while, until she came close to forgetting how easy it was to ignore what she was afraid of and to forget what was smart and made sense. And then River stopped and pressed his forehead to hers, his chest rising and falling.

"I'd better sleep on the couch," he said.

"Right." She straightened her clothes, feeling a bit shaky herself.

When he didn't move right away, she gave him a moment to collect himself and went to the main room.

Liza was snoring lightly on the couch, and Trip was at the coffee table, his face aglow from the laptop.

He winked at her. "Trouble sleeping?"

"Hush," she said.

Trip looked back at the screen, his brow furrowed.

"What's wrong?"

"We haven't had any response to the messages we left." He turned the computer screen around to show her, clicking through open tabs. "Nothing. We're messaging into a void."

Liza spoke from the couch, her sleepy voice muffled by a pillow. "Have you tried the show's streaming site?"

"The *Cut Off* site? Yeah, nothing. It's as dead as everything else. No updates for days."

Liza propped herself on her elbows. "The Skyms are still streaming. If the internet is working, the video must be uploading somewhere." Liza thought for a moment. "Can you access the backchannel, the one the producers are able to see? That's what we always started with." She spun the laptop to face her and started typing.

River emerged from the bedroom, his hair damp from washing his face.

"Everyone's awake," he said, sitting on the couch next to Liza.

"Good," Liza said, still typing. "We need to talk. Even if no one responds, they could still show up. Until they do, we need to figure out our next move."

"How do we do that?" Cam said.

She pushed aside the computer and motioned for the notepad on an end table with the Cedar Springs resort name at the top. Cam tossed it to her. She wrote down: *What We Know.*

Something had apparently happened in the outside world that made their rescue impossible. It had also caused the internet to shut down, making communication impossible as well.

Trip glanced up from typing. "The internet's still there. We can post on it, and people can *access* it, but for over a week no one has. At least that I can find."

"Okay," said Liza. "What else do we know?"

The place, the island, somehow made their fears come true, or materialize in physical form. Or the virtual-reality technology gave them incredibly realistic, multisensory delusions.

"Is it just this place," River asked, "or is it happening everywhere, to everyone, and that's why we can't contact anyone? Worldwide panic and manifestation of fear?"

"We should put on the list that it's getting worse," Cam said.

"It is." Liza nodded. "But . . . why is it getting worse?"

Cam wasn't sure, but she spoke, thinking out loud. "Every day, every minute, we're more scared. If what's happening is based on our fear, it'll continue to get worse. Maybe the more scared we are, the worse it'll get."

"Plus," Trip said, "we're out of plane pills. We gave the last one to Cam, and that fake River dumped the rest."

"Okay," Liza said. "Maybe we don't need the pills. You guys have to control yourselves, that's all. Control your fears."

"We haven't been particularly successful with that so far," Trip said.

"And why are you just talking about us?" Cam said to Liza. "Don't you need to control your fears too?"

"It hasn't happened to me yet. None of my fears have manifested."

"You know, you're older than us," Cam said.

"No kidding," she replied.

Cam continued, ignoring Liza's derisive tone. "Didn't they say the technology was more effective on young people? The younger the better, they said. So if the VR technology is causing all of this, then you're less susceptible because you're old."

"Thanks." Liza made another column on the page. "So. Let's hear all your deep dark fears and figure out what we're likely to be dealing with."

"Start with what we already know," said Cam.

"Trip, for you we've got spiders and your dad. Cam, you're afraid of earthquakes and River—or men in general—being abusive jerks. And River . . ."

River had stood when she started the list, unconsciously distancing himself from the rest of them, hands jammed in his pockets. Liza continued. "River's afraid of attack dogs and of being abandoned."

"You're not off the hook, Liza," River said, his jaw tight. "Or are you not interested in sharing your own fears, and you maybe want to keep some things for yourself?"

Liza moved on, disregarding River. "What else?"

"Isn't that enough?" River said.

"No, it's not. We need to know what we might encounter, and like Cam said, fear of fear will make it worse. If you guys can cultivate some self-awareness, we can try to prepare. So what else are you afraid of? Clowns? Snakes? Zombies? Public speaking in your underwear?"

Trip dropped his head on the table. "Great, now we're all thinking about scary clowns."

"Yeah, this isn't helping," River said. "We should find ways to *stop* thinking about the things that scare us, and distract ourselves from our fears."

"That's called denial," Liza said. "Guess what, your parents died, and one make-out session with Cam isn't going to cure your abandonment issues."

Cam's raised an eyebrow. "Every reality show needs a bitch, right, Liza?"

Liza shrugged as if her words hadn't been cruel. "What do you want me to say? It's true."

"That's not truth. You read a file, that's it," River said, his voice hard. "You're not a psychiatrist, you're not a therapist, you're not even a friend. You don't know me."

He turned, heading for the door.

Liza called after him, "River, I don't think it's a good idea for you to separate yourself from us again. Do you?"

He stopped, his back to them. He stood there a moment before his hand fell from the doorknob; then, without speaking, he returned and slumped in a chair. He hadn't left, but he wasn't happy about it. He sat there, antsy and closed off from the others, locked in his own head.

"Let's focus on what we can do," Cam said to Liza. "You know the resort and where we are. What should our next move be?"

"The resort has a golf cart. It'll be light soon, we can explore the grounds. They offer boat trips, so I figure we find something better than the little thing we arrived on. If we head south, I bet we can get to Seattle in a few hours."

Trip chewed his lip. "We're out of pills. What if something happens?"

Liza shook her head. "I don't know. Breathing exercises?"

He gave her a withering look.

"The only thing to fear is fear itself, right?" Cam said.

River studied his fingernails, lost in thought. He looked up and caught Cam watching him. She shrugged. What else could they do? None of them had a better plan. Although he didn't smile, his face softened.

Liza peered out the window. "We should head out once it gets light."

"Nope," Trip said. He was still on the computer. "I'm not going anywhere. I want to keep working on this. I think I can get it, I just need more time. Plus, there are spiders outside."

"There were spiders inside yesterday," Cam said.

"Well, they seem to have set up camp outside, so I'll stay here, thanks all the same."

"Because splitting up worked so well yesterday?" River said. "We all go, or none of us does."

"We can't stay stuck in this hotel until we die," Liza said. "I don't know if anyone's coming to save us. We need a way off the island."

"I'll go with Liza," Cam said.

"No way, it's dangerous out there," River said.

"It hasn't been particularly safe in here."

"No," River agreed, raking a hand through his hair. "That's why we should stay together."

"Listen," Liza said. "I don't care who comes with me, but I'm going whether Trip comes or not. River, if you want Cam to stay inside, then you come with me."

River looked at Cam, an entreaty on his face. She pulled

him into the hallway and he immediately leaned her against the wall, their foreheads touching. The back of his fingers brushed down her face and over her collarbone.

"I'll stay with Trip. We'll be fine here," Cam said. His kisses started at her temple and then ran down the side of her face to her neck.

"No," River murmured. "Stay here, with me. I spent half the night combing the island. If Liza wants to explore, she can go by herself."

"You know she shouldn't."

"I don't care."

"Yes, you do."

He sighed. "Fine, I'll go."

She held his chin and turned his face to the side. "You're bruised."

He nudged her hand away. "It's nothing."

"It's from when that thing hit you. That means—"

"I know what it means." He held her eyes, intent and serious. "Be careful. Promise me."

"I will," she said. "You be careful too."

He kissed her then, and, despite everything, it felt in that moment as if nothing could ever hurt them.

It wasn't true, however. It might have been foolish, but she'd hoped their fears were exactly that—fear. Scary visions that were otherwise harmless. Their other injuries they'd caused themselves, from falling or from running away. But they weren't deluded, it wasn't in their minds. River's bruise was from a fist, evidence that they were at the mercy of some twisted version of reality.

She let herself pretend that River's kiss could make it all go away, but her fingers brushed the dark mark left on his jaw, and she knew better.

Anything that could leave a bruise could also kill.

CHAPTER 19

"You want to drive?" Liza asked.

River and Liza had found the golf cart in a shed north of the hotel, the key hanging from a pegboard on the wall.

"Not particularly," River said. In any case, she was already in the driver's seat and putting the key in the ignition, so it wasn't a genuine question.

She sped up the narrow road, no wider than a sidewalk, that ran past the bungalows and then over the hill, the hotel disappearing behind them. Liza's Skym zipped along beside them.

She steered the cart with authority, seeming to know where she was going, so River sat back, propped his leg on the dash, and took in the surrounding hills. The tide was higher than when they'd first arrived. The end of the pier where they'd tied the boat was partially submerged, and it hadn't been that way when they'd docked.

He didn't want to be traveling around the island with Liza. Whatever he'd thought of her before, since she'd stopped putting on the act she'd maintained in the beginning, she'd been insensitive and calculating. Most of the time, she seemed to view the rest of them as employees to be managed, not as real people deserving consideration. She knew a lot about the show, however, and touring the grounds of the resort in a golf cart was a chance to get more information.

"Tell me about the technology the show implanted in us."

"What do you want to know?" Liza jerked the wheel to the left, dodging a boulder blocking the path. The golf cart continued to bounce along.

He wanted to know everything, basically. The answers to the questions he should have asked before coming on the show. Looking back, he couldn't believe he'd let them inject him with something he knew nothing about. Everyone involved with the show had been so blasé, it had been easy not to question it: the producers, the other contestants, the woman in the lab coat who'd shown up with the needle and six forms for him to sign. Like an idiot, he'd held out his arm and let her poke him, thinking nothing of it. It was a new technology, but they were minors, and it was just a TV show. He figured a TV show wouldn't do anything to put them in danger. And now here they were, weeks later, stranded and fighting off nightmares. It was connected, it had to be, but he couldn't figure out how, and unless they had a better understanding of the technology, they'd never know how to fight it.

"I know the technology is something in our brains, but how does it work?"

"I don't know, River. That wasn't part of my job. The folks who worked on that side of the show were neuroscientists and physicists, microelectronic engineers, not low-level producers like me. I barely passed introductory physics."

Her chin was raised defensively. She might not be lying,

but she was dodging the real question, and probably her own responsibility in the show's grand plans and high-tech visions.

"But you know more than the rest of us. What were you told about the show?"

"I was told the same thing as you guys, and the viewers when it was advertised. It's a 3-D virtual-reality experience, with full visual immersion. That's where Trip's app came in. We needed his platform to stream the content over the internet to the visors everyone bought. We were shocked when he accepted our bid. Others were offering more, but you've met Trip. He knows what he wants, and what he wanted was to be on our show. We needed to cough up extra liability insurance when he didn't pass our psych requirements. Normally, we'd avoid casting someone with anxiety issues on a stressful show like this, but he signed some extra waivers and seemed game, plus we thought he'd be interesting to watch. Which was true —he was a great cast member. He knew the role that worked best for him—spoiled rich kid out of his element, cheating to get by. It played great on camera."

"So how does Trip's app work with the injection?"

"We were injected with ions, and as I understand it, the ions have a specific signature for each contestant, which connects you to your Skym. It's like a radio signal, but it's capturing perceptual data sent from the brain itself. Trip's app streams the signal in real time to the visors. The general audience can watch the show traditionally, on TV or regular streaming, but the people who bought the visors experience a lot more, because of the ions and your brain waves."

River sighed, frustrated. "I don't get it."

"Trip might be able to explain it better. I do know that it's incredibly innovative technology, changing television and entertainment as we know it. It was going to change everything. With the visors, the viewers see and hear everything you do, all in 3-D. I tried it before coming on the show. It was so much more than sitting in a theater at a 3-D movie. It was like standing in the middle of the wilderness. You could see and hear everything, the trees and the birds. It's amazing."

"We have a technology that sophisticated, and the best anyone could do with it is make a reality show?"

"Listen, one of the bidders for Trip's app was a porn site that couldn't wait to get its hands on the tech. Another makes cartoons for kids. The military wanted it too. Be happy our vision won out. Anyway, we have to start somewhere. Don't dismiss the power of entertainment so easily. What we have is a new technology, still being tested, and a reality show is the venue where that testing can happen. We have a platform across the whole world, and the world can see how it works, understand the implications, and figure out the best use for it."

The trail took them past a cottage tucked in the trees, a hidden bungalow probably for a guest seeking extra privacy. The building sat near the water, and on the sand was a colorful line of beach towels, four of them. Rainbow, orange, pink, and blue, with a picnic basket, a bottle of wine, and four glasses, only one still standing upright. Another abandoned scene. Another sign they were alone. As familiar as the landscape was to River, that familiarity now felt layered with a sinister menace. Their own fear had become a presence, something that followed them into every dark corner of the place.

"Even if we accept that somehow this tech is tapping into our fears and manifesting them in the real world," he said, "what are the odds it also somehow shut down communication systems, or caused a global catastrophe?"

"Seriously, zero," Liza said. "There's no chance. It simply doesn't work that way, or have that kind of scope. Honestly, it's the same thing with our fears becoming real, physical things. It's not possible. I suppose a delusion could be created, and our senses are making us believe what we're seeing, but the brain isn't that easily fooled. And there's no way we'd all be able to share the delusion."

"Then how do we explain what's happening?"

"You know what I think? I think something completely unrelated and devastating happened in the outside world, and we just happened to be on a haunted island when it did. Because why the hell not?"

"I don't believe in haunted islands."

"Well." Liza stopped the cart and set the parking brake with an irritated yank. "That's the thing about haunted islands. You don't have to believe in them for them to exist."

She'd parked in a circular drive surrounded by tall firs at the base of an overlook. The hotel was above them, looking down at the bluff, and the ocean was before them, slate gray with swirling white eddies. River stepped out of the cart and scanned the water. The tide was even higher than it had been earlier. Driftwood and ropes of rubbery kelp littered the pebbly beach.

"Look, out that way," Liza said, pointing to the left where a small inlet notched the shore. "That'll get us to the mainland."

There was a marina, a few fishing boats, and what Liza was indicating—a two-tiered yacht the size of a small house.

"Can you drive that thing?" he asked.

"What's to know? Forward, backwards, steer. If we can get it out of the marina and to open water, it's not like we'll hit anything."

The plan wasn't bad, and in the end Liza was right. River didn't believe the island was haunted, but they needed to get off it and find out what was happening back home. They needed to find people, and help.

The air cooled as a breeze came off the water. River tucked his hoodie close against the chill.

"Okay," he said. "It sounds easy enough. We should leave today, as soon as possible."

"It will be easy, right? I mean, it's a big boat. Boats that size are pretty safe."

River looked back at Liza. "They are."

Her fingers fluttered against her throat. "When they're that big, they don't usually tip over."

"No, they don't. Liza, what's going on?"

She continued as if speaking to herself. "We got here on that little console boat, and that was fine."

The breeze picked up again, slicing through his thin jacket.

A flock of birds rose from the trees, taking flight in irregular bursts that streaked the sky, heading inland.

The noise of rustling pebbles drew his eyes back to the water. A wave came in high, reaching the top of the beach, then drew out again, exposing the rocky shore, the sand and silt, as if the sea inhaled and then held its breath.

"Liza, something's wrong."

Her fingers slipped up her neck and tugged at her hair. "Everything's wrong, River, or haven't you noticed? Somehow I'm the one in charge of keeping a bunch of teenagers alive, and apparently that means captaining a huge goddamn boat across the Pacific. How is that fair?"

She had seemed so confident only a moment ago. So why did everything suddenly feel wrong?

"It's not fair, I get it. But listen, we need to stay calm."

The tide continued to recede, uncovering a ridge on the ocean floor, dropping fish to flop in the mud.

Liza's gaze locked on the water. "Don't tell me to stay calm," she said, an uncharacteristic waver in her voice. "What's happening, River? Why is the water doing that?"

"I don't . . . I don't know. But we should go."

She looked ashen. "This isn't me. I didn't do anything."

Liza, who'd spent their time together manipulating them for the show, taking charge, and talking about fear as if it was something only for children, now looked terrified, and that was enough for River to want to get the hell out of there.

"It doesn't matter. Let's go."

"It was just a thought. Not even a thought, a feeling. It was only for a second!"

"What thought?"

She took two steps toward the expanding shore. The yacht rocked violently. "I thought about the boat sinking. I thought about being trapped inside."

"Jesus. Stop this, Liza. Stop thinking!"

"I don't know how to do that."

"You do!" He gripped her shoulders, held her eyes. "Remember in the hotel, when that guy just vanished? Trip told Cam he wasn't real, and she believed him. He vanished. Remember? You can make this stop."

"Cam had the pills!"

"The pills don't matter. Close your eyes, it'll be okay. Nothing can hurt us if you calm down. I need you to breathe, all right? Deep breaths, in through your nose and out your mouth. Everything is fine. Okay? It's fine. It's not real. It can only hurt us if we're afraid."

She didn't close her eyes. Instead her gaze settled just past his shoulder. She stared as if her mind were being pulled outward as forcefully as the water. Her expression—sheer terror —turned his body, inside and out, to ice.

It wouldn't work. He'd never convince her this wasn't real, not with the tide dragged back and back as if it would never stop, as if it would draw the water out until the sea was empty. He'd never seen the ocean act like this.

River ushered her away from the edge. "Get in the cart. We've got to reach high ground."

Sweat blotched her forehead. "How can this be happening? We're on land, nowhere near the boat, or water for that matter. This couldn't have been me!"

"It's a tsunami, Liza. We don't need to be near water, the water's coming to us."

An abrupt rush of air sucked outward, and the force of it seemed to shake Liza from her trance. She ran, and River ran with her.

Liza jumped into the driver's seat and jerked the cart into motion while River was still climbing in. He gripped the crash bar and fell back when she gunned the engine. He kept his eyes on the sight behind them, the exposed ocean floor growing rapidly, impossibly. The squawk and screech of birds drowned out the tiny electric engine sputtering uphill, back the way they'd come.

The cart was too slow.

"We won't make it," he said.

Liza's lips pressed into a thin line. Her leg straightened, flooring the pedal. "Like hell."

"Liza, we won't make it!"

She looked back and her body seemed to shrink like a wilted branch. "Oh God."

The treetops behind them collapsed, tipping and crashing to the ground. Seawater and boulders came barreling toward them. A wave crested from nowhere, rising from the water as if it was alive, a monster roaring for them both, ready to swallow them whole.

Liza wasn't steering anymore, but it didn't matter.

They bumped along the road wildly for a few yards, and then the wave hit them and they were lifted with the tumbling surf, thunderous as a barrage of cannon. As if in slow motion, the path rose up until they were looking straight down on it, and then it rushed toward them, the cart diving like a roller coaster. Liza screamed, but her voice was carried away by the gusting wind. River closed his eyes and held on.

The cart ripped away from him with the force of a freight train, and his fingers held nothing as it spun away. Water swallowed him. Silence filled his ears and he was alone, tumbling and churning in a blender of rocks and trees, sand and black ocean.

CHAPTER 20

Cam stood by the window of the hotel lobby looking down at the Springs. It was just as well Trip had decided to remain inside. The spiders were livelier than they'd been earlier, covering the patio like the shifting shadow of a cloud. It made her shiver, as if she could hear their scrabbling through the glass. Trip had set up the laptop on a table in the lobby, and Cam had made a decent breakfast in the kitchen from powdered eggs and canned peaches. She'd also made a mug of tea.

River and Liza had left a while ago. She'd watched the golf cart head down the hill, and now she was bored and anxious, listening for the sound of the cart's wheels crunching on gravel.

"You've been on there for a while," she said to Trip, plopping down at the table and resting her chin in her hand. "Found anything?"

"You try breaking into a backchannel site for an international reality show. Liza got me in with a code, but that only gave me access to her account."

Liza had been out of line earlier, bringing up River's parents. Liza's motives had been questionable from the beginning, and her style of communication sucked, but she hadn't been wrong. River wanted to pretend none of this was happening because it didn't make sense to him and he couldn't fix it. It was scary, and nobody wanted to deal with scary, but when fears became real—things that could truly hurt you rather than just provoke abstract anxieties—there was no choice but to confront them.

Cam had always imagined herself a fighter. She would never be trapped, would never fall apart, and she wouldn't let anyone underestimate her. What did that mean out here, however, in a creepy place like this? Did knowing your fears and weaknesses come with some understanding, some knowledge that would make you more able to counter them?

The wind whistled against the building, and the tall pines wavered in the breeze.

"Got it!" Trip shouted, making her jump.

Cam dragged her chair closer to see the computer. "You're in?"

"It's the backchannel *Cut Off* site. Look, there we are!"

He pointed to the screen where they hunched over the computer, an image of both of them watching themselves watch themselves in an endless loop through the camera of Trip's Skym.

"That's so weird."

"Isn't it? Look, there's Liza and River in the golf cart. How come your camera is black?"

"River stuffed it in a closet."

"There are three screens showing footage," he said. "My Skym, which is showing the two of us, Liza's, showing her and River, and yours, stuck upstairs in the closet."

Cam shoved him with her elbow when he smirked about her Skym. Trip knew full well why River had hidden it, but he didn't have to sound so amused. She should probably rescue the thing. Not that she cared much about filming anymore, but Trip and Liza seemed to.

Trip took them away from the main screen and searched the site for something that would tell them what had happened, or if anyone had updated or been in contact since everything had gone wrong, but there was nothing. He exhaled and slouched back, defeated.

"Nothing. I was sure this would work. What the hell?"

Cam pointed to an advertisement on the right hand of the screen. "What's that?"

"Looks like some kind of ad for the resort." He hit play and they watched as a young man in a cardigan sweater with a shiny white smile walked along the resort's veranda with a mug of coffee and talked about the amenities at Cedar Springs. While he was talking, a message square popped up on the screen. "Hey, what's that?" Cam said, handing the computer back to Trip. Text unrolled across the screen.

WE'RE ALONE. WE'RE THEONES GONE. HELP HELP HELP
HELPWE HELP HELP HELP HELPUSHELP. HELPME HELP
HELP HELP HELPWE'RE HELP HELP HELPGONE HELP
HELP HELPTHE HELP. HELPHELP HELP HELPNOW HELP
HELP HELPTHEONES HELP HELP HELP HELPIAM HELP
HELPALONE HELP HELPTHE HELP HELP HELPWE HELP
HELP HELPTHE HELP HELP HELPNOWGONE HELP HELP

HELPHELP HELP HELP HELPTHEONESHELPHELPHELPHELP
HELPMEHELPHELPHELPPPP

"Jesus," Trip muttered.

"'We're alone.' What does that mean? Who's 'we'? Is the message for us?"

Trip shook his head, also mystified. "It must be for us. It only popped up when we accessed the site." He typed in the reply line *Where are you?*

An answer came back:

WE'RE ALONE. WE'RE THEONES GONE. HELP HELP HELP
HELPWE HELP HELP HELP HELPUSHELP. HELPME HELP
HELP HELP HELPWE'RE HELP HELP HELPGONE HELP
HELP HELPTHE HELP. HELPHELP HELP HELPNOW HELP
HELP HELPTHEONES HELP HELP HELP HELPIAM HELP
HELPALONE HELP HELPTHE HELP HELP HELPWE HELP
HELP HELPTHE HELP HELP HELPNOWGONE HELP HELP
HELPHELP HELP HELP HELPTHEONESHELPHELPHELPHELP
HELPMEHELPHELPHELPPPP

The same message continued for two more pages, the same variations, the same note of hysteria.

Trip typed furiously.

Cam swallowed. "Someone's trying to communicate with us."

"Or trying to communicate with the show," Trip said, still typing. "We can't know who 'we' refers to."

"Whoever it is, they're obviously in trouble."

"They can join the club."

Trip stopped typing and leaned in close to the screen. He opened his mouth to say something, but then a rumble came from outside and Cam felt a flush of relief. River and Liza were back.

She went to the window, and the rumble grew until the glass began to rattle, and then an Adirondack chair was hurtling toward her like a plastic lawn ornament in a tornado. It was being carried, lifted on an enormous wave. With just enough time for her to wonder what the hell was happening, the room exploded with water.

CHAPTER 21

Everything in the water became a projectile, bullets striking right and left. He couldn't tell which way was up, and he was thrashed by everything the wave had picked up along the way —a beach chair, a tackle box, a room-service tray. A branch caught his shirt and dragged him down. Pain stabbed his side. Fighting the current, he reached up with a gasp before being sucked down again, until he was tossed like a sock in a washing machine.

When he finally broke the surface, he choked out a mouthful of briny sea and surveyed the wreckage. The choppy, violent current had picked up splintered trees, which poked like crooked teeth from the sludge and spume.

A mattress rushed past and he flailed for it, hauling himself onto it as a crude raft. It hurtled forward until his eye caught a flash of pink. Liza's hair. She was face-down, her body inert on the swirling river. He yelled her name but got no response. He drew closer and reached out from the mattress as far as he could, barely hanging on. His fingertips brushed her shirt, and he struggled to get a firm grip. With a wordless sound of frustration and effort, he finally hooked her arm and pulled her toward him, turning her face from the water. Her eyes were closed, her mouth hung open.

"Liza!"

He dragged her up so she lay next to him. In all the turmoil, he couldn't tell if she was breathing. He felt helpless, unable to do anything but say her name while they hurtled forward, speeding past deadfalls of leaves and branches.

"Liza! Liza, come on, wake up!".

He couldn't see land anymore, or the resort. Was it submerged? If so, how could anyone survive?

She was unconscious, her lips blue. He should try CPR, but there was no way to find purchase on the mattress and keep her from falling into the water. He held on, his arms clutching her tightly. They wouldn't last long like this. His strength would give out. For now, however, he wouldn't let go. He'd sink with her before he'd let himself give up.

With no warning, as if with a sigh, the water stopped. The debris sank, the tide drew back, and the mattress floated into gently swirling eddies. Wet hair clung to Liza's forehead. He swiped it away.

"Liza? Liza, it's stopped. Come on, wake up. Please."

She didn't stir, didn't seem to be breathing. He set his teeth, trying to ignore the pain in his side, Liza's blue lips, the icy cold of her skin, and the despair that hovered just along the edge of his mind. He shook her, angrily almost.

"Hang on, Liza, please." He closed his eyes, his forehead resting on hers, and heard his voice whisper the word over and over, *please*, speaking as much to himself as to her.

And then she vanished. He was alone on the mattress, his arms empty.

"Liza!"

He must have passed out and not realized it, let her fall. But he'd been holding her so tight, and he hadn't lost consciousness, he was sure of it. It didn't make sense.

He dove into the water, thrashing through the debris. It was too murky to see anything, too cluttered. He yelled her name. He yelled until his voice was hoarse. His limbs quivering with exhaustion, he clutched for the mattress, fingers digging into the spongy padding, and floated, still desperately scanning the horizon for any sign of Liza. There was none.

Sunlight sparkled on the capped waves. The day had turned bright and sunny, as if all that chaos hadn't been real, as if he could go back to the resort and find Liza there, scowling and drinking bourbon.

Blood dripped into River's eyes from a gash on his head. He felt like he'd been outmatched in a fight, thrashed, kicked, and pummeled, but the cold held most of the pain at bay. He felt numb.

Time passed, and he wondered if this was it, if this was how it was going to end. Cam and Trip were gone. The Skyms were gone. There was no show, no audience, no help or rescue. No going home. He would die like this, wet and cold, surrounded by water and the chaotic remnants of a shattered island and a sinking, broken wilderness.

He lost track of how long it had been. An hour? Two? Time ceased to matter as the effort of hanging on drained his muscles and resolve. He couldn't hold on much longer.

Underneath the sound of lapping waves came a vibration.

Maybe it was another tsunami. But the ocean was calm now, the sky clear. Even so, it didn't matter. The water had taken everything, and if it wanted to take him, it would.

The noise grew louder. River opened his eyes, and his first sight was the golf cart bobbing past, beaten, dented, still somehow puttering along, its motor churning. But the vibration was too loud to be the golf cart. The rumble shivered through the water until he felt it in his bones.

And then he saw it—a small seaplane motoring against the horizon, coming straight toward him.

After everything, someone had come. Rescue had arrived. It was too late, of course. He was the only one left.

The plane worked its way clumsily through the debris, waves splashing up its sides. The door opened, and there was Cam. Waterlogged, pale, as torn up as he was, and then, behind her, Trip, his mouth quirking up ridiculously.

"I need to rescue you again?" he said, and River finally let go.

■ ■ ■

River collapsed on the floor of the plane's cabin.

"You're bleeding," Cam said.

Trip was still at the open door, scanning the water's surface. "Where's Liza?"

River shook his head, unable to say the words. Cam blinked, at first not comprehending, and then her face clouded. Trip grimaced and turned away.

"No," Cam said. "It's not true. She's out there. She must be." Cam was shivering.

"I had her. We were on the mattress," River said, sitting up. "She disappeared."

"What?" Trip said.

"She just . . . I don't know. She was there one second, and then she was gone."

"You mean she fell in," Cam said gently.

"No! She was unconscious, but I had her. I wouldn't have let go."

"She can't be gone," Trip said. "People don't just disappear."

Cam's expression darkened. "We did last night. And Brandon, too, he disappeared."

"The guy in the trailer?" Trip asked.

Cam nodded. "Nobody said anything, but we all saw it. He disappeared. One minute he was on the couch, and then he was gone."

"He was dead," River said. He dropped his head in his hands. "I thought you guys were dead too."

"When the wave hit the resort, it flooded the lobby. We escaped through the kitchen and found the plane in the boathouse. We're okay."

None of this was okay, though.

He felt like he was still out there treading water, trying to stay afloat on a soaking raft, the horizon receding farther and farther back with no end in sight.

The moment the ocean had calmed, he'd known. The tidal

wave was caused by Liza's fear, and she wasn't afraid anymore. She was gone. The fear had won. He hadn't been able to save her.

Cam and Trip should be dead too. The wave hit the resort. They should have drowned, just like Liza.

Stop.

Stop thinking that way.

He caged his fingers over his eyes and willed his mind to shut down, to ignore its own screeching noise, loud as a fire alarm blaring through his brain.

It was too late, though. It was there on Cam's face already, in her rapid blink of surprise, a hand clutching her chest as her breath hitched.

"Cam?"

He moved toward her. Her back arched and she fell to the floor. Her eyes rolled up as she gasped for air.

"Trip!" River's voice sounded foreign in his ears, too loud, too scared. "Trip, help!"

He'd let himself fear her death, and now she was choking, drowning on nothing. That's what happens here. The island was cursed, their fears came to life, and now Cam was going to die.

Her head dropped back as she lost consciousness.

CPR, he needed to do CPR. Chest compressions, head tipped back, two breaths, more compressions. He should have done it for Liza, should have at least tried.

"I know this," he muttered, even as a distant part of his

mind repeated, *You did this. She was fine, and now this. It's you.*

He counted in his head as he pumped her chest.

"That won't help," Trip said.

"Let me do this!"

One, two, three, four.

Trip was right, it wasn't going to work. Hadn't he read that somewhere? CPR never works, it was something people were taught, but the statistics were bad. She would die. She might as well be dead already, and it was his fault. Maybe if they had pills, but those were gone.

What did it matter? He may as well be trying to convince Liza the wave didn't exist even as it came barreling toward them. Pills couldn't change this, no chemical could fix it. It wasn't a glitch in his brain, a broken way of thinking. It was real. Not just real, but *likely*. People died all the time, every day. Important people, beautiful people, loved people. Cam wasn't special. She was only special to *him*, and that didn't change anything. Death wasn't an irrational fear, not an anxiety like monsters under the bed. That River feared Cam's death was simply a way to prepare for the inevitable.

And that's what it was, inevitable. Everyone died.

Cam would die.

Her lips were already blue. Just like Liza.

"Damn it, River, stop!"

River fell back from her body as if he'd been struck. He was making it worse. He pushed himself against the wall and

235

linked his fingers behind his head, covering his ears with his arms as if that would keep his thoughts contained in his skull.

The plane lifted in the waves, tipping precariously. Trip stumbled and River's stomach fell with the floor as the plane began to sink, the ocean sucking it down with a force stronger than gravity. They'd be pulled into the center of the earth, and some small, secret part of him was relieved.

"Jesus, we're going under," Trip said, but his voice was far away.

The plane groaned as pressure built on its hull. Waves slapped the sides, rising up over the window. It reminded River of being in an aquarium, though the water was churning and it was too dark to see beyond the glass. The plane door buckled and water sprayed into the cabin as the creaking metal drowned out Cam's desperate, wheezing breaths.

Trip went to the cockpit and came back holding a fire extinguisher. He stood over River, looking down at him, his face unreadable.

"Sorry about this, buddy," he said. "But we're out of pills."

River opened his mouth to tell him that a fire extinguisher wasn't what they needed, not when the problem was all this water, but before he could speak, a bright pain flashed across his eyes and the world went black.

THE
MAINLAND

CHAPTER 22

Everything hurt. Her throat, her head, along with every tiny muscle in her body she'd never bothered to think about before. The plane was rocking violently.

Trip was trying to help her, but was also yelling. "Come on, Cam, get up, we've got to go!"

He was in the cockpit, and water churned outside the windows as the engine rumbled and spluttered. River slumped sideways in a leather seat, the buckle holding him in. He was unconscious.

"Is he okay?" Cam asked.

"Probably," Trip said.

Probably wasn't exactly what Cam wanted to hear, but at least River seemed to be breathing. Better than she was. Her lungs were on fire.

"What happened?"

"I had to knock him out before we got sucked down to the bottom of the ocean. Not as gentle as plane pills, but apparently effective."

The plane gave a forceful jolt.

"We're sinking. Buckle in!"

A roar filled the cabin. Cam stumbled to a seat.

Mirroring the luxury of Cedar Springs Resort, the plane

was nicer than anything she'd flown in before, with its shiny imitation-wood trim, tufted leather seats, curtains, and carpeting. All of it swayed and rattled now as the plane improbably fought its way to the surface. Cam doubted it was possible, but so many impossible things had already happened that once the plane sloshed out of the water, she was willing to accept that the rules she believed about the world no longer applied. They bounced hard, lifted up, then bounced down once more, and her heart pitched into her throat. They skimmed the ocean, cutting through white surf, picking up speed, until, with a final stomach-flipping lurch, the plane lifted into the air. And stayed there.

Cam wanted to close her eyes and pretend none of this was happening, but she couldn't take them off the island. Or at least what was left of it. The water had continued to rise.

They'd spent weeks on that plot of land in the ocean, first in the wilderness and then at the resort, and the tidal wave had demolished it. There was nothing left but floating boards and driftwood, an overturned boat, and an underwater resort, only the top floors remaining visible. The sole indication that a mass of land existed under the surface was the white-capped surf and still-crashing waves churning along the top. The distance grew, the land shrank, and then the water engulfed even the roof as the island sank into the sea.

They were leaving with nothing but the torn, soaking clothes they wore. They were beaten and battered, scared and lost.

Liza was gone.

It didn't feel real. She should be on the plane with them

right now. That she wasn't felt like a mistake. Cam kept looking up expecting to see her, only to be met with an empty space where Liza should be. It was like a word on the tip of her tongue, and the more she struggled to remember it, the further it skipped away.

She and Trip were alive, though, and River. That was something.

Once in the air and flying straight, Cam went to sit next to Trip in the cockpit. She'd lost her Skym in the tsunami—or it had lost her, which felt more accurate. She'd never taken it out of the closet.

In the close quarters of the seaplane, the last remaining Skym bopped against the ceiling.

Cam had questions. Trip's hands gripped the yoke firmly, and his steady gaze focused on their path. He seemed comfortable, sure of himself.

When she sat down, he gave her a subdued grin. "Impressive, yeah?"

"Pretty impressive."

"Think River will forgive me?"

"If we survive the flight, he'll get over it."

Cam couldn't remember all that had happened once they'd gotten River into the plane. She'd been talking to him, trying to process what had happened to Liza, and suddenly she couldn't breathe. The next thing she knew, Trip's voice was in her ear, and her body was gripped by a vicious convulsion that left her feeling like she'd run a marathon.

Cam sat quietly for a few moments. Trip flew at a low

altitude, and the ocean sped beneath them in a blur. The sky had cleared, and clouds billowed above.

"Where are we going?"

"I don't know that it matters. Liza said we were north of Vancouver Island, so I'm heading south, to the States. I figure some pissed-off air-traffic controller's going to start yelling at us any minute. Once we find people, we'll be okay."

That's what they'd said about the resort.

"Trip?"

"Yeah?"

"What if there is no pissed-off air-traffic controller?"

"We go to Seattle," Trip said without hesitation. "Specifically, Fort Harris, a military base. The message that appeared on the *Cut Off* site? The one that said 'We're alone'? I saw where it originated from. Someone's there. That's as good a place to start as any."

The voices Cam had been hearing in the wilderness for so long, and at the resort, had fallen silent. She'd become so accustomed to the sound that now she almost missed it, like a white noise, the sound of rain falling while she drifted toward sleep. The plane was quiet except for the rumble of the engine filling her ears.

Sunset spread across the sky, coloring the ocean orange and red. After a while, darkness fell and the ocean turned black.

Cam peered out the window. "Shouldn't we be over land by now?"

"We are," Trip said, pointing to a string of highway lamps in the distance. "See?"

"Where are the cars?"

"There aren't any." Trip had already noticed, even if he hadn't pointed it out.

There should be streams of cars heading down the highway, with white lights on one side of the road, red on the other. Cars meant people. Cars meant civilization.

And where were those air-traffic controllers?

"I guess we go to Seattle," Cam said.

After a little while, the Space Needle hovered on the horizon, straight as an arrow, lit up against the night sky.

"Keep an eye out for an airport or a large open space where we can land."

"Okay," Cam said. "How many flying lessons have you taken exactly?"

"I got six months under my belt. For the first time in my life I had some money to burn, so I thought it'd be fun. Never flown this kind, though. I don't think it's too different."

Trip's confidence, while not especially contagious, seemed genuine.

"You sure you can land this thing?"

"Sure," Trip said. "Easy-peasy."

"Don't you have to land it on water?"

"It's a seaplane, but it's amphibious. I can land it anywhere if I have enough room."

"How'd you end up taking flying lessons? Didn't your mom have a fear of flying?"

While Trip talked, he circled a lit parking lot. "Something about her being afraid to fly meant that I never picked up that particular anxiety. But yeah, she takes five or six of her plane pills just to set foot on a runway. I used to tell her, if we're going to crash, we're going to crash. No sense worrying about it."

"Of course, worrying about it here will make it happen."

"True. You're not going to worry about it, are you?"

"Honestly? I'm too exhausted to worry about anything right now. Even the fact that you're about to land this plane at a Safeway."

"It looks like it's near the military base. You might want to strap in."

"Right."

Cam sat one seat away from Trip and buckled the belt tight.

The wheels screeched on pavement and the whole plane shuddered from side to side.

"It's too fast, Trip."

"We're fine."

The store hurtled toward them at alarming speed. The nose of the plane was about to crash through the storefront glass.

"Trip?"

At the last minute he pulled up, laughing nervously to her. "All part of the process. Quit making me nervous."

Cam bit her tongue as Trip made two more passes at the parking lot until finally, on the fourth try, the plane landed with a booming thud that jolted into Cam's bones. She closed her eyes tight, because of course they were crashing. In a world where fears became real, how could they not be? A series of thuds and the noise of shattering glass made her open her eyes and look out the window. The plane's wing had swiped an entire row of cars. They went careening across the lot, headlong into other cars and toppling lampposts. Cam's hands locked to the armrests, her fingernails biting into the soft leather.

Just when she thought she might scream, Trip shouted, "Here we go!" The plane corkscrewed over the pavement. The store, highway, and traffic lights flashed past the window in a dizzying carousel until the plane didn't so much stop as sever a tree in half and crunch into a wall.

They were off the island, and they had landed. They had, somehow, survived.

For all Trip's cool self-assurance, the relief on his face once they'd come to a full stop made Cam realize that his display of confidence had been for her benefit. He cut the engine, and silence fell over the plane. Then Trip opened the hatch.

The voices came back stronger than ever. The sound wasn't coming from the trees anymore, it was coming from everywhere, from the heavy air and streaming lights. Cam covered her ears.

"What's wrong?" Trip said.

She shook her head. "You don't hear that?"

"There's nothing to hear. Look around."

Cam looked, and what she saw made her stomach drop.

The parking lot was empty. It was evening, and dark, but a place like that should have been bustling and moving. And a plane shouldn't have been able to land without drawing a crowd, not to mention the police.

The air was damp, and mist lay thick on the ground. Cam and Trip stood wordlessly on the pavement, their disappointment at not finding a bunch of late-night shoppers hovering between them like the fog.

"Let's pick up some food," Trip said. "But we'll stay close to River. We sleep on the plane, and check out the military base in daylight."

The Safeway felt eerie and wrong, so they grabbed what they needed and left quickly. After the dark, abandoned store, Cam was relieved to climb back into the quiet of the plane, if only because it felt protected when no place else did.

Cam curled into the seat next to River, who hadn't stirred. She rested her head on his shoulder and he turned toward her without waking.

The world outside was empty.

Where had everyone gone? If something terrible had happened, where were the bodies? The tanks and guns littering the streets? The grocery store was intact, so there'd been no looters, no emergency stockpiling. Everyone was simply . . . gone. They were as alone as they'd been on the island, and this time there was no place left to go. Nothing was going to suddenly be okay.

Cam slept, and she dreamed of the voices. They brushed past her, like undertones lost in a soupy mist. She woke in the morning with a start to find River missing from next to her, the blanket that had covered him crumpled in his seat. Trip was still asleep.

She found River in the back of the store, his shirt off, placing a last strip of tape over a bandage on his side.

"How are you feeling?" she asked.

Without looking up, he tore open a plastic bag of blue shirts and put one on. The tattered Cedar Springs shirt lay discarded on the floor.

"I'm good."

He made his way to the front of the store, stopping briefly to pick up a new deck of cards along with a road map of the area. He slipped the cards in his pocket and opened the map, studying the crisscrossing lines.

"Trip said you live nearby," Cam said.

"My uncle lives in Seattle. My parents' house is a forty-minute drive."

"Trip found a signal coming from the military base. We might find someone today."

River said nothing.

"It's weird that no one's here."

He folded the map and left the store, outpacing her in the parking lot as he headed back to the plane.

"River, hold on. Talk to me for a second."

He stopped and waited for her to speak, his face impassive.

Her stomach turned as if she were still in the air on the lurching plane. "What's wrong with you?"

"Nothing."

"You're acting like something's wrong."

"Don't worry about me. We have plenty to deal with already, don't we? Let's focus on finding out what's happened to everyone."

A patch of red had bloomed at the side of his shirt, turning the blue fabric dark purple.

"You're bleeding again."

He twisted to take a look. "Damn. A branch caught me in the water. I thought I patched it."

"Here, let me help."

He waved her off. "I've got it."

"I'll get more bandages. I can—"

"Seriously, Cam, it's not a big deal. I've got it."

The sting was less in his words than in the way he said them.

"What the hell?"

His gaze dropped to his feet for a second before he faced her again, resolute. "Liza's dead."

"I know that."

"Liza's dead, and I almost sank the plane, with all of us in it. I almost killed you and Trip. With everything happening— earthquakes, dogs, spiders, tsunamis—it's too much. I won't put you in danger again."

"It wasn't your fault. We shouldn't apologize for what we don't control—isn't that what you said?"

"You don't get it, Cam. I'm not apologizing. I want us safe, and I can't worry about anything else."

He'd had the same haunted look when she'd reappeared at the resort.

Cam crossed her arms. "And 'anything else' refers to us? To me?"

"No, I . . ." He let out a frustrated breath. "You almost *died*, Cam. It's safer if we back off."

"Back off from each other, you mean." He didn't answer, only pressed his lips together. Yes. That was exactly what he meant. Cam nodded. "Okay. Fine."

"Cam, it doesn't mean—"

"No, it's fine," she said again. "No problem."

River pinched his fingers to his eyes, searching for something to say to make it better, but Cam didn't care what he might say. From the beginning she hadn't wanted to get caught up in anything.

Back when Cam had still been playing the game, trying to stir up trouble and get the others to tap out, River had entertained them with card tricks. She'd found it irritating at the time. She was trying to win a million dollars, and he was distracting them like children at a birthday party, as if he didn't care whether he won or not. The real annoyance, however, was that it had worked. He'd shown her the card she'd picked, his smile knowing and pleased at the little burst of surprise she couldn't keep off her face, and just like that, her resolve had cracked, a fissure in her determination that she would do this on her own, with no help and no attachments. And then the game had turned into an actual fight for survival, and there she was, making out with some boy as if the world weren't falling apart, right before he dumped her in an abandoned parking lot. All because of pretty eyes and a dumb card trick. What a sucker she was.

Trip stepped from the plane and walked toward them. "What's going on?"

"Nothing," Cam replied. She turned to River. "It's fine. Go back in the plane. Eat something. I don't feel like talking anymore."

He looked like he wanted to start the whole conversation over, but she wasn't about to let him. Better to stay in control. She was in charge of her own life and made her own decisions. No one did that for her.

River gave a tight nod and headed back into the plane.

"What was that about?" Trip asked.

The mix of anger and fear and wanting to cry became a snarled mess that Cam had no idea what to do with. "I thought he was different."

She found herself in a hug, but that only made her want to cry more.

"Maybe I whacked him too hard with that fire extinguisher," Trip said, trying to make her laugh. When she didn't, he added, "Or not hard enough?"

Cam shook off the threatening tears. There was no time for her to fall apart, even if everything else was. After all they'd been through together, she thought River owed her more, but whatever. He could do what he wanted. She didn't have to care.

Trip headed toward the store. "Think I can find coffee in there?" When Cam didn't follow, he came back and ushered her along. "Come with me. It's too creepy by myself."

Cam went, not wanting to be back on the plane anyway. Nothing was right here. Whatever had happened on the island must have happened here too, must have happened everywhere.

That meant Benji needed her. She couldn't waste energy on anything else. She was ready for all of this to be over, one way or another. They'd find the military base today, and hopefully, some answers.

Walking through the store was no better in daylight. It reminded Cam of the restaurant at Cedar Springs. The produce section had become a mountain of slick black mush, and the fetid smell of rot at the meat counter turned her stomach. After Cedar Springs, they didn't want cookies and sweets anymore. They had escaped the island and survived a plane crash, but there was nothing to celebrate in this uninhabited place. Trip rolled a shopping cart through the aisles and they filled it with canned meat, soup, bottled water—food that would keep them going despite the unknown, despite their fear, despite the strange, alien atmosphere surrounding a place that should have felt safe and familiar.

"Hey, look," Trip said, snatching a box of Oatmeal Creme Pies from an endcap display. "I love these things. My mom packed them in my lunch all through middle school." He opened the box, tore away the cellophane from one, and handed it to her. "Here, eat this. You'll feel better."

Cam remembered the brown sugar sweetness and creamy filling of the one she'd eaten on the island after she'd found Trip's camp. At the time, it had been the best thing she'd ever eaten. That felt like a million years ago.

"I can't believe you snuck these onto the show. And got away with it."

He unwrapped one for himself and looked at it wistfully. "At least for a little while. Until Liza burned it all down. She was pretty badass, huh?"

Cam took a bite. At first it was sweet like she remembered, but the more she chewed, the more it wasn't at all like that time in the woods. It didn't make her feel better. If anything, it was a reminder of how much had changed, and how bad things were. They'd made it to the mainland, but they hadn't found people, and their situation was just as dire as it had been on the island. They were in danger, and the world felt like it was collapsing around her. Sweets wouldn't help. The thing tasted like cardboard on her tongue.

Cam stared at the cookie, the space behind her ribs feeling as empty as the shadowed corners of a room. "Liza should be here."

Trip put an arm over her shoulders. "I know."

He took another slow bite. Immediately his lips screwed into a grimace. He coughed and spit on the floor. What came out wasn't partially chewed cookie, however. It was a mouthful of sand. He dropped the box, spluttering and hacking.

Cam blinked as the half-eaten cookie in her own hand dissolved, filtering through her fingers in tiny granules. At the same time, the box Trip had dropped collapsed into a little pile of sand. Streaks of color from the cardboard — blue, white, and red — mottled the grains.

"The hell?" Trip said, still spitting and wiping at his tongue.

"This is bad," Cam said.

The towering pyramid of boxes in the display buckled and

sand scattered across the floor with the shushing sound of a deflating balloon, covering their feet up to their ankles. One by one, the packages in the aisle behind them dropped into color-streaked streams of falling powder, and then the shelves themselves crumpled until the tiles of the Safeway floor resembled a mislaid beach.

Cam wavered, her feet swallowed and slipping in the growing mounds.

"Let's get out of here," Trip said.

They tried, but it was impossible to run. With each step Cam's feet disappeared. Her shoes filled, her lungs grew heavy, her eyes watered.

Trip fell, and his legs were immediately covered. She grabbed his hand and he struggled up, coughing and red-faced, his eyes streaming from the coarse grains that she could feel too, like sandpaper behind her eyelids. Each shelf they passed dropped into a cascade of sand. She led him blindly to the door, but when her fingers closed on the handle, the door and wall both crumpled, burying them in a flurry of dust. Cam lost hold of Trip. She tried to scream, but sand filled her mouth. It continued to pour down, covering her head. The weight of it trapped her limbs until she was frozen in place, unable to move even an inch in any direction. Panic flared through her blood like electricity.

Someone closed on her arm and pulled. She was dragged, grit scraping into her skin. The moment her face was free she gulped in air, pulling dry particles down her throat, but she didn't care because it was *air*. Trip was to her left, and River was in front of her, tugging her free. She tried crawling forward, but each spot her hands and knees touched turned to pools of sand that slithered under her. They were floppy dolls in a giant shifting sandbox.

"Car!" River choked out, pointing to an idling sedan parked in the fire lane.

Cam fought her way through, but it was like moving in slow motion. Every surface she touched disintegrated, and she could barely see two feet in front of her. She finally escaped the sand and made it to pavement, where she ran for the car. For a split second she was sure that touching it would make the whole thing disappear like everything else, but it didn't, and she dove inside next to Trip in the back. River jumped in the driver's seat and gunned the engine.

They sped across the parking lot. She and Trip twisted around to watch through the rear window as the world flattened into nothing. The grocery store was gone, replaced by a smooth heap of sand. A light pole fell apart from the top down, raining a fountain of debris.

River's gaze focused on the rearview mirror. "It's chasing us."

He was right. The path behind the car was a moving stream, and it was gaining on them. He turned onto the main road, and the path of sand turned with them and followed.

Trip eyed the crumbling street. "We can outrun it. Speed up."

"Don't you get it, Trip?" Cam said. "We can't outrun this any more than we can outrun ourselves. I felt like everything was falling apart, and now it is. We can't stop this."

"You can," River said. "This is happening because of us, and our fear, but we control it. It's like the tidal wave, if it can come out of nowhere, it can go away. It's not real."

Is that how this worked? Believe it's not real, and it'll go away? Just don't be afraid? Or maybe Trip should knock her unconscious, too. Maybe that was the only thing that could save them.

The line of sand behind the car had widened. It took over a fast-food restaurant on one side, a doughnut shop on the other, as if the grains were eating away at the world with tiny sharp teeth.

Cam shook her head. "It's real. Look at it. It's destroying everything. There's nothing we can do." She spoke too quietly for River to hear, but Trip was next to her in the back seat.

Just as softly, he said, "We're all afraid—we're afraid of spiders, and relationships, and things falling apart. Of course it's real. But we can't lose hope. It's not that we're not afraid, we just have to get through it. There's always a way out. Always."

The world behind them was a haze of beige. It surrounded the car on either side until they were driving on an island of pavement. The car fishtailed, its tires spinning and kicking up what remained of the road. A tree fell in front of them and River jerked the wheel just as it exploded in a shower of dust over the windshield.

Billowing clouds blocked out the sun, but a bright flash caught Cam's attention.

"Trip, look."

He glanced up, and his face fell. "My Skym."

"It's moving fast. Can it stay with us?"

"It reads the ions we were injected with. It knows I'm here. It'll follow as long as it can. All the sand in the air, though" —he shook his head—"it can't be good for it."

Even as he spoke, the Skym wavered in the sky. It dipped low, struggling to stay airborne. A billboard fell, dousing the Skym in more sand. It dove sharply, then smashed into the ground, scattering bits of glass and metal.

Trip made a sound like he'd been punched in the gut, and that was it. The last remnant of the show was gone, lying broken and abandoned on a sand-covered road.

They passed a highway sign, and Cam caught the words just before they crumbled: FORT HARRIS MILITARY BASE. That was what they'd come here for, to find answers. The Skyms and the show didn't matter, not anymore. Somebody was there, someone who knew what had happened and what they should do. It was their last chance, but it was a chance.

"Take the next exit," Cam said.

The world continued to disintegrate around them. River leaned into the steering wheel, his eyes narrowed in focus. They zigzagged left and right as he dodged the drifts piling onto the road.

This was her fear, then—this collapse of everything that made sense. Their fears had started out so specifically: dogs, spiders, bad men. This was different. It was far-reaching and impossible, and would swallow the whole world. Perhaps the heart of every fear was right here—despair that the world wasn't orderly and sensible, that it was held together with nothing but hope, as weak and useless as a bit of tape holding on a limb.

Cam clung to that hope. It was all she could do.

"There," Trip said, pointing as they came to the exit.

River turned the car and drove it up the ramp, then merged onto the next road. Slowly, the furious pelting noise quieted, and after they'd driven a ways, the storm dropped behind them.

Trip slumped forward but his head dropped back. "See?" he said. "You did it, Cam."

Cam watched as the sky, shut out by the storm, opened to clear blue. They were eight miles from the military base. Eight miles from, hopefully, some answers.

CHAPTER 23

The sand cleared and the car stabilized as they drove. The roads beyond the Safeway were messy in their own way, however—crowded with empty vehicles and clusters of pile-up accidents. Some cars had simply come to a stop or drifted from the road entirely. They passed a minivan that had rolled off the highway, crushed the bushes in the median, and ended up inside the broken window of a flower shop.

Whatever had happened, it had happened completely, and suddenly.

River had been lucky to find a car with keys dangling in the ignition. That kind of carelessness would have surprised him, except that the cars he'd searched in the parking lot had been just like the tables in the dining room at Cedar Springs. Drinks, purses, fast-food meals, phones with dead batteries, all littered the seats as if they'd been placed there and then abandoned along with the cars days ago.

River's head hurt, and after running from the sand the puncture in his side had opened again where he'd patched it with tape. The painkillers he'd washed down with muddy coffee weren't helping much. He didn't mind the pain, though. Focusing on it gave him a sort of clarity. It kept his thoughts from wandering. So far, only disaster had come from any of their wandering thoughts.

The military base turned out to be a small, grassy compound with buildings of white brick, a row of fluttering flags, and a decorative cannon out front. River pulled into a lot behind a wide, low structure that looked more like business offices than the site of secret military operations. They exited the car, dumping sand from their pockets, emptying their shoes, brushing it from their hair. While the others dug through cars for an access badge to get in the locked door, River gazed back toward where they'd come from. A dense haze blurred the edges of the sky with a strange transparency in the early morning light. They'd outrun the sand, but it still swirled like a monstrous body a few miles away, substantive and large. It seemed to crawl closer with each minute.

"Got one!" Trip called. He slid the badge through the scanner and the door clicked open.

"Do you know where we're going?" Cam asked.

"I have a hunch," Trip said. "There's a department on this base called Remote Experience Training, and here's the thing —they're the people who tried to buy my ThreeDz app."

"They're the ones you didn't sell to?" Cam said.

"Right."

"And someone from that department has been trying to contact the show?"

"Not just contact. The message we saw on the *Cut Off* site was a call for help. A pretty desperate one."

In the hallway, a directory listed the offices.

"H-535," Trip murmured, scanning the names. "Fifth floor."

Trip led them to a stairwell. A bank of elevators could have taken them, and the electricity seemed to be working, but none of them wanted to close themselves in a metal box when there'd be no help from outside if it malfunctioned and trapped them.

River held the door open. Cam went through after Trip, but she didn't make eye contact with him. In fact, she had a distracted look, as if she was straining to hear faraway sounds. He touched her arm to get her attention, and when her gaze landed on him, a coolness settled over her.

"I'm sorry about earlier," he said. "I feel like the sand happened because I pushed you away. I was trying to do the right thing, keep us safe, but . . . I guess I don't know how to protect us from our own minds."

"It's not your job to protect us, River. And it's not all about you. Liza's gone, and she's not coming back. That triggered the sand as much as anything."

"Still, I should have handled things better."

"You don't have to explain yourself to me."

"I know, but—"

"Listen, I just want to go home and be there for my brother. That's what matters to me, *all* that matters. Nothing—not sand, tidal waves, or even you—can distract me from that."

He nodded. "Right. It shouldn't."

He would help her find her brother, do what he could for

her, but anything more than that . . . How many times did it have to go wrong before he figured it out? It was too dangerous.

Cam took a moment to study him in that removed, calculated way he'd noticed when they first met, then slipped past him. He stepped out of her way, and the movement caused pain to shoot through his side, enough to make him wish he'd pocketed more painkillers earlier.

They reached the fifth floor and found H-535, a sign identifying it as the office of the Remote Experience Training Facility. It was in a long hallway, one of three gray metal doors with square glass windows. The rooms were dark, and the building felt eerie. Every noise they made—their footsteps and voices—seemed so much louder than it should have. Beneath the silence, the whole place thrummed like a giant pulsing engine. The place was empty, but it was hard to shake the feeling of being watched.

The keycard didn't work on the door. They stood in the hallway, pondering a trip back downstairs to search an office, find a keycard with a higher clearance.

"How would we know where to find it?" Cam asked.

"Can you tell what the clearance is for the card we have?" Trip said.

River leaned against the wall, drumming his fingers on his arm. This could take hours. He went down the hall and found a hammer in a utility closet, tucked away in a custodian's toolbox. He returned with it and smashed the window of the door with a couple of blows. He reached in and yanked it open.

The room was bigger than he'd expected. Computer screens lined every wall, controlled by dozens of keyboards and thousands of buttons and switches. A row of tanks stretched across the white grated floor, all of them bolted down, with tubes and wires protruding from them, and hoses looping out from the floor.

The deep mechanical thrumming was louder in here. It was coming from under their feet. Beneath the grate floor, a massive machine pulsed with energy, sounding like a hundred fans running at once. River had no idea what it was. Thousands of beams, plates, and wires radiated out in widening circles, like a giant blinking web of circuitry and metal spanning the entire room—even past the room, as the machine disappeared under the walls of the lab.

The tanks anchored to the floor looked like mini submarines, or iron lungs with windows on top of their closed, hinged lids—in any case, they were the right size for a person to lie down in. River wondered if they were, in fact, meant to hold people, and why.

He peered into the first tank in the row. It was empty.

"There's no one here, Trip," he said.

Trip already sat at a computer, typing at high speed, his eyes racing across the screen.

"But somebody sent that message from here. I figure they'll show up."

Cam opened a cupboard. A row of vials lined the shelf. They were filled with clear liquid, and each had a label. She picked one up. "This has my name on it."

River looked through them. "There's one for each of us. And these other names . . ."

"Those must be the other contestants," Cam said, bewildered. "I never heard anything about the military being involved with the show." She flipped through the binders on the lab desks. "Far as I can tell, they were working on virtual-reality technology to train soldiers. There's a whole section here on military surveillance using VR and another on PTSD. Trip, do you think they wanted your app to work on all this stuff?"

Trip didn't look up from the screen. "They didn't just want my app, they needed it. It looks like they went ahead and took it, reverse engineered it. Bastards didn't pay me a dime." He typed some more. "They were piggybacking their own customized tech onto ThreeDz, running an experiment to somehow communicate with the ions we were injected with and the *Cut Off* virtual-reality programming."

"What's this machine under the floor?" Cam asked.

"It's a particle accelerator." Trip scanned the computer screen. "What the hell were they doing with a particle accelerator?"

River looked over Trip's shoulder, but the screen showed strings of lines and numbers that meant nothing to him. "Did they use your app illegally?"

"Not exactly. The tech was readily available for viewers once the show went online. It's just . . ." He kept searching, a crease forming between his eyes. "Instead of using the visors the show was peddling, they built their own engagement system to stream the content. Like, their own visors, I think?"

Cam's head came up from the binders. "Not visors." She looked at the tanks that filled the room. "People."

There were twenty tanks lined up neatly down the center of the room, like coffins in a funeral-home showroom.

Trip stood from his chair. "Jesus."

They peered into each of the tanks until Cam shouted from the other end of the room, "Here!"

They converged on the tank. The readout lights, like those used on hospital monitors in emergency care, blinked red, blue, and yellow, and the window on top of the tank fogged over with condensation.

A man with short-cropped hair floated inside, eyes closed and unconscious, his head and body submerged in a pale, whitish liquid.

Cam searched the hatch seals, looking for a way to open the thing. "I can't find a latch. Trip, can you figure it out?"

A panel on one side blipped lines across a screen, displaying blood pressure, heart rate, respiration, blood-sugar levels, and other vital signs. The readouts indicated the man inside was not dead, but unconscious or drugged.

Trip inspected the buttons and switches and reached up to press one.

"Hold on," River said, stopping him. "Is that safe? We don't know what we're doing, who he is, or what the hell this tank does. What if it's keeping him alive? What if he's connected to the particle accelerator? If we don't do this right, we could kill him."

"I don't think we have a choice," Cam said. "There's no

one else on the base. No one in the whole city. If we don't get him out, who will?"

"What if he can get himself out?" River said.

"Look." Trip tapped the screen embedded in the tank, scrolling through the readout of vital signs. "It says his name's Jacob Lawson. He's thirty-four, a lieutenant, and a scientist through MRL. That's the military research lab. There's a record, and it goes back a while. If he could have gotten himself out, don't you think he would have?"

"How far back does the record go?" Cam asked.

Trip reached the end of the scroll and looked up. "It's been days. Maybe weeks."

Cam's hand settled lightly on the tank. "He's been in this thing for that long?"

"I guess so. There's nothing to indicate he's been out."

"He must have been in there when the producers disappeared," River said.

"Not just the producers," Cam said. "Everyone. If we don't get him out, no one else will."

Why were the other nineteen tanks empty? Why make so many and then use only one?

The tank was indeed a life-support system, Trip explained as he continued to inspect the device. If the tank wasn't disconnected in the proper order, it could be catastrophic for the man inside. It took a while to figure out the mechanics of the thing, but Trip eventually pinpointed a series of buttons on the side that indicated the appropriate procedure. The first few caused three of the pipes to hiss and retract, and the next resulted in a thick yellow liquid shooting into the tank. He turned a knob next, and something went wrong. The monitors beeped frantically.

"Damn it," Trip muttered, pressing more buttons.

The man jerked and thrashed against the glass.

Cam yelped and jumped back. "Do something, Trip."

"I'm trying!"

The machine screeched, and the lights on the panel flared bright red. The man's eyes had opened, but they stared unseeing for a moment, and then his fists beat the glass. The tank gave a deep hydraulic sigh and the lid popped up. River took the man's feet and Trip his shoulders, and they lifted him out. He wore gear of dark-blue rubber, similar to a scuba outfit, and he was slick with the fluid he'd been immersed in, a viscous substance that glopped and smeared on the floor.

The man rolled onto his stomach and heaved the fluid.

Cam knelt next to him, her knees getting wet in the blobs of liquid. "What should we do?"

River shook his head. "What can we do? Wait for it to pass."

The man dropped onto his back as he stopped spasming and breathed heavily.

For all they knew, Jacob was the only person left on the planet besides the three of them. And it seemed like he might have answers.

"Thank God," Jacob croaked.

"Can you walk?" Trip asked.

He nodded and lifted himself up. Trip and Cam helped. He was weak on his feet, and his shoulders hunched forward.

He pointed his chin to a door off the lab marked MEDICAL BAY, a brightly lit room with a row of beds, lockers, and medicine cabinets. He peeled off the blue outfit and left it in a pool on the floor; then, naked and unselfconscious, he toweled himself dry. On wobbly legs he crossed the room to a numbered locker and took out fatigue pants and a gray T-shirt.

"Listen," River said once Jacob was dressed. "What do you know about—"

Jacob held up a silencing hand. "I know you guys have questions. But I need something to eat first."

His voice came out a gravelly rasp. He obviously hadn't spoken in a while.

Cam gave him a bottle of water and microwaved beef stew she found in a kitchen cupboard. Jacob sat in a folding chair drinking in hearty gulps and chewing slowly. Trip and Cam seemed content to wait patiently, their eyes fixed on Jacob, trusting he had all the answers they hoped for. River felt restless, holding his tongue while Jacob took his time getting settled.

Trip blurted out the first question. "You put the panicky 'help' message on the *Cut Off* site, right? That was you?"

Jacob slanted his mouth. "I've trained real hard in how to avoid getting *panicky*, Trip. The tech I was connected to transmits information from the outside. It wasn't designed to send a message in the reverse direction. When I tried, it was like typing with most of the letters hidden and the words floating in a swamp and multiplying beyond my control. I know it looked garbled, but that was the best I could do."

River tilted his head. "How do you know Trip's name?"

"Oh, right. There's a lot you guys don't know. But yes, I know all of you. Pretty well, actually."

"What's that mean?" River was getting impatient.

Jacob took another bite of food. "It's real," he groaned through a mouthful. "It's really real."

"It's from a can," Cam said apologetically.

Jacob shook his head with force. "No, I mean it's not VR food, it's not make-believe cookies eaten by someone else. You can taste a thing, smell a thing, but your brain knows the difference. It seems real, but it's not real. This"—he tapped his spoon on the bowl—"this is real."

"You're sure?" Trip asked.

"Believe me, I can tell."

Trip stumbled to sit in a chair and bowed his head. "So this *has* all been real." He looked up as if appealing to Jacob to say he was wrong. "That's what you're saying—it's real?"

"Yeah, Trip. Definitely."

Cam glanced back and forth between them. "What are you talking about?"

"I know we talked about it before," Trip said. "But in the back of my head this whole time, with all the crazy stuff happening, I couldn't help thinking we're stuck in a simulation. Like we're test subjects in an experiment, hooked up in tanks like Jacob, and this has all simply been computer code."

"Oh." Cam looked a bit stunned.

River had dismissed that idea immediately when Trip had first brought it up back at the resort. He'd been worried the whole time that they were in a simulation? Of course, that was how his mind worked. He studied computers and VR technology. But there was no such thing as virtual reality so convincing you couldn't tell if it was real or not. If there was . . . how were you ever supposed to trust anything?

"That's good, then, right?" Cam said. "That we're not actually stuck in a virtual-reality simulation?"

Trip shrugged. "That depends on what you think 'good' means. If this was a simulation, maybe Liza wouldn't really be gone. If it was an experiment, at least we'd be safe, and there would be someone to unplug us when it's over, same as we unplugged Jacob. But this guy says it's all real, so now we have to try to explain all the things we've seen, and deal with what's happened. Not to mention where everyone disappeared to."

Jacob blinked at Trip, then gazed again at Cam and River. "Right. You still think everyone disappeared."

"They have," River said. "You haven't been out there. Seattle's empty—I'm guessing everywhere else, too. There's just a wasteland. And the internet's deserted, has been for weeks. Everyone's gone. We're the only ones left."

"No," Jacob said. "You don't get it." He dropped the spoon into the empty bowl of stew and put it aside. "It wasn't everyone else who disappeared. It was you."

CHAPTER 24

Jacob wasn't willing to sit around for long. Once he'd finished eating, he set to work in the lab, typing commands into a console and doing some kind of maintenance on the tank he'd only recently been rescued from. He drained the liquid, connected new tubes and hoses.

"We have to get moving," he said. "We have to get back before it falls apart."

Jacob crossed the room for another part, but River stepped in front of him, blocking his way. "What are you talking about? Back where? And before what falls apart?"

Jacob only paused for a second before brushing past. "I'll explain, but let me keep working."

Jacob talked while he hurried back and forth, his hands moving quickly and knowledgeably over the machines.

He explained that he was the second in command of a military research project that had begun a year ago. He certainly didn't look much like a bookish scientist—a physicist, apparently. Though he did look like the kind of guy who'd get excited about something adventurous and high-tech. Even while he worked and spoke, he smiled easily, like he was open for anything, always searching for the next thrill. At the same time, so many days in the tank had taken a toll on him. His skin was pruny and pale, and dark shadows ringed his eyes, which were distant and preoccupied.

The project first tested basic virtual reality before moving on to the new VR visors marketed by *Cut Off*. Jacob directed the volunteer soldiers, and they reported back to him the effects of interacting through the visors, experiencing the VR just as the rest of the *Cut Off* audience was experiencing it. The soldiers joked about their easy mission, calling the project "Reality TV for Science."

After a while, Jacob informed the soldiers of the true nature of the project. They graduated to an entirely new system, one built by the military research lab: multisensory virtual reality.

"They hooked into the new VR through sensory-deprivation tanks, and it was an incredible escalation. In the beginning it was only computer simulations, and they were riding roller coasters and skydiving. When I tried it myself"—Jacob took a breath, as if remembering the exhilaration—"I could feel the wind on my face and my stomach drop. It was wild. Some of the soldiers couldn't handle it. There was a lot of vomiting after those exercises."

He suddenly clutched the edge of a tank, out of breath from all his movement. So many days spent enclosed inside the metal tub had left him weak. Cam handed him another bottle of water, which he drank.

He smiled warmly. "Thanks, Cam."

There was something strange about the way he said her name. It was so familiar, as if they were old friends. She might have thought it was simply because he'd watched the show as it aired and thus felt like he knew her, but it was more than that. There was a significance in his tone that she couldn't overlook.

He continued with his story.

The project — Jacob's project — involved the contestants on *Cut Off*. The show presented a unique opportunity to expand the scope of the military's new combat training.

"Imagine," Jacob said, "an army whose experience is entirely accessible to commanders, even from a distance. Soldiers would be able to train in the very environments they'd be serving in without ever leaving home. A general could tap into the experience of any soldier at any time. He could be on the ground in a combat situation, while remaining completely safe. Not to mention the opportunities for infiltration and espionage, tracking targets twenty-four/seven, with no one the wiser. We had no choice but to take advantage of the *Cut Off* technology and access Trip's app in the Skyms."

The soldiers were injected with what were called *sympathy bots*, which were clusters of entangled particles. The soldiers would engage with the show while submerged in the tanks, thus experiencing the wilderness not only through their eyes and ears, as they had with the visors, but through every sensation possible: sight, sound, touch, taste, smell.

The sympathy bots were designed with a unique signature, so each soldier would connect with a specific contestant.

Jacob pointed to the cupboard of vials. "If you were wondering why your names are on those vials, that's why. Those vials are full of sympathy bots. The ones I was injected with connected me with Cam."

Cam had been standing close to Jacob, concerned about how tired he might become and how much he was trying to do after the harrowing experience of being trapped in the tank. When she heard that Jacob had connected to her, that he'd had access to *every sensation possible*, unconsciously she took a step back.

The connection probably explained his familiarity with her.

"You were watching only me the whole time?" she said.

Jacob shook his head. "Not *watching*, Cam. That's how the visors worked. This technology is different. I would *be* you, experience and feel everything you did, from your perspective. I'd see and hear what you did, like everyone else who watched the show, but I could also smell, taste, and feel what you did."

Cam watched River struggle with his thoughts even as she tried to parse her own. Before she could figure out what to say, River said, "Why would you get the injection of sympathy bots? I thought you were testing on soldiers."

"I spent a lot of time designing this program, working on the technology, and experiencing it step by step with the soldiers. There's no way I'd let someone else be the first person to try it for real."

"You had no right," River said. "You can't just go into someone's brain like that."

He spoke with so much conviction, and she understood his outrage. At the same time, she hadn't expected privacy when she'd signed on for the show.

Jacob shrugged at River's indignation. "I'm not concerned about what's right or wrong here. I was in charge of important research. I was doing my job. The fact is, the show gave the public access to the technology, and our research project took advantage of it, enhancing it in new and exciting ways. There wasn't anything illegal or subversive about it. And it wasn't supposed to affect anyone but those of us in the tanks. You wouldn't have known one way or the other, except something went wrong."

Trip was engrossed in Jacob's story, his chin in his hand.

Cam and Jacob had never met, never touched, never talked, yet he'd known her longer than River or Trip had. She needed to remind herself that she didn't know him at all.

"So what went wrong, exactly?" Trip said. "And what did you mean, *we* disappeared?"

"Okay," Jacob said, taking a minute to think through his answer. "Dr. Barker—she's my partner, and the person in charge of the project—wanted to take our virtual-reality experiments further. She's a visionary, willing to take chances and thwart protocol to get her ideas out there. She got access to the exact configuration of the ions used by the show, the ones we used to create the nest of sympathy bots for each contestant."

The machine under their feet filled the air with a constant drone. Beneath that, Cam could still hear the voices. Had she been hearing Jacob this whole time? Was the whispering in the trees somehow tied to Jacob's brain connecting to her sensory experience?

"What happened?" Trip said.

Jacob closed his eyes briefly. "Something . . . unexpected

happened. When I stepped into the tank, Dr. Barker, the soldiers, the other scientists, all crowded around me, taking notes. It was a party. We had champagne. We were excited to see how it worked in action. Every screen in the room was streaming *Cut Off*, and more soldiers lined up, immersion suits on, ready to hop into their own tanks and connect to their own contestant once we had a successful link established. After that, it's hard to explain. Dr. Barker activated the particle accelerator, which would trigger the connection between my brain and Cam's. And here's the thing—it worked. Suddenly I was standing in the wilderness. I *was* Cam. The problem is, I was only supposed to be in there for a couple hours, but then days went by. I figured it out around the same time you guys did. Everyone had disappeared."

"Right," River said. "Everyone disappeared. Except you said they *didn't*, so which is it?"

Jacob turned to Trip. "Do you know anything about entangled particles?"

"A little. It's like a quantum physics thing, right?" Trip said.

"Yes. Entangled particles are connected in such a way that action on one particle has an instantaneous effect on another, even when they're apart, whether across a laboratory or at the distant ends of the universe. No one knows how this can happen, and it seems contrary to all the laws of physics, but . . . there it is." Jacob shrugged. "So I was in the tank, and what was supposed to happen was that I would fully immerse. Cam's perceptual data would become my sensory experience."

"My perceptual data?" Cam said, hugging her arms around herself.

"Yes," Jacob said. "I know it's weird. It was weird for me, too." He gave her another one of his warm smiles. "It was only supposed to be for two hours. I'm glad it was you, at least, and not one of the others. There was this one guy on the show who kept drinking his own urine. Even when he had plenty of water to drink. I guess he was trying to make himself famous by being a spectacle. So listen, I'm glad I was connected to you, Cam. You made it bearable while I was stuck in that tank."

"Okay, great, I didn't drink pee," Cam said. "But your firsthand sensory hookup with me didn't make the world disappear."

"That's what took me a while to figure out. *We're* the ones who disappeared. This place we're in, it's not the real world." He held up a finger to Trip, who was about to jump in. "And it's not a simulation, either. I don't know. My best guess is that the particle accelerator somehow created a brand-new world, and it put us on an alternate plane of existence, like a parallel dimension. And we're the only ones in it."

Parallel dimension.

Trip's and River's expressions conveyed different reactions to this information, somewhere between annoyed skepticism and wide-eyed disbelief. Cam had never heard of particle accelerators or entangled particles, and she'd never thought about parallel dimensions. It seemed impossible to comprehend what Jacob was talking about.

"You mean," Trip said, "we're not in the real world? We're not in *our* world?"

"I can't know anything, Trip," Jacob said. "It's a theory, an educated guess."

"And in this dimension," Trip said, "our fears are real?"

"You mean like the sand and the spiders?"

"How do you know about that?" River asked.

"You keep forgetting, I was there. I've been there the whole time, with you guys. But it was impossible to communicate and let you know."

Cam asked the question that had been nagging her. "I heard voices in the woods, and then at the resort. And I heard them again when we landed. Was that you, somehow? Were you trying to talk to me?"

Jacob's smile, seemingly reserved for her, dropped instantly. His face turned hard. "You heard voices?"

"Yes. Like whispering. All the time. That wasn't you?"

"I couldn't talk to you. I was connected to your brain waves, but you weren't connected to mine, so it'd be impossible. You've been hearing voices the whole time?"

She was hearing them louder in Seattle than anywhere else. Jacob's look was so stern, however, that she let it go. "Yeah," she said, flustered by his penetrating gaze. "I guess it was just in my head. Never mind."

Jacob shook off his sudden intensity. "If I'm right, this world exists because of Cam's consciousness, so it's a world controlled by consciousness, and everything here is the manifested reality of our thoughts and emotions. Does that make sense?"

"No," River said. "None of this makes sense. There's no such thing as parallel dimensions. That's something made up in the movies."

"Not really," Jacob said. "The possibilities of what we can do with this technology are endless. The biggest unsolved problem in physics is the nature of quantum reality. And I'm good at what I do, but Dr. Barker is a genius. If anyone could make such a thing happen, even by accident, she could. She's all business, but the day before I went into the tank, we had a few drinks at a bar downtown and ended up talking about our technology for hours. We let our imaginations run wild, without worrying about evidence or grants, labs or experiments. We considered what this thing" — Jacob waved his hand, indicating the monstrous computer under the floor — "this particle accelerator is capable of. We talked about multiple parallel universes — the multiverse — and we didn't invent it; it's not like it's new. The many-worlds theory has been around since the sixties. Dr. Barker knows as well as I do that the mathematics that account for the theory are impressive, and let me tell you, she's not one for flights of fancy."

River crossed his arms. "You're talking about alternate planets populated by smart apes, things like that?"

"That movie was the future, not a different dimension," Cam said.

"That's not what I'm saying anyway," Jacob said. "There are millions of parallel dimensions, but my theory is that this dimension was *created*, independent of the rest of the multiverse."

Trip shook his head, confused. "What?"

"River," Jacob said, "you have those cards?"

"I lost them in the tidal wave."

"Didn't you pick up new ones at the Safeway?"

River's lips twitched and Cam nudged his side. "Come on, he's trying to help."

River sighed. He peeled the cellophane off the brand-new deck and handed them over.

Jacob tapped the deck. "Imagine each of these cards represents a separate, parallel world." He flipped up the five of clubs. "This is a world where a meteor never killed the dinosaurs." He held up another card, the jack of diamonds. "This is a world where the Nazis won World War Two. And this," he said, showing them a six of spades, "this is a world where some small, insignificant thing happened differently from our home world. Where, say, you decided you wanted bacon and eggs for breakfast instead of your usual bagel with cream cheese. So instead of grabbing something as you walk out the door, maybe you go to a diner. It's not that different, right? But maybe there are ripple effects. You have a conversation with the waitress about how the weather's turned cold, and on the way home she drives to the store to buy herself a new winter coat, and maybe she gets into a fender bender in the parking lot. Little ripples, little waves in our existence. Some of them can turn into a huge swell, and some simply flow along with no significant repercussions. The point is, every decision, every accident, every choice, becomes a new timeline." He fanned the cards on the table. "It becomes a new card."

Trip picked up two of the cards. "So if our real world is this nine of hearts, then where we are now is like this ace of spades or something?"

Jacob shook his head. He took the card box from River's hand and fished out the card left inside—the joker.

"The timeline we're in now is like this: a wild card. It has no value or suit or property of its own. Its properties are determined at the discretion of whoever holds it. In this case, that's us. Me and Cam, specifically."

River's brow furrowed. "What do you mean, 'you and Cam'?"

"Think about it," Jacob said. "It was Cam's consciousness that created this whole world—a consciousness-driven world. And everyone still in the game was pulled along with it. This world was generated *independent* of the rest of the deck. That's why, when our fears feel most real and tangible, they become something real here."

"Great," Cam said. "So if only my love of candy was stronger than my fear, we'd be trapped in a candy land right now?"

"This world was created because of your consciousness, but we all seem to have an impact on it, not only you. Think of it like this—the particle accelerator is the sun, a giant furnace that generates massive amounts of energy. If you hold a magnifying glass up to the sun, it can create fire. That fire is this new dimension that never existed before."

"And Cam is the magnifying glass," Trip said. "Like a conduit."

"That's what I'm thinking. Listen, I don't have all the

answers. When you're dealing with this much energy, poking around with the fundamental laws of physics, strange things can happen. This is exactly the kind of thing Dr. Barker would obsess over. If we can harness what's happened here, the implications are staggering."

River crossed his arms. "You're talking about this world like it's an abstract concept, an exciting experiment, but we're stuck here. We could have died. Some of us *did* die. You messed with our . . . consciousness, or sympathy bots, or whatever. We're not soldiers, we didn't volunteer. Your project cost people their lives."

"What happened to Liza is tragic, and Brandon, too. We never meant for anyone to get hurt. But listen, my life's also at risk. I didn't just experience what you've been through from Cam's perspective. I had my own fears to contend with. I am —or *was*—deathly afraid of wasps. When I finally figured out how to navigate the VR, it became a nightmare where my fears came to life. Every day they attacked me."

Cam hadn't really thought about the fact that Jacob had been alone this whole time. Sure, he'd been with the four of them, but they hadn't known he was there. He'd spent days in that tank, not knowing whether he'd live or die, apparently immersed in his own fears. It sounded terrifying.

"That must have been awful," Cam said.

"It was. I learned something from it, though. When I wasn't hanging out with you, I practiced fighting my fears, fighting the wasps. Eventually, I had it under control, no more attacks."

"What do you mean, 'hanging out with me'?"

"I figured out how to move through the VR. I could immerse in the show with you, but I was also able to create new spaces within the program. I learned to control my experience, almost like you would control a dream. I bet you could do it here, too, Cam, if you tried."

The determination and strength in his eyes gave her hope that they'd get through all this. He'd been alone, conquered his fears—learned how to tame his wasps—and now he could help them. Perhaps controlling fear was a way to control this strange world they were in.

"I don't know what else explains any of this, so let's say your parallel dimension theory is true," River said. "What I care about is how we get back."

Jacob had taken a break from his work on the computers, talking to them while a tube sucked the whitish fluid from the tank's basin. River's question seemed to jolt him back into action. He extracted a hose from the wall and dropped it in the same tank he'd been in, then pulled a second hose for the adjacent tank. They both filled gradually with new, gurgling fluid.

"That's the other thing I was doing while I was stuck in that tank—trying to work that out. I have a theory. If some quirk in the VR created this dimension, our best bet is to recreate the conditions that caused the problem to begin with. If Cam and I go into the tanks at the same time, our minds can function as entangled particles, establishing a channel of communication that might give us the means to navigate back to the real world. Someone out here can activate the particle accelerator. It might work."

River shook his head. "No way. I don't understand a word you just said, but no way is one of us getting in those tanks."

"She has to. It's the only way I can think of. It was Cam's consciousness that created this world, and we need to recreate the parameters of the experiment."

Cam watched the white fluid pouring into the tanks from the hoses, a tight feeling in her stomach. "What would I have to do?"

"Here's my thinking. We want to end up in the real world, our home dimension." Jacob illustrated his point by separating out individual cards from those still spread on the table. He separated the joker next. "Here's where our consciousnesses and our physical bodies are now. We recreate the conditions that brought us here, and then, in the tanks, we use the virtual space to navigate our way home. Reverse what happened."

"It sounds complicated," Trip said.

"In the tanks, Cam and I can create a new, independent expanse of consciousness that we control. I want to act quickly, though. The island is gone, it's underwater. Eventually, what happened there will happen everywhere. This world will continually fall apart, and if we're still here when it does . . . Has anyone looked outside lately?"

All of them turned to look out the window. The skyline of Seattle was obscured by a massive sandstorm. The haze had thickened in the distance, rising up from the buildings in a swirling dance. It was eerie and unsettling—those empty buildings, the way the lines of the horizon didn't join quite right, like they were crooked, and something about the cloud made them verge on transparent. Whether it was sand, or an earthquake, or a tidal wave didn't matter. Something was eating its way toward them. Something large.

Jacob's eyes creased as he watched the crumbling landscape. "At best, we run from one place to the other, constantly chased by our fears. At worst? Now that we know this world is a construct, it's all the more likely to fall apart, and we die."

"You can't know that," River said. "This is such a load of crap. What you're talking about is dangerous, and you have no idea what will happen."

"You're right, River, I don't know for sure. But I believe this will work. Anyway, we don't have much choice." He brushed his hand toward the window. "We can't stay here."

The tanks were filled with fluid now. Jacob lifted out the hoses and tapped more buttons. He seemed to think they'd get going immediately, but Cam's head was spinning.

"Is it dangerous?" she asked.

"It's more dangerous to wait for what's coming. But it'll be okay. Remember, Cam, you can learn to control your fears too, like I did. I'll be there, in the VR with you, to help."

"I don't like this," River said.

"I'm not going to lie, there are no guarantees. I'll admit this project was the realization of some big ideas, and apparently even Dr. Barker and I didn't understand the repercussions of what we were doing, because we certainly didn't predict any of this. But as long as Cam and I are together, her safety is my top priority. I promise you that."

Cam looked at the two open tanks, side by side. "If I really am the only one who can help us get back, I guess I have to try," Cam said.

River's jaw tightened at her words. But how could she not try? If it would get her back to Benji, what else could she do?

Ever since that first earthquake, which she'd caused, she'd felt powerless and scared. Jacob held out the prospect of doing something that would help. River might not be happy about it, but he would put himself at risk in a heartbeat for the rest of them, so who was he to say she shouldn't do the same?

"This thing you're talking about doing in the tank," Trip said. "It'll work for everyone? We'll all get back to the real world?"

"Like I said, I think so. The world we're in is specific to us. An accident. This dimension is transient, and it will cease to exist without us. We'll be okay as a long as we find our home dimension, the real world, before that happens."

"What if we don't get home?" River said. "What happens to us?"

Jacob shrugged. "Our consciousness ties us to this world. If it collapses, we'll go with it."

"So what does everyone think happened to us?" Cam asked. "What did they see on the cameras?"

"From their perspective, we probably disappeared. Just like you thought everyone disappeared here."

"They must be looking for us."

"If you disappeared, search parties would scour the island.

When I went into the tank, by the way, the show was a huge hit. Can you imagine so many people watching while you guys vanished?"

Benji would have been watching the show. He didn't have any VR visor to watch with — they couldn't afford one — but he'd be watching, and worried. He'd be freaking out, actually. He'd been excited that she was going to be on TV. All the kids at school talked about it nonstop. She would return a celebrity, he said, and he'd show her off to everyone. If they'd disappeared, with everyone watching, surely everyone was talking about it constantly on the internet and on TV. She could just imagine Benji glued to every headline. She hoped Aunt Pam would shield him from some of it, not let him get too upset.

"What about the military?" Cam said. "They know what happened, the how and the why. Aren't they doing anything to fix this? The least they could do is tell our families we're alive."

"They don't know that we're alive," Jacob said. "We disappeared, remember? They don't know this world exists."

River eyed the prepared tanks. "You want to do this right now. Today."

"It's not like I'm looking forward to getting back in that tank," Jacob said. "Honestly, I was beginning to unravel in there. But who knows how much time we have. I'd like to get moving."

Cam wanted to go home — to the real world, to Benji — and she was more than ready to get away from this terrible place, but everything was moving so fast.

Jacob held her elbow, seeming to understand. "There's still

some programming I need to do, and I'll need to fire up the accelerator. Take a minute, get something to eat. You don't have to hop in the tank right this second."

"Okay," Cam said. Her hands vibrated with nervous energy.

"Not too long," Jacob said. "We want to get home, right?"

River followed Cam into the hallway. He leaned against the wall, looking at her with tight eyes.

"What?" she said.

"You're really doing this?"

"I don't have a choice."

"Of course you have a choice."

"Jacob seems to have a handle on what's happening."

River drew a hand through his hair. "He and this Dr. Barker are the very people who got us into this mess."

"He wants to get home as much as we do. You have to believe that, at least."

River's head tipped down, a quick nod. He wasn't agreeing with her. He was taking in the information that she trusted Jacob enough to submerge herself in a tank and join him in an unknown, possibly dangerous state of consciousness.

He was also probably thinking about that violent version of River she'd made appear on the island, and how she now evidently trusted a guy she'd just met more than she trusted River. He didn't understand that her feelings for him were the very thing that made trusting him so terrifying. She understood Jacob's motives because they were the same as hers: to get back home.

Trusting River, on the other hand, felt like a much greater risk.

Trusting River meant heartbreak.

River went back into the lab.

When she was alone again, the strange voices returned, their words just out of reach. Jacob had reacted to her mentioning them, as if he suspected where they came from. Surely they weren't a delusion, surely there was an explanation.

The voices never quieted now. And they were getting louder.

CHAPTER 25

In the hallway, Cam had barely looked at him. It was better that way, and he'd caused it, but her aloofness left a hole in his gut. He'd wanted to talk to her. Everything in him fought against trusting Jacob. The man was full of information, revelations, and theories, and he seemed to have an answer for everything. Cam wouldn't listen to River, however, not after the conversation they'd had at the Safeway.

In the lab, Jacob typed on a tank's keypad. Trip followed Cam to the kitchen on the premises, but River stayed behind with Jacob. He picked up some papers on a desk and flipped through them. They contained charts, strings of numbers and code, words he either didn't understand or had never seen before, like *neuristor*, *nanos*, *biometrics*, and *teraflops*. Instead of reading more, he swept up his playing cards from the table and shuffled them together, keeping his eyes on Jacob. Jacob felt his stare and paused.

After a moment of awkward silence, he said, "You don't trust me, do you?"

"Should I? If you and your Dr. Barker had left us alone instead of trying to invade our minds, we wouldn't be here."

"I know it's been hard. I know what it was like out there in the wilderness. We were alone, and it was scary."

"*We* were alone? You weren't out there. You may as well have been watching a TV show that we starred in."

Jacob touched a litmus strip to the liquid inside the tank, then inspected the results. "I felt everything, same as you. Hunger and pain. Every taste and smell and sensation. I've been with you every step of the way."

"You've been *spying* on us every step of the way."

"However you want to see it, I know you guys, and I know Cam. That's why I'm confident she can get us home. She's a strong person."

"You know her the way a stalker knows his target."

"I'd say I know her a bit better than you do."

"No, you don't."

"I know you, too, River. I may not have been able to see and hear what you did, not like I could with Cam . . ." Jacob talked about Cam as if she'd agreed to whatever connection they had, as if he had some kind of relationship with her. Jacob continued. "Settle down. I'm only asking you to give me some credit. I was there, remember. Every glance you shared, every word . . ." His lips twitched. "Everything. I was there." When River bristled at that, he said, "Oh, don't worry. I went some-where else when it got . . . private. But I know your feelings for her, and I have insight into your relationship that you're not capable of." Jacob tipped his chin at River's hands. "You'll bend your cards."

River looked down at the deck squeezed in his fist. He slipped them back into the box.

It wasn't really anything Jacob *said*. If River tried to explain this conversation to the others, it would sound harmless, like River was the one being unreasonable. Jacob's tone made it sound like they were discussing the weather, but River heard the well-hidden danger coloring the edges of the man's voice. He wasn't entirely sure even Jacob knew it was there.

"If anything happens to her, if she gets hurt, or Trip—"

"It must be hard, always feeling the need to save everyone. Maybe take a break, give someone else a chance. Maybe Cam is perfectly capable of saving herself."

"We need your help. I won't pretend we don't. But if you try anything . . ."

Everything in Jacob's body language relaxed, and suddenly he was an affable, open friend. He punched River lightly on the shoulder. "Listen, don't worry. We're in this together, we'll get out together, right?"

"Whatever you say."

Something was up with Jacob. Something more than him having been in the tank for too long.

River turned the box of cards in his hand. "If only one of these cards is the real world, how do you expect to find our home dimension? I could shuffle this deck a million times and it'd never come up the same twice. If the multiverse is what you say, there must be a million—a million million—dimensions out there. It'll be impossible."

"I believe Cam can do it. I believe she'll sense where it is somehow. She's got to. It's our only shot." Jacob typed a final command into the second tank and closed the lid, giving it a quick rap with his knuckles. "I'm going to head downstairs and make sure everything's ready to go with the accelerator. As soon as Cam's in a suit, we're all set."

After a while, Trip came in, fidgety and excited.

"Hey, man," Trip said. "I ran into Jacob on the way back from the kitchen. He's been showing me the particle-accelerator control room. I've never seen anything like it."

River wished he could help in a concrete way, like Trip could. He was out of his element, though, surrounded by computers and programming notes. He'd been able to help them survive in the woods. Here was a different story.

"Do you think all that stuff Jacob said about different dimensions is real?"

Trip shrugged. "When you're using a particle accelerator and dealing with high-energy physics, crazy things can happen. Man, if we can journey across dimensions and alternate universes . . . imagine the possibilities. Maybe there is a multiverse out there, endless worlds, each one taking a different path from our own."

"They're like the scientist who detonated the first atom bomb. All they cared about was trying their new toy. They had no concept of the danger or the consequences."

Trip thought for a moment. "I guess so. But that's how science works, isn't it?"

"Did Jacob say anything else while you were down there with him?"

"No. He was showing me how to engage the particle accelerator once he and Cam are in the tanks."

"You think it's creepy that Jacob's been watching us this whole time, don't you? It can't just be me."

"We were on camera, at least until things changed. Everyone was watching us."

"Not the way Jacob was. The visors were 3-D and immersive and all that, but in the end it was just a fancy way to watch a show. Whatever Jacob was doing in that tank went beyond anything we agreed to. He couldn't just see and hear what she did. He experienced the world *as* Cam—all her senses, what she felt and tasted."

"And you're jealous?"

"Come on, Trip. I'm not jealous. I wouldn't ever want that."

"So you see it as, like, a privacy issue."

"More than privacy. Think about it: if who we are is the sum of our interactions with the world, who do we become if someone else is able to violate that experience? And what right do they have to do it? Sure, we signed on for cameras, and yeah, the virtual-reality stuff, but we never agreed to share our fundamental selves."

"That's heavy," Trip said. "And definitely, it's a violation. But you heard Jacob: we were never supposed to find out about all that. They didn't care, as long as they got to experiment on us. To them, we were rats in a maze."

"Their maze got Liza killed. And it could still kill us."

"What'd you say to Cam?" Trip asked after a moment. "You're both acting strange. It's all very businesslike, except for you staring at her when she's not looking, and the way she's trying to hide how miserable she is."

"It's possible she's miserable because we're trapped in a fear-based alternate dimension."

"I mean, sure. We all are. But don't tell me it's not obvious. She's too proud to admit it, but I'm pretty certain you ripped her heart out."

River sighed. Cam had reverted so quickly to her defensive self, guarded and careful, just like she'd been when they'd first met, and of course that was what she'd done. He'd counted on it. He needed her to keep her distance, because it wasn't in him to do it. She'd wanted to trust him, and he'd promised that she could. He'd broken that promise. Regardless of the reason, she wouldn't forgive him.

"On the plane, when she collapsed . . ." The words stuck in his throat. He tried again. "She's not safe with me."

"None of us are safe, no matter what you do."

"Trust me, it's better this way."

The light outside shone like burnished metal in the sky. River squinted into the distance.

"Do you see that?" Trip said.

The dense haze blotted out the landscape. Mount Rainier wasn't visible anymore. The Space Needle in the city center wavered on the horizon. Rays of light broke through it like glass. The air cracked with static and the top of the Space Needle tipped, then slid down, breaking apart as it fell. Slashes of brilliance lanced into the distant buildings. The city was breaking apart.

"If we're really doing this," River said, "we should do it now."

■ ■ ■

Cam stood by the window. Another building split and shattered in place. The electricity in the air had sharpened. They could feel it, a sensation of energy crawling over their skin like a swarm of insects. River pushed the thought from his mind. It was no good thinking about bugs in a place where they could swarm as soon as they were imagined.

On the island everything had happened in such quick succession, furiously and fast. This was something else. With the collapse of downtown, it was as if the sandstorm had merged into a collective miasma of fear, and now it was rolling across the city.

Jacob commanded the room, directing Trip to start up the tanks. He wore his blue outfit already, the upper half hanging down around his waist.

"Cam," Jacob said, "come away from the window. Help Trip with the other tank."

Cam had dressed in the locker room, and now the blue rubber suit covered her from ankles to wrists. Her hair was wet and slicked back. She clutched her hands nervously, and River wanted to go to her, help somehow, but he held back.

What they were doing was dangerous and unpredictable. When Jacob had been in the tank, a whole world had been conjured from nothing but experimental machinery. What would happen when Cam was in there with him?

The tanks blinked and beeped to life as Trip followed the procedure written out in a manual Jacob had provided.

"What's it going to be like?" Cam asked Jacob.

He went to her and rubbed her arms comfortingly. "You'll do fine. Just remember, you're in control. I'll show you what to do once we're in there." He zipped up the rest of his body suit.

"What's the liquid?" Trip said.

"It's a fluorocarbon," Jacob said. "An oxygen-rich fluid. It allows your lungs to absorb oxygen from liquid rather than from the air."

"So you breathe that stuff?"

"It's a pretty drastic adjustment, but once it's working you don't notice it anymore. In the VR experience, it's like you're breathing air." Jacob bent his legs so he was level with Cam. "You ready?"

Cam nodded. Jacob helped her climb into the tank, and she sat up in it while Trip entered the final settings. River approached and inspected the controls. They were too complex to make sense of, but he wanted to be near her.

"I don't know how to do this," she whispered to him.

He held her gaze. "You don't have to. We can find another way."

She shook her head. "No. We're out of time." As if she was convincing herself, she said, "It's okay. I'm okay."

Trip rested his hand on the lid. "You ready?"

Cam lay down. The fluid enveloped her until only her face remained visible. She looked at Jacob in the adjoining tank. "You're sure I can breathe this in?"

"That's the way it works." To show her, he leaned back. The fluid covered his head. It bubbled around him as he inhaled.

Cam blinked rapidly, took two deep breaths, then sank into the liquid.

Trip closed the lid.

CHAPTER 26

The world tilted.

After Cam took her first breath in the tank, the world skewed badly enough that she wondered if they were too late, and whatever was shattering downtown Seattle had finally reached the military base. And then she was lying down in the tank but she was also standing on her feet. The blue rubber suit clung to her skin, and the soft fabric of a white dress fluttered around her. And those feelings were true at the same time.

For the first time since the plane, the whispers stopped. Wherever she was, it was silent.

With a wave of vertigo she took in her new surroundings —a blank white room without doors or windows. Jacob stood nearby, wearing his fatigues and gray T-shirt.

She hadn't known what to expect, but it wasn't this.

"This is weird," she said. "It's like I'm in two places at once."

"What do you mean?" Jacob asked.

"I feel a little sick, actually. Like I'm in two worlds, and in one I'm eating butterscotch pudding, and in the other I'm eating fish, and they're mixing together in my stomach."

"Huh," Jacob said, considering her. "The VR is meant to be immersive. You can tell your body is in the tank right now?"

Cam nodded. "You can't?" She braced herself against the wall. It resembled bathroom tile. She could feel it under her fingers, cool and smooth, and as much as she told herself it wasn't really there, it didn't matter. It *felt* real. But so did the warm, sloshing liquid that bubbled through her fingers. "It really is making me queasy."

"You'll acclimate," Jacob said.

After several minutes, though the warring sensations remained, she did start to feel better. The rubber suit and the dress no longer stood at such odds; her awareness of being suspended weightless in liquid came to terms with gravity pressing on her body.

"Okay," she said, "what are we supposed to do?"

"I want you to concentrate, Cam. Think about your house, your family. The things that you miss."

"There's no place like home?"

"Something like that. Just focus. I'll do the same thing. I've had more practice in the VR space. If you can find home, I'll make sure it becomes something real here."

She closed her eyes.

What was home, though? She'd barely seen where Aunt Pam lived, so that didn't feel like home. And not Brad's house. They didn't live there anymore, and it had never been theirs anyway.

She'd barely started, and already she was failing. If she couldn't picture her own home, how could she get back to it?

He'd said family, too, however. That was Benji. She missed him, his chattering voice, constant and too loud until she had to wear headphones just to find quiet for a minute, his messy room that smelled like crayons and sneakers, his tight, infrequent hugs.

"Cam," Jacob said.

She opened her eyes. A door had appeared in one wall of the room.

"Is that . . . is that a door home? How did that happen?"

Jacob grinned. "I *knew* you could do it. I knew we'd be great partners. That was perfect—you did it so easily. Incredible."

She shrugged, mystified. "I wasn't thinking about a door. You're sure I made that?"

"When you told me about the strange voices, I knew. I should have been hearing everything you did, but I never heard any disembodied voices. You're somehow connected to the real world in a way that the rest of us aren't."

"What are you talking about?"

Jacob went on excitedly. "Imagine a wall separating us, in this dimension, from home. I think for you the wall is thinner. It's more like a veil that lets in light and sound. Those voices and whispers in the trees are the veil lifting a little, and only you can sense it. Think about it. You were probably hearing search parties in the woods. You couldn't see them, but you could hear them. They must have blanketed the place. The airplane was silent because in the real world it was empty. You heard people staying at the resort. You heard crowds in Seattle, because Seattle is still there. That's why you're the one who can find the real world for us. I've been searching for some kind of portal back for days, and you did it like—" He snapped his fingers, shaking his head in amazement. "Damn, just like that." Speaking more to himself than to her, he paced back and forth and said, "It was your neural signature the program latched on to, your specific consciousness that created this world. That must be it. Don't you see? That's why you can get us home."

"But . . . home is through a door?" It was pretty underwhelming when it came down to it. Were they supposed to walk through the door? And that would be it—this would all be over?

"This is virtual reality. You can sense the real world, and I can help you manifest your understanding of how to finally get there. So together, we manifested a door. Makes perfect sense. Now." Jacob spread his palms in invitation. "Open it."

Cam walked to the door and curled her fingers around the knob. "What about our bodies? We're still in the tanks."

"That doesn't matter. We can't separate our bodies from our consciousness. We'll disappear from the tanks like we'd never been there. Come on, Cam. Let's go."

"What about the others?"

"They're fine. They'll be right behind us. You pulled them through with you the first time, you'll bring them back, too."

The knob on the door was white like the walls, a porcelain handle, polished and real to touch.

How would the others follow? There was no door for them to walk through, even a door conjured in their minds. If what mattered was consciousness, where was River's consciousness now? Or Trip's? Not here.

"But how can—"

"Jesus, Cam, just open it!" Jacob paused, then with noticeable effort modulated his voice. "It's the only way. All you have to do is turn the knob."

She dropped her hand from the door. "You can't, can you? You need me to do it. But we can't leave without the others."

Jacob took a moment to summon patience. "It's not ideal, I get that. When we're home, I'll brief Dr. Barker on the situation, and we'll find a way to get them back. With cutting-edge technology at our disposal, and the most brilliant minds the military has to offer, we'll find a way. You can't ask for more than that."

"You said yourself, this world is falling apart. It'll take River and Trip with it. They'll die."

A small, unsure voice spoke from behind her. "Cam?"

She spun around.

Benji.

Benji was in the room with her.

She ran to him, folded him in her arms. "What are you doing here?" She held his face in her hands, kissed him, practically smothered him in another hug.

"Let go, Cam. I can't breathe."

"Sorry, kid." She took him in, ruffling his hair like an annoying mom, but she couldn't help herself. "I can't believe it's you." She asked Jacob, "How is he here?"

"You have control over this place. You focused on him and brought him here."

She looked Benji over, wanting to memorize him, take him

in. It felt like she hadn't seen him in forever. Since he was born, she'd been there.

Something poked out from under the short sleeve of his shirt. She pushed the fabric aside to find a bruise on his skin in the shape of fingers. "Benji, what's this?"

His eyes were wide and worried. "Aunt Pam. It's nothing. She gets mad sometimes is all."

"*She* did this?"

"Come on," Benji said. "Let's go home. Come home with me, and I can live with you. I want to live with you, Cam."

"I'll be back soon, I promise."

"She's coming, Cam," Benji said. "She'll be here any second. We have to go."

Cam's heart beat furiously. "Who's coming?"

A rush of dizziness swept through her, and then Aunt Pam was there, in the room with them. She had on the same suit she'd worn at Cam's mother's sentencing in court. Stern, sharp lines creased her face. "What the hell are you doing?" She grabbed Benji. "I didn't say you could leave the house."

"Stop!" Cam pulled Benji back. His face was red and his mouth twisted in a grimace. Aunt Pam was upsetting him, and now Cam was upsetting him too. "It's okay," she said, clutching him to her.

Aunt Pam jerked him back. They were going to have a tug-of-war with Benji in the middle. *Just like Brad,* Cam thought. It wasn't fair. Benji shouldn't have to go through this again.

"Jacob, what's happening?"

"Your fear, Cam. This is your chance to confront it,

conquer it, like I did with the wasps. It took a long time, but I managed it. If I did, you can."

A gun appeared in her hand. She dropped it as if it were a snake about to bite her.

"Pick it up, Cam. It's the only way."

No.

No, she wouldn't do this.

"I can't."

"Don't give in to the fear. You'll never get out of here unless you overcome it."

The gun was in her hand again. Again she dropped it, but before she could, somehow it went off. Aunt Pam fell to the floor, blood pooling around her.

Benji took Cam's hand, pulling her to the door. "Come on, Cam. We have to go. They'll take me away from you otherwise. We have to go now."

Blood covered Cam's white dress. Was it Aunt Pam's? But how had it gotten there? It dripped down the bodice, the gauzy cotton sticking to her skin. The gun was back in her hand, the smell of gunpowder sharp in the air.

Benji's hand was warm, and hers was sweaty in his. Her other hand was slick with blood against the heated metal of the gun.

Benji's hair fell in his eyes. It was too long. When was the last time someone cut it? It was uneven, just like in his third-grade picture. The night before picture day, Cam had tried to cut it herself. She hadn't known what she was doing and had really botched it. It looked like that now. And he was wearing the same shirt from that picture too, even though he'd out-grown it over a year ago. It fit him fine now.

Her body was here in this room, but in the lab she twitched violently. Fluid from the tank sloshed around her, and Trip and River's voices came to her, muffled and distant, speaking to each other in heated tones. She couldn't tell what they were saying.

"Stop," she said.

Aunt Pam disappeared. Benji disappeared, and Cam's hand dropped, empty. The gun, and the blood, were gone.

Jacob leaned against the wall, arms crossed. "Open the door, Cam."

"You saw my file. I didn't make that figment of Benji appear. You did. The picture of Benji in the show's binder is from last year, his third-grade school photo. That's all you had to go on. I'd never have imagined Benji that way. He's in fourth grade now."

"Open the door, Cam," Jacob said again, his voice cold.

"No. There must be another way."

"There's not. I'm getting out of here, one way or the other. You can come, or you can stay here and die."

Just as suddenly as the gun had vanished from her hand, an axe appeared in his, the blade fire-engine red, vivid against the stark white walls.

He strode toward her, his eyes dark and determined.

CHAPTER 27

After Trip closed Cam in the tank and connected the particle accelerator, River paced the room until Trip's scowl made him take a seat at one of the blinking consoles.

He sat for a few minutes, then was up again. Out the window, the buildings downtown protruded against the sky like broken bones. The destruction was moving closer. What would happen to them once that gnawing, shattering energy reached the lab? Would they split apart, shiver into a million grains of sand, and cease to exist? If their bodies were here, in an alternate dimension—which must be true if they'd disappeared from home—where would their bodies end up when they died? They would appear in the real world, presumably. Brandon had died behind a locked door while a Skym watched, and River remembered the impression, in the last second of footage, that his body had vanished. River had held Liza in his arms and then, just like that, she was gone. Had she disappeared in the very moment she died?

It was like the dimension they were in was trying to expel them, spit them out.

Well. They'd end up back home one way or another.

"For God's sake, sit down," Trip said.

"Are we supposed to just wait? We don't even know what we're waiting for. How long is this experiment supposed to take?"

"They'll be okay. Jacob's done this before, remember?"

"He's done *this?*"

"Well, no, I suppose not. But he's a scientist. And he was in the tank a long time before we showed up."

"Right. Long enough to become unhinged." Cam's tank beeped. "What's that?"

Trip studied the machine. "Her heart rate's up. It's expected. Nothing to worry about." Trip's eyebrows drew together, however, and River checked the screen as well.

"That's high."

"A little," Trip said. "Give it a minute."

River had been restless since they'd arrived at the compound. A sense of disaster loomed over him and this world like a shroud, making him edgy and uncertain. But seeing the numbers on the readout settled him. He'd do what was necessary. He was here, and if Cam needed him, he'd help.

If nothing else, he could do that.

Liquid sloshed in the tank as Cam's body jerked. Her heart rate spiked again.

"Something's happening." Trip tapped the screen, calling up more numbers and graphs. He went to Jacob's tank next. "His numbers are high too."

"Should we pull them out?"

"No." Trip scratched his head worriedly. "Give them more time."

The window on the far side of the room cracked and spiderwebbed.

"Uh-oh," Trip said.

The window gave way with a pop, and shards scattered across the floor like marbles. A breeze from outside swept the room.

A building across the compound crumbled in on itself.

Trip tapped the screen on the tank again. "Come on, Cam," he murmured. "Get it done."

The lights on the tank's screen blinked red, beeping frantically. Cam thrashed inside.

River tried to understand the flashing numbers. "Is she awake?"

"I don't think so."

"Those numbers are too high. She could go into cardiac arrest."

"We can't pull her out. If we give up now, we all die, her included."

"If she dies in that tank, none of us will get home anyway. Get her out, Trip."

Trip's fingers flew over the tank's buttons as the monitor continued to flash and blink. Instead of the lid opening, however, a message appeared on the tank's screen.

I REPROGRAMMED THE TANKS AND ALTERED THE REMOVAL PROCEDURE. ONLY I KNOW THE PROPER SEQUENCE, AND

IF YOU TAKE HER OUT WITHOUT IT, SHE'LL DIE. IF
YOU TAKE ME OUT EARLY, SHE'LL DIE.

I'M SORRY TO DO THIS. I NEEDED HER AND THIS WAS
THE ONLY WAY. I'LL DO MY BEST TO TAKE HER WITH
ME. THAT'S UP TO HER.

—JACOB

Trip's eyes blazed. "Son of a bitch. We trusted him!"

River opened a third tank in the row and dropped in the hose extracted from the wall. It filled with fluid.

"Get this ready," he said, already stripping his clothes. "Where are those scuba suits? I need one."

"You can't get in a tank! We have no idea what other programming Jacob's done to screw us."

"Guess I'll find out when I get there."

"How do you know it won't kill you?"

River stopped and took Trip by the shoulders. "Then help me. Figure it out, and fix it."

"I can't! These tanks, these programs—it's too complicated!"

"How can you say that, Trip? This is what you do. They needed *you* for all this to work. You created ThreeDz. Doesn't that allow communication between VR programs and people? Do to me what they did to Jacob—connect me to her."

River hadn't listened to all of Trip's ramblings while they'd hiked through the woods, but he'd picked up some of it.

Enough to know that Trip was better at this stuff than anyone River had ever known.

"But . . ." Trip said. He was looking for an argument about why he couldn't do it, and at the same time, his mind was seeing figures and numbers, working it out. He scanned the room. "You know, ThreeDz collects and transmits information because of the injections we got. We have those vials in the cupboard, so if we . . ." He trailed off, deep in thought.

Trip had started on the problem. He'd figure it out.

River found the blue suits hanging from pegs in a closet on the far side of the room. He shed the rest of his clothes and stepped into one, then picked out the vial marked CAMERON in the cupboard. He handed it to Trip with a syringe from the drawer below.

"Can you do this?"

"This is happening too fast. Give me a chance to work it out first."

"There's no time." River pointed at the shattered window. Trees outside were snapping and wavering, slashes of light cutting through them, their branches falling to the ground and shattering like glass, trunks split down the middle. The world was breaking apart. Nothingness hacked through it like a knife.

"At least let me reprogram the tanks, work out the VR system so I can communicate with you while you're in there."

"How long will that take?"

Trip scanned the numbers on the screen. "I don't know. It's VR, so it's just data, but there's so much of it."

"Work it out while I'm inside."

River didn't wait for Trip to take the needle from him. Instead he plunged it into the muscle of his own arm and pushed the plunger, just like the woman in the lab coat had done before the show. He imagined the microscopic particles rushing through his blood. They couldn't know if it was enough, or too much, but it was too late now.

"River, please . . ." Trip's throat bobbed as he swallowed. "What if I can't?"

River's hand closed on his arm. "Of course you can. You're good at this stuff."

River tugged the rubber suit up his chest and zipped. He climbed into the tank, and the warm fluid enveloped his lower half.

River leaned back. "Close me in."

The liquid was thick and gelatinous, jiggling more than flowing around his legs. How was he supposed to breathe this stuff?

As Trip lowered the lid, River drew in several deep breaths, subduing the sudden worry. What if this didn't work? What if he couldn't help? "Jeez, Trip. This is a hell of a bad idea, isn't it?"

Trip's mouth slanted in a smile. "Idiot."

"It's just . . . she's alone in there."

"I know."

"I'll bring her back, and we'll find our own way out, all three of us."

"Right." Trip's grin was strained. "We don't need Jacob

or his fancy . . . education and experience. We'll figure it out ourselves."

"Will you be okay here alone?"

"Don't worry about me. Just come back before the world ends."

River gave a quick nod. "Promise."

Trip closed the lid. The rushing noise of the particle accelerator silenced as liquid covered River's ears. He struggled against the instinct to hold his breath, then he inhaled.

■ ■ ■

Liquid filled his lungs. It was terrifying, like drowning. He was back on the island, plummeting into the depths of the ocean, jagged shards of coral reaching toward him as he sank.

His stomach dropped, and then he was, in fact, on the island, but now at the resort. He was sitting on the beach in one of the Adirondack chairs, clear blue waves lapping at the sand. It was sunny and warm. He wore swim shorts, and Cam sat next to him in a red bathing suit and floppy sun hat, smiling.

A waiter bent down to offer a tray of drinks with fruit poking from the top. Cam took one, so River did too. It tasted like oranges.

She sipped the drink, then put it down. "Swim with me."

The weather shifted. A dark cloud, far out to sea, rumbled inland. The waves turned choppy, shifting to slate gray like paint spilling into the ocean.

"The water's getting rough, Cam."

She laughed, tossed her hat to him, and ran. Her feet splashed in the surf, then she dove in and swam until she was a distant figure cresting the surface of the sea. She waved.

River sipped his drink again. It was bitter now, so he put it down.

Cam was too far out.

"Cam," he called, standing. "Come back!"

Her laughter carried over the waves, which were breaking higher now. Water sprayed against rocks in a fan of frothy white. He took three steps and the sea lapped his bare feet.

He couldn't see her anymore.

"Cam!"

An arm flailed upward. She cried out.

She was drowning.

He ran.

Droplets flew around him as he entered the choppy surf and dove, slicing beneath a towering crest. He surfaced and swam long strokes across the expanse of ocean. In a minute he'd reach her.

Hold on.

She cried out again, her voice choked and spluttering as she submerged and floundered.

The water turned thick as honey. It clung to him, pulling him down. He struggled for each stroke, dragging his arms through the surf. He had to get to her, but he was sinking, his chest tightening with cold. The water seeped into his bones and he went down. His lungs filled, the surface shimmered above him, and the ocean went black.

■ ■ ■

He was on the island, at the resort, sitting on the beach in an Adirondack chair. Soft blue waves lapped the sand. A waiter bent down, offering a tray of fruity drinks.

Cam laughed. "Come on. Let's swim."

She ran out into the waves, and the water turned dark.

CHAPTER 28

Jacob lifted the axe above his head like a demented lumberjack and swung. Cam backed away, and the blade smashed into the door. He tipped his chin at her, and before she had time to think, she was in a chair, her arms held in place by an invisible pressure. Ropes appeared and moved on their own, winding their way around her wrists. She struggled against them, but then the ropes turned into snakes, and wordless terror flared in her throat.

Jacob blinked at the snakes. "I didn't do that," he said. "You're the one who made them snakes. I'm not a monster."

Cam tried to breathe, but her lungs felt full of rocks. Jacob took another swing at the door. Wood and tile shattered.

"You can't leave us here."

"I wanted you to open the door, Cam." Regret dripped from his voice. "I thought you'd at least do it for Benji. Your file said he was the only thing you cared about, and now he'll be alone. Tell you what." He swung again. "I'll tell him you died saving me. That'll mean something to him, I think."

"Don't you go near him!"

Jacob rested the axe on the floor, considering her. "It's kind of true, though, isn't it? I've been killing myself trying to find a way out, and I never did. I'm still not sure how you managed it. You saved my life. I know that. And not just getting me out of the tank, or finding this door. I'd have been alone without you. I'd have lost my mind."

"I don't think I made that door, Jacob."

"Listen, Cam, it feels like I've spent years in here, and that's the first time I've seen a door. It had to be you."

"The door is wishful thinking. Maybe you never found the way out because you don't care about anything except saving yourself. Nothing connects you to home if all that matters is your own skin."

He lifted the axe again. "I'm the one getting out of here. Survival's got to count for something. You guys, constantly running, hiding, and . . . Christ." He shook his head. "All that screaming. If you'd stopped for one second and thought about it, or quit taking those stupid pills, you'd have figured out the same thing I did. *You're* in control. It's your own mind building these fears up, and with a little self-awareness, a little goddamn determination, you can fight it. Instead you spend your time moping about Mr. Blue Eyes and running from damn spiders. Look at those snakes you conjured up."

The snakes tightened around her wrists when he pointed to them, the distaste clear on his face. Their tongues slipped out and they looked at her with black, lifeless eyes, like beads. She shuddered as one of them circled her arm, its cold scales sliding across her skin. Jacob took a break from hacking the door and knelt in front of her.

"They don't have to be snakes. I told you: *I* didn't do that.

I thought of ropes. Go on. Turn them back into ropes. Try, see what happens."

Cam didn't know what game he was playing. The tiles on the door were chipped and cracked, and in one spot the axe had broken through and splintered the wood beneath. When he succeeded in breaking the door open, what would happen? He'd walk through, be home again, leaving the rest of them lost forever in a disintegrating world?

She stared at the snakes, but seeing them didn't make them less real, so she closed her eyes.

"Good," Jacob said. "Now concentrate."

She squinted at him. "How do you know I won't make it all disappear, and then tie you up?"

He gave her one of his warm smiles. "You could, I bet. But I've been at this longer than you, and I had a lot of motivation. Look." He held out his hand, palm up, and a wasp appeared like a magic trick. Its low buzz made Cam think of the Skyms.

"How'd you do that?"

"Fear is easy to manifest. It's our strongest emotion. It takes a little more work, more motivation, to control fear and defeat it. That's what you kids lack, you know. Motivation. But you must have a little now. Come on, Cam, try."

"Shut up and give me a second."

He sat back on his heels and waited. Cam closed her eyes again.

There are no snakes.

It wasn't going to work. Telling herself there were no snakes only made her think of snakes.

They're only ropes.

But why not make them disappear altogether? Imagine there were no snakes and no ropes at all? Leave them behind the same way the exit on the highway had let them outrun the sand. They were so tight, though, squeezing against bone, bruising. They were *there*, it was impossible to imagine otherwise.

Jacob heaved a sigh and went back to work on the door, ignoring her as if she'd disappointed him. The wasp flew out of sight.

From nowhere a phone appeared at her feet. It had a brown case and a tiny, peeling sticker of Spider-Man. It was Trip's phone. She glanced at Jacob to see if he'd noticed, but he was still busy chopping away at the door. She scooted closer to the phone and, using her feet, flipped it over. A series of texts showed on the lock screen.

Cam

It's Trip

I'm texting you on my app, like Jacob messaged us at the resort, just enhanced. We injected River with the sympathy bots so he could connect to you. It gave me the idea that if I was injected too, all of us could communicate

It sucked sticking myself with a needle

Are you okay?

Jacob's batshit fyi

He made it so we can't get you out of the tank

Answer me

Cam?

I thought this would work. Is it not working?

Cam?

She couldn't release her hands to reach the phone. She had no way to answer.

More wood splintered under the blade of Jacob's axe. The phone vibrated with another text.

River followed you into the VR. Is he there?

We both have the same particles as Jacob. The sympathy bots. River should be able to connect to you.

Are you there?

Cam, everything's falling apart here. Like the walls and stuff

It's getting worse

Cam reached with her foot, trying to drag the phone closer.

Jacob came over, picked it up, and scrolled through the texts. "Huh," he said. "A virtual-reality phone. That's clever. Though I don't see how it's supposed to help. Anyway, Trip can't do you any good. Come on, Cam. Self-reliance. Determination! That's what you need. Without that, no one can help you." He dropped the phone and started in on the door again, giving her up as hopeless.

I'm looking at the VR program. Jacob altered it somehow, created a sort of loop, like a trap. I think River's stuck. I'm trying to fix it.

Jacob slashed at the door, sweating. Shards of porcelain and wood littered the floor around him. With a powerful swing, he opened a large hole in the door, and the air in the room whooshed out. Cam's hair whipped around her face. Jacob swung again, and again, until most of the door broke away and flew outward. The storm of wind pulled at him, sucking him toward the door.

Bracing himself, he turned back to Cam, his voice raised over the racket.

"Come with me, Cam. We've been through so much, shared so much. I don't want to leave you like this."

"Aren't you worried I'll get home and tell everyone that you left us here to die?"

"All this . . ." He waved his arms around the white room, his short hair grazed by the gale. "Information as valuable as

322

this sometimes requires sacrifice. It's imperative that one of us return to tell them what happened. It's my job. That doesn't mean I like it. I hope you believe me."

"Untie me before you go, at least. Let me be with them."

"You're stuck here, Cam. I reprogrammed the tanks. I couldn't risk them taking you out before we found the way back. I didn't think you'd be able to find it that easily. By now that world is a mess, you don't want to be there anyway. It's falling apart. Your consciousness isn't enough to hold it together anymore. It wasn't supposed to exist in the first place."

Cam looked past him, at the black, blustery space outside the door. "I don't know where that door leads. It doesn't look much like home."

He glanced at it. "You're the one who made the door. Does it lead to the real world or not?"

"That's just it—I don't know. Jacob, it looks dangerous."

Jacob scratched the stubble on his cheek, a moment of uncertainty on his face. "I guess I'll find out soon enough. If I stay here any longer, I'll lose my mind." He laughed humorlessly.

He turned back to her, his hand grasping the doorjamb. "I am sorry about this. I've been with you guys the whole time, in the woods and at the resort. But I'm not about to sacrifice myself just to stay here and die with you all. You can't expect that of me. Honestly, I don't understand why you're willing to do it."

She didn't want to stay and die with anyone, but she couldn't abandon her friends. And she hadn't given up. Like Trip said, there's always a way out. She had to believe that. That door wasn't it—at least, it didn't *feel* right. If they couldn't find a way out together, well . . . at least they'd be together.

The wasp Jacob had manifested flew past her ear, ambling clumsily through the air. But then there was a second wasp. It entered the room just over his shoulder.

"Jacob . . ." Cam said.

"Good luck, Cam. I hope you change your mind before it's too late. If you would just concentrate, you can get out of those ropes any time you want."

Another wasp followed the other. The two of them floated through the room, impervious to the whipping wind. Jacob hadn't seen them yet. He turned to the void outside and inhaled. He took a step, then jerked his hand from the broken door frame with a hiss.

"Ow. Shit."

With one hand clasped over the other, his gaze landed on yet another wasp traveling into the room. Fear fell on his face like a mask.

All at once, hundreds of wasps swarmed, surrounding him in a black cloud.

The snakes coiled from Cam's wrists, turned back into rope, and then dropped away, vanishing once they hit the floor. She rubbed her arms, bringing the feeling back to her numb fingers.

Jacob swatted wildly at the insects. The wind pulled violently, and he dove for the door, tripping as he dropped toward it. He grasped the door frame, screamed as his palm landed on a cluster of wasps, but he held on.

Cam ran to him, took his hand. He was pulled halfway

out the door, and she'd been right. The door was nothing—there was no world on the other side of it, only pitch-black nothingness and more terror. His legs flew out behind him as a tornado of air dragged him into the void. Trying to shield her face from the stinging wasps, Cam clutched at his arms. His fingers clawed for her, digging into her skin. Bright panic shone in his eyes.

"Help me!" he yelled.

Cam pulled, struggling to drag him back inside. Needles of pain shot through her skin as wasps stung her, and then the quick barbs blossomed into a poisonous agony.

He was torn away from her, the force of the wind sucking him outside. She hung halfway into the nothing that was beyond the white room, about to get sucked out herself. He wouldn't let go, and she willed herself not to give up.

The wasps swarmed him. He opened his mouth to scream, but a black cloud of insects flew down his throat. The last inch of his fingers slipped, and suddenly he was gone, the wind sucking the wasps with him as he went. The last image before Cam scrambled back from the edge of the door was his blistered, swollen face, his mouth wide in a soundless scream.

She didn't realize she'd been screaming until the last vibration of it died in her throat.

She was shaking, tears were burning down her face, and her hand was swelling. Her breath hitched. The only place that felt safe was the farthest corner of the room, as far from the door as she could get. The wind continued funneling in and spinning like a cyclone, and then it was carrying with it grains of sand that pierced her skin. A few remaining wasps floated about, their wings flicking against the walls. She wanted to scream again, it was building in her chest, but if she started, she wouldn't be able to stop.

The phone was on the floor. She grabbed it and hit reply to Trip's text.

> **Trip! Get me out of here!**

Trip answered immediately.

> **I'm here. Jacob's tank is empty. He just disappeared. What happened? Does that mean he's home?**

> **Jacob's dead. Maybe his body is home, but he's dead**

There was a long pause.

> **Are you okay?**

> **I'm scared**

> **Me too.**

> **What about River?**

> **Something's wrong. His vitals are all over the place, and they're getting worse**

> Can't you get me and River back to the lab?

There was another long pause.

> It's bad here, Cam

> What do you mean?

> The room is breaking apart.

> I don't want to be alone

> I know. I'm working on a way to get you and River back. Find him. The sympathy bots should be working. Find River.

> How?

> You're in a VR program, and so is he. This isn't a phone you're texting on, you know. It's not like the VR has a phone plan. It's data. You can find him. It's just data, Cam. You control it.

Jacob had said the same thing to her, that she could control this world if she tried hard enough. But in the end, even he hadn't been able to do it. The wasps had returned and carried him away. In his last moments before he died, the image he'd conjured was the same fear he'd always seen, the one he imagined he'd conquered.

He'd been lying to himself. Fear never went away. It ate you up from the inside, coming to the surface no matter how far you pushed it down.

If Jacob couldn't control this world, with his tough-guy confidence, his scientific mind, and his years of military training, not to mention the weeks he'd spent learning how to manipulate the VR, how could she hope to? She was too scared, and that fear took over so easily. It seemed like the more she tried to control it, the stronger it became.

Cam, are you there?

I'm here.

Listen, the ions in your body created an entire world, one based on your consciousness. Your understanding of it is what defines it. Try to use that to control the VR.

I can't control anything in here.

Jacob thought she'd created that door, but it had been him and his wishful thinking. Even the image of Benji had been Jacob's, not hers. The only thing she'd made happen were the snakes, and before that the sandstorm, and on the island the earthquakes and that violent version of River. She hadn't been able to control any of it.

> Okay, don't think of it like control, then. It's perception. It's data. Use the phone.

The wind was a cyclone in the middle of the room now, and wasps swarmed in the center, their numbers growing. Whether she found River or not, this wasn't where she wanted to die.

> Cam, the ceiling's caving in

> > Don't leave me, Trip

There was no answer.

> > Trip? Are you there?

Cam stared at the silent phone.

Buzzing filled her ears as the whirlwind of wasps grew and sand piled up in the corners of the room. She was cold, and the wind didn't stop. If anything, it became stronger, dragging her toward the broken door. Would it end faster for her to go through the door herself? Or would she only be entering some-place worse, with all her fears centered in one place?

She stood and crossed the room, fighting her way through the mounting pressure. It was still black outside the door, like looking into space. She thought about the stars above the Springs at the resort. They'd scattered the sky, and River had been in her mind that whole evening. She'd been drawn to him, and he'd filled her thoughts completely. They hadn't even kissed yet, and he'd been all she could think about.

She opened Trip's phone and created a new contact: RIVER

She tapped the word *call* next to his name and put the phone to her ear.

The walls around her dripped and pooled at her feet like melting butter. The white tile flickered with color and light. The slow hum of the wasps shifted and grew louder, until their buzz morphed into the sound of crashing waves. Her stung hand didn't hurt anymore. She clutched for the door, feeling dizzy, like she was about to fall over and tumble out into the void, but the door wasn't there. Instead she felt River's arm under her hand, solid and warm. The ocean was beside them. They stood on the U-shaped beach at the resort. Rainbow umbrellas dotted the sand, waiters carried drinks, and children played in the distance.

"I found you," she said, but he didn't look at her, didn't see her. Her own voice screamed in the distance; then her hand dropped to her side as he left her and ran into the ocean, disappearing into the blue waves.

CHAPTER 29

The waiter bent down to offer the tray of drinks. River didn't want one. They smelled bitter and rancid, like overripe oranges, but Cam took two and handed him one.

"The water's so nice," she said after taking a sip. "Let's go swimming." She tossed her floppy hat on the chair.

He put his own drink aside without tasting it. "A storm's coming."

She laughed. "It's nothing. Come on."

She ran to the water, kicking up sand behind her. Clouds rolled in, tumbling over the sky like spilled ink.

He followed her, dread threading through his chest.

"Cam!"

The only answer was her careless laugh tripping over the water.

And then she was drowning, and he was running, and it was happening again, like it always did.

"River."

Something stopped him, and that was different. He couldn't let anything stop him, however. He had to get out there, ignore the fear. He had to save her. This time he would save her.

"River, stop."

Cam was here, holding his hand, but she was also calling for help out there. How could she ask him to stop?

"What are you doing here?" he said.

"Trip is in trouble. The lab is collapsing. The whole world is collapsing."

"You'll figure it out. And Trip's good with the technical stuff."

"But there's no time. And we're in the lab too, River. We're in the tanks. Remember?"

"I have to go, Cam."

"Don't."

"I have to. You're drowning."

"My toes aren't even wet. I'm not drowning."

He glanced out at the ocean to see Cam's flailing arm. "You will, though."

"River, look at me. I'm here, right in front of you. I'm not out there."

It wasn't any good. She wouldn't understand.

"I must've gone out there a hundred times. You drown every time. I can't save you. A hundred times, and not once have I saved you. What else can I do?"

"You can stop."

"Don't you get it? If I stop, you drown."

"You already said I drown every time, no matter what you do. You can't stop it. So let me drown."

"No." He jogged toward the water, but uncertainty slowed him down. She went after him, caught up.

"You don't have to do this. You're killing yourself."

"I have to try." He rubbed his eyes. They were irritated, raw with salt and sand. "I can't save you. I can't save anybody, but I have to try. What's the point of anything if I don't try?"

His hands balled into fists. She lifted one and he unclenched it reluctantly. Her cries sounded in his ears, mingling with the screech of seagulls and playing children. He wanted to run — to swim and not stop until he reached her.

She flattened a hand on his chest, drawing his attention back.

"I'll die, River. You said yourself, I always do. In the end, everyone does, don't they?" An inarticulate protest rose in his throat, but she stopped him. "Tell me, would you regret knowing me if I were gone?"

"What do you mean?"

"It hurts when someone dies. But would you wish we'd never met, because then it wouldn't hurt?"

"Of course not."

"Then stay here, sit with me."

"That's not enough."

"It has to be enough. It's all we have."

The breaching crests drew lines of foam on the water, so dark now it was black.

"It's not fair." He cleared his throat to cover the break in his voice, but it was no use. He couldn't hide from her.

"No. But you can't change it. All you can do is be here, now. With me."

He wanted to fall to his knees, to give up. It was too hard, it hurt too much. Instead, he surrendered. A shuddering groan escaped his lips and his head dropped. He buried his face into her hair and she pulled him close, her arms tightening around him to stop his trembling, and for one second—not long, but it was enough—for one second he wasn't worried about what came next.

The world tilted like a sinking ship, and then it jumped.

They were in a black space. He was weightless, floating, and the blackness was all-encompassing. At first he thought he was back in the tank, but he couldn't be in the tank. Cam was with him. He couldn't see her, but her body was pressed to his, and her heart beat against his chest, echoing his own.

"Cam, where are we?"

"I don't know."

"The beach is gone."

"We were never really on a beach. It was a program that Jacob made into a trap. Trip must have stopped any new programs from running. I thought we'd end up back in the lab, though, and be able to get out of the tanks. Instead we're here."

A jolt of alarm rippled through him. "Trip! We have to get back to him. I promised." God, how could he have forgotten? Trip was still in the lab.

"I don't know where we are, or how to get out of here. How am I supposed to get back to Benji?"

River didn't know what to say. Everything was gone, and they were lost.

"I'm glad you're with me," Cam said.

"Me too. I wish Trip wasn't alone."

He still couldn't see her, but she was real and solid in his arms. Her skin and the air around her were cool and smelled of honey. He felt for her face and tipped up her chin. Their noses touched first, finding the place where their lips would meet.

They floated.

They were nowhere and everywhere at once. Were they wearing blue plastic suits? Or T-shirts from the island? Or did they wear no clothes at all, because they had no bodies, no skin or bones, or eyes to see? He couldn't tell.

The sympathy bots had to be working, because where he ended, she began. Though he must have a body, because every stirring, rushing feeling a body could have coursed through him at once like a tide, drawing him closer to her. And somehow, in this place, they kissed, and it was more real than any real world could ever be.

She pulled away before he was ready.

"It's loud here. Can you hear it?"

"I don't hear anything. I'm not even sure I have ears."

"It's so loud."

"Is it like what you heard in the trees?"

"Jacob said those voices came from home, that it was search parties in the woods, shoppers in the grocery store in Seattle, soldiers at the military base. The veil is thinner for me because it was made through me."

"The veil?"

"The veil between worlds. That's what Jacob called it."

"Where is Jacob?"

"Gone."

"Oh. And you hear home? Can you get us there?"

"Not just home. And I'm not just hearing all these worlds, I feel them too. I feel like I'm in a hundred places all at once. A thousand."

"That sounds confusing."

"It is. But also, somehow, it isn't. We're in the tanks. I can hear the walls falling down outside."

River couldn't hear or feel what she did. He only knew she was there, right next to him, and he didn't want to let go.

"Is one of the places you feel our world?"

"There are so many worlds," she sighed. "I can see them. I can't believe how many . . ."

"I can't see anything."

"Look," she said.

His stomach lurched, and what was left of his body—or whatever part of his body existed—dropped, and the world jumped.

CHAPTER 30

River lives alone in the wilderness. It isn't for the show *Cut Off*. The show never happened. When his parents died, he left his uncle and moved to Alaska, spent that whole summer building a cabin, cramming the crevices with clay and moss. He lives off the land, faring better than most, but he's lost whatever drive he had to make the place welcoming and comfortable. He's rawboned and sick, hasn't eaten for days. The snow on the ground drifts inside with the wind. His teeth chatter and he shivers near a meager fire, but he doesn't care. It's been this way for so long, the thought of warmth is a distant memory, a joke. He could find more wood, build up the fire, but the cold is gratifying somehow. It helps him focus on staying alive for another day, and the day after that. It helps him not think about anything else.

Jump

Cam files in and picks up a tray. The sleeves of her gray sweatshirt fall over her hands, and the matching sweatpants stay up only because she cinched the waist. The prison-issued sweats are about three sizes too big. Except for the risk of losing the pants in the middle of the crowded dining hall, she doesn't mind. They're comfortable, kind of like pajamas, and better than the bright orange jumpsuit in the county jail.

A couple of girls at the front of the line are getting heated about who they think should win some reality show everyone's watching in the common room.

DJ steps in line behind her. "They're offering art class next week. Will they let you sign up this time?"

"Probably not."

Classes are only for nonviolent offenders and girls who've been in for over a year with good behavior. Cam has a while yet.

DJ is in for violating probation and failing her drug test. She says it isn't fair, because the probation violation was for running because she knew she'd test dirty, so really it should only be one violation. DJ has been a good friend, though. It's not her fault circumstance caught up with her, any more than it is Cam's.

Visiting day is coming up, and Cam's excited to see Benji. Her mom will cry the whole time. Mom feels guilty, of course. It should have been her who went away. It was better that Cam confessed, however. Cam's a minor. She got off easier, and if mom was in prison, who'd take care of Benji? So Cam sticks it out. It sucks is all, to listen to mom cry about it every visit.

DJ pushes her sleeves up, revealing the scars down her forearm. They aren't from the drugs, but from cutting. Cam wonders sometimes if it helps. DJ describes it like a release, something she does when she can't find drugs, or when she was trying to quit the drugs. A release sounds nice.

One of the girls arguing about the reality show throws her tray and tackles the other girl. The dining hall erupts into chaos. Cam hides under a table.

Jump

River is in trouble again. He talked back to the sergeant and got stuck running drills. He'll end up working the kitchens over the weekend if he isn't careful, and he can't afford that. He's supposed to meet up with Terrell and Caleb on Friday. They plan to head into the city. Caleb knows a few girls at the local high school and they're going to hang out by the lake. Terrell can get ahold of some six-packs, and Caleb says the girls are up for partying. There isn't anything better to do, and River would just as soon get drunk with a random girl and take his mind off the mess of his life for a few minutes. It's handy that a military-school uniform impresses public-school girls. He never mentions to them that he only wears the thing because he flunked out of junior year and his uncle put his foot down. It wasn't all bad, though. If he quits getting so pissed and landing himself in trouble, he can see himself sticking it out, maybe even joining the army for real when he graduates. He never thought that was where he'd end up, but there really is nothing better to do.

Jump

Cam pours gravy over a mound of mashed potatoes on a plate

heaped with roast chicken and peas. Mom decorated the dining room for spring even though it's still cold outside and the gas fireplace fills the house with warmth. Green and yellow silk flowers fill a vase in the center of the table. Gary brought her real flowers, but she put those on the mantelpiece next to the family picture of the four of them in Disneyland a few years ago, the same trip where Gary proposed. The park was too crowded for Cam, but Benji had a great time. He and Gary rode the worst roller coasters while she and Mom took pictures and ate popcorn.

"Eat the peas," Mom says to Benji, who makes a face.

"You know he never does," Cam says.

"What's the rule, Benji?" Gary's feigned gravity barely hides a grin.

Benji recites. "'Try it twelve times, and if you still don't like it, you don't have to try it again.'"

"Exactly!" Gary says.

Benji rolls his eyes. "Twelve times. Where'd you even get that number?"

"Hey," Gary says, rubbing his hands together. "The *Cut Off* finale is tonight. Only River and Brandon left now! Whose turn is it to wear the visor?"

"Cam's," Benji says, pouting.

She smiles. "It's okay, kid. You can wear it this time."

Cam leaves for college in a few months. These dinners are what she'll miss most.

Cam, what's happening? These places aren't home.

There are so many versions of our world. So many. I can hear them all. Can you hear them?

How can I know what I'm thinking and feeling in these other places? Those versions of me . . . they're different.

They're different, but we are still them. They are who we would be if things had gone differently, if we'd taken a different path. You can't hear all those worlds?

No.

Look.

Jump

Seattle is a jungle. A steamy knot of leaves, larger than any human, casts shadows on the ground. A beetle the size of a pickup truck lumbers onto a trampled path.

Jump

River, Cam, and Trip are on a stage with several other contestants, being asked interview questions by Liza, who's hosting the show. River and Cam don't know each other. They nod hello and pass by. They never met on the show, and only saw each other for the first time backstage, but too much is going on for them to pay much attention to any one person. Neither of them won *Cut Off*, but they did pretty well. The audience likes them, though River a bit more than Cam.

River hates being onstage, but for Cam it's sort of fun. She isn't looking forward to getting back to real life.

Liza introduces an ad for *Brandon in the Wild*. The clip runs on a giant screen behind them. The audience claps and cheers as Brandon paraglides from a cliff followed by a couple of Skyms.

Jump

Cam and Benji are eating fast-food hamburgers in Mom's old Nissan. After Mom disappeared, Cam threw clothes in a suitcase, took the car, took Benji, and ran. No way would she let her and Benji be split up, or let Benji get stuck in foster care. It's cold in the car, but she's glad to have it. Her mother didn't ditch them with nothing, at least.

Sometimes at night, when Benji's asleep, she wonders if Mom will ever come back. How could she leave them like that, without even saying goodbye? It's not like her.

Unless something happened. Brad was real mad when she ended it with him, and who knows what he's capable of . . .

Cam tries not to think about that.

Jump

River won *Cut Off*. He's a celebrity. He's thinking about moving to Alaska, getting away from it all, but he's not even sure that would work. The producers laugh, tell him even up there reporters will hound him and helicopters will buzz the cabin day after day. He misses being in the wilderness. Here there are too many cameras, too many people following him wherever he goes. It's not what he signed up for.

Jump

It's winter, and the air is colder than anything either of them has felt before. It's winter, and it has never been anything but.

Jump

Seattle, along with most of the northern coast of the Americas as far as the Aleutian Islands, is under the Pacific. When the tsunamis didn't stop after the first year, the federal government washed its hands of the region—temporarily, it declared—and the surviving areas were taken over by speculators, private companies, and gangs. There hasn't been electricity for over two years.

River cooks rabbit over a fire in the Licensed Zone. He's alone. He doesn't have the energy or interest to look out for anyone else.

Cam is in a parking lot with Benji. They won't last much longer. She knows this. Benji can't survive another bout of bronchitis, not when antibiotics are so hard to come by. She hates watching him suffer.

When they see the guy crouched alone over a campfire, roasting a rabbit, she thinks about her gun. It used to be Brad's, but he died in the first quake, so it's hers now. Benji needs to eat, and she bets that guy carries medicine. He looks like a prepper. She draws the gun from her pack and tells Benji not to watch.

Jump

River's parents are alive. They're at the house, all of them together. Mom and Dad sit on the front porch bickering about some rule in a card game, and River and Terrell toss a Frisbee in the yard. River caught a few perch earlier, and his dad's going to grill them. They'll spend the evening eating fish and picking out the tiny bones. His dad will toss Terrell and him a beer each, and wink, as if his mother didn't see.

It's normal.

It's *Before*.

There was never any *After*.

River is happy.

It doesn't mean his life isn't complicated. He has worries, a few things distracting him, his parents are a hassle sometimes. It doesn't mean everything is perfect.

It only means this one thing.

His parents aren't dead.

He's not broken.

Do you want to stay?

We can stay?

If you want.

If we stay, what happens to him?

Who?

That other version of me.

That is you, though.

Would I become him? Or would I take his place? Would I remember doing it?

River, he is you.

It wouldn't be right, to take away what he has.

You're the same person. You can't take something from yourself. It's yours.

We're not the same person. I'm not him anymore.

Okay. We can leave.

Wait. Stay. Just one more minute.

Okay . . .

Are you ready now?

No.

Do you want to stay?

No.

Jump

This place is different.

    Cam and River are not here.

    Trip is not here either.

    They disappeared without a trace weeks ago, and Brandon's body was found dead in a trailer. Headlines talk about THE *CUT OFF* FOUR, THE *CUT OFF* TRAGEDY, THE *CUT OFF* MYSTERY, and also THE *CUT OFF* CONSPIRACY.

Producers insist they have no further information, and no idea what happened or how the technology could have failed so catastrophically. Search parties have combed the island for weeks. They found abandoned camps, but no sign of anything or anyone else.

Kidnapping, alien abduction, and terrorism are the prevailing theories, though some think the contestants are only hopelessly lost. Hard to imagine on an island, but what other answer is there? People don't simply vanish. The government is involved now. They've had to restrict the island, which in the first few days became overrun with volunteers and curious tourists. They've launched the most extensive manhunt in history. The producers have provided Skyms to assist in the search. An international audience of millions watches, day and night, analyzing every movement in the woods. Everyone wants to be the first person to see one of them alive.

Most people think they're already dead, in any case.

Some believe the mystery is merely part of the show, an attempt to pump up ratings. They're waiting for a big reveal in the finale.

Cam.

I know.

Is it . . .

I think it is.

We found it.

Home.

CHAPTER 31

Home

It must be. Cam could feel it. She could hear it — it sounded like home. Benji was here. He was scared, with no idea what had happened to her, and every day the whole world was asking — where had they gone?

This world was home.

Now that they'd found it, they couldn't stay without Trip. Cam had no idea what to do.

She was with River already, he was right there, and even though they weren't actually touching — on some level she knew that — she was wrapped in his arms, and his warmth coursed through her. They had kissed before, and become lost in that kiss. He would be with her wherever she went. She carried him with her.

Trip was another story. She had to connect with him somehow, and that felt more complicated.

Jacob had said she had control over this world, but she thought perhaps he was wrong. Nobody *controlled* any of it. Although she had done something Jacob couldn't do. She'd found all these worlds. His door had led to nothing, but she'd found home.

How had she done that?

It wasn't enough to *want* something. Every version of herself in every one of those worlds had *wanted* the same thing —to keep Benji safe. But in most of the worlds she saw, Benji wasn't safe, and neither was she.

River had wanted to keep her safe, to keep her from drowning. He had killed himself trying over and over, but she'd still died.

If it wasn't about control, and it wasn't about want, what was left?

What had she told River to get him out of the endless loop he was in?

"You told me to let you drown," River said.

He didn't use words to say it. Out here, in this black space full of worlds, they didn't need words, just as they didn't need lips to kiss or hands to touch.

"That dimension we got stuck in was never supposed to be there. It was a mistake. An entire world was created because of a mistake. I don't know how to fix this."

"You can't fix it. Just like you can't keep Benji safe any more than I could save you from drowning. We can't save each other."

"So what are we supposed to do?"

"We don't *do* anything. All that matters is that we're together. I'm here with you, we have each other, and that's enough. You have Benji, and he loves you. That's enough. It has to be."

"But Trip is trapped in the lab, and it's falling apart. I won't be like Jacob. I won't abandon him."

"You created that place, and that world. Do you think it matters if he's there, or in a resort, or a forest? How did you find me?"

"I used Trip's phone. He said it didn't matter that it wasn't real. It's all only data."

What would Trip say? That maybe the dimension they were in wasn't a virtual-reality program, but it was still a kind of data. Data that could be rewritten and reworked, changed by the way she thought about it and the choices she made.

There's always a way out. Always.

"Find him," River said.

His hand left hers, and then something slipped onto her palm. The phone. Cam felt the buttons on the side, and the peeling sticker on the case. She ran her finger down the smooth glass, and it turned on. A light shone in the darkness, white and blinding. The tip of her finger disappeared into the screen, swallowed by the glare, and then her whole hand was through the glass and her mind felt like fingers reaching out into the dark, feeling for something hidden. The screen of the phone grew until it was as large as the window of the tank, and River's hand was still in hers, and she was in a million different places at once. In one of those places, she was pounding on the lid of a tank, in a Seattle that didn't exist, a Seattle that was splitting into pieces and crashing around her. She couldn't tell if she was breathing air or the fluid from the tank, and she realized it no longer mattered.

The lid lifted, and there was Trip.

"Cam, Jesus. What happened? Where's River?"

He started to lift her out, but she took his arms. Her wet hands left blotchy marks on his sleeves. "You have to come with me."

Jacob's tank was empty, split open, spilling viscous liquid across the floor until it reached the grate and dripped down into the particle accelerator, which popped and sizzled. Flames lapped the walls of the locker room on the left, and a deep gash cut through the ceiling. Half the tanks were unmoored from the floor and lay scattered across the room.

Trip braced himself as the building shook, and his feet slipped on the slick floor. An arc of light slashed the walls, splitting the room in half.

"Now, Trip."

He didn't argue. He climbed in, squeezing next to her in the tank.

"What are we doing?" he asked.

"Just stay with me. It'll be okay. It's only data, right?"

"I mean, yeah, it's data. It can still kill us."

As if to prove his point, a chunk of the ceiling dropped onto the body of their tank, putting a massive dent in the metal.

"Not helpful, Trip."

A bank of computers slid across the room and crashed into the legs of their tank. Cam pulled the lid closed while they wobbled precariously. The fluid covered them both. Trip struggled briefly against the fluid in his lungs. She held him tighter, closed her eyes, and everything tipped and crashed to the floor, the fluid sloshing around them both.

She was with River. His hand, warm and strong, rested at

the curve where her neck met her shoulder. His thumb brushed idly behind her ear.

She was in a white room with a wasp bobbing nearby.

She was on a beach.

She was in a prison, and at a park with her family, and at home with Benji.

She was in an upside-down tank with Trip crushed against her, his heart beating wildly.

She was in a thousand worlds at once. Some were better, some were worse, and some—far more than she wished—were nightmares.

What world she was in didn't matter. How could it? She had no control over that.

In every world, only one thing was the same. She was Cam.

Not perfect. Sometimes pretty flawed, actually. But doing her best.

That was all that mattered.

That was enough.

CHAPTER 32

To Cam it was a feeling, a call to Trip—*I found you*—that took her where she needed to be.

To River, Cam remained in his arms, warm and present. Then lightning flashed across his eyes, splitting a pitch-black sky. He was nowhere, floating in nothing, but that brilliance rose up from a million different places and came together as one, the place where his and Cam's bodies met, right down the middle of them, binding them together with light.

And then he was drowning, and he had enough time to think, *Not again*, before a lid lifted. He climbed out and fell to the floor, then immediately rolled to his side and vomited the liquid in his lungs. He heaved a ragged breath of air.

He looked up to see the same lab as before, the empty tanks, but now soldiers circled above him, guns drawn. People in lab coats frowned down at him.

The soldiers spun around when thumping came from the tank behind them. They didn't make a move toward it, so River scrambled to his feet and broke through the line of men to lift the tank's lid and find Cam and Trip in a tangled knot inside. In a moment, all three of them were huddled on the floor. They were coughing, covered in slime, and gripping one another so fiercely it hurt.

The soldiers lowered their guns, but the surprise and fear on their faces gave River some brief satisfaction. He wasn't the only one confused around here.

Cam's voice was in his ear, hoarse and wet. "We're home."

River was wearing the blue suit he'd worn into the tank. Had he been in the tank the whole time he'd been floating in nothingness? It had felt so real. It had been real, hadn't it? When they'd been in that black space, his body had been weightless and unmoored. Now gravity crashed into him. It sat low in his stomach, leaving him slow and heavy.

As if reading his mind, Trip said, "Was that for real?" He jerked a thumb at the team of soldiers still behind them and the scientists rushing throughout the lab. "What's up with these guys?"

Cam whispered back, "We appeared here, like from nothing."

Despite everything, Trip's eyes lit up. "We're like time travelers. Like the first people on the moon! They have no idea. I bet they're still looking for us in the woods."

A man approached. He smoothed his tie with a clean, manicured hand. He crouched down, and the movement caused a syringe to poke from his coat pocket.

"Hello," he said. "May I have your names, please?"

River resisted the urge to keep his eyes on the syringe. No sense in letting on that he'd seen it. "You know who we are."

"Yes, of course." A condescending smile tipped the man's mouth. "It's only to verify, for our records."

Cam pulled away from River. "Maybe your guys can put these guns away before we start verifying records."

"Certainly." The man flicked his wrist in the general direction of the soldiers, and immediately the guns were holstered. "You're Cameron, yes? Your family is nearby. I imagine you'll want to see them."

"Is Benji here? Why? How?"

"All your questions will be answered, but first we need to go over a few things." The manicured hand slipped into the pocket with the syringe, and River tensed. "If you don't mind, I'd like to get started by taking some blood."

"No!" Cam used River's shoulder to push herself upright. Her fingers bit into his collarbone as she struggled to stand on the slippery floor. "Who the hell are you? Where's my brother? Why do you have him?"

If this was going to be a fight, it'd be a difficult one. They were exhausted, dressed in nothing but rubber suits—except for Trip, in his soaked T-shirt and cargo pants—and the armed soldiers stood nearby, clearly ready to act at a moment's notice.

"Cam," River warned, pulling her back down while staring pointedly at the men with guns.

Cam lowered her voice, but remained wary. "No names, no blood, no nothing until I see my brother."

From the back of the crowd of people, a woman with thin wire glasses and a narrow face spoke. "That's fine, Nicolas. I'll handle it from here." She emitted a smile that had a sort of calculated warmth. Not insincere, but deliberate, and slightly nervous.

She came over, placing a hand on Cam's shoulder. "We only want to help. Of course you'll see your brother, and soon. You have my word: you'll all be back where you want to be in no time at all."

"No offense," Cam said. "But your word doesn't mean much. Who did you say you were?"

"Of course, I'm sorry. I'm Dr. Celeste Barker. I work here, in the science division. We study the uses of virtual reality for military application."

Cam shrugged the woman's hand off. "Your partner left us to die."

"You're talking about Lieutenant Jacob Lawson."

"Is he here?" River asked.

"He's dead. His body showed up in a tank a little bit before you. I don't know what happened to him, and I'd very much like to. No one here is going to hurt you. We want to ask your permission to run a few tests. Afterward, perhaps we can talk. I'd like to hear your story, know what you've been through. I'm sure it's been harrowing, but we would be unendingly grateful for your cooperation."

"Man," Trip said. "Nobody's going to believe this. We'll blow their minds."

"Yes," the woman said, her warm smile dropping briefly. "You'll find you've become quite famous because of your mysterious disappearance. Your story will be of great curiosity to the general public."

Cam was still suspicious, but calmer. "After, I can see my brother?"

"Yes," Dr. Barker said. "I promise. Would you like to rest, to eat first, before we talk?"

"No," Cam said, at the same time as Trip said, "God, yes."

Trip was bruised and scraped up, Cam had dark circles under her eyes, and they were all dripping with fluid. It was drying in a sticky film on River's skin and hair, and he felt like he'd been twisted in a million directions at once, like a wrung-out towel.

Cam was anxious to see Benji, but no one was going to let them go, at least for a little while. The chance to get cleaned up was appealing.

"Fine," Cam said.

Dr. Barker gave them army-green shirts and pants and pointed them to the locker rooms. The three of them were separated, and River didn't know what happened to the other two, but when he peeled out of the blue suit, a lab worker collected it and folded it into a sealed, beeping box. They ran a clicking wand across his skin like the kind that measures radiation. They scraped skin cells and flakes of dried tank fluid from him before they let him step under the hot spray of water and scrub away what remained of the woods and ocean and tank.

Dr. Barker convinced an impatient doctor to delay a physical exam until they'd had a small meal she'd arranged in a cozy, quiet room. When Dr. Barker entered to join them, she said, "I've brought someone you might like to see."

River caught a flash of pink hair and a nose ring before Trip and Cam rushed from the table.

"Liza!" Cam cried.

He stood, struggling to comprehend. Liza came to him and wrapped her arms around his neck, and he held her just as tightly as he had when they'd floated in the waves.

Every word he knew vanished except the ones he said in her ear. "I tried to hang on."

She held his face to look into his eyes. "It wasn't possible to hang on. And I'm okay."

Even while she held him, he hadn't believed she was real until he heard her voice.

"You died."

"I did. And then my body showed up on the beach at the resort. There were people there. They did CPR, brought me back."

Cam and Trip touched Liza's shoulder and hair as if making sure she was really there.

"I guess I wasn't immune after all," Liza said. "My fears came true, same as you guys."

River smiled. "And you thought you were too old."

She tried to scowl, but couldn't even pretend irritation.

"What's up with this lady?" Cam whispered, tipping her head to Dr. Barker.

"She's okay. Hear her out."

Dr. Barker ushered them back to the table of food.

"We'd been searching for you in the woods. The contestant Brandon McCay, he died, and we found his body early on. Then Liza appeared on the shore by the resort, and she told us what you'd been through. When Jacob showed up dead in the tank, I rushed back to the lab. I've been working nonstop since you all vanished."

"Jacob said the world we were in was consciousness-based," Cam said.

"If that's true, maybe when your consciousness ceased to exist, your body was returned to a permanent dimension. Liza was lucky they were able to bring her back."

As much as they were wary of Dr. Barker, she spoke to them kindly, joking with them, telling them about the project. She recognized their guardedness and was patient. She was obviously eager to hear their story, but she let them take their time in telling it, listened as they told Liza what had happened after they'd thought she'd died. Their stories unfolded, slowly at first, a little confusingly, sometimes bringing back the same feelings of fear and terror in the telling as when they'd lived it. Dr. Barker answered their questions carefully, understanding their confusion.

After they'd eaten, and after the exams and questions, she brought them all together in her warm mahogany office.

"I'm hoping," she said, removing her glasses and folding her hands, "that before you go home, before you see your families, we can talk about what happens now, and how we'll move forward. If you don't mind."

CHAPTER 33

CUT OFF POST-DISASTER SPECIAL

"HOME"

ON-CAMERA INTERVIEW: RIVER ADAN AND CAMERON JAIMES

INTERVIEW CONDUCTED BY EXECUTIVE PRODUCER DARLENE
  AMARI

AMARI: You've been back for a little while now. How has it been? Was it a shock to return to civilization and find yourselves the subjects of one of the biggest mysteries of our century? It's as if Amelia Earhart was found.

RIVER: If there'd been social media when Amelia Earhart disappeared.

AMARI: Social media has played a significant role in the attention paid to this story. Your disappearance was watched live by millions, and rewatched countless times, dissected by an audience intent on cracking the case. You two, Trip, and Brandon McCay were our finalists, and Elizabeth Rojas had just joined the game as a sort of host —everyone else on the show had tapped out at that point. All of you seemed to vanish into thin air, right before our eyes. That disappearance certainly lent an air of mystery to the drama. And then of course there was the tragic discovery of Brandon McCay, and then Liza washed up on that beach.

CAM: Of course, from our perspective we didn't disappear. It only looked like we did on camera because of the breakdown of the Skyms.

AMARI: Right, the Skym malfunction. You've seen the footage. For us, one minute you were on camera, on our screens, in our visors, and the next minute you were gone. Poof! All of you at once. It was only after that that the four of you found each other, but by then you were lost, yes?

RIVER: That's right. Although it wasn't so much that we were lost as that you guys—the producers—couldn't find us. The Skyms were supposed to provide our GPS locations, and they couldn't.

AMARI: Because of the malfunction.

RIVER: Yes.

CAM: Yes.

AMARI: Even the American military searched the island for weeks. How did they miss you?

CAM: Beats me. We were out there.

RIVER: It's a hilly, tangled sort of place. It might be easy to miss someone even if you're just a few yards away.

AMARI: Tell your fans—how did you manage to survive all that time? Alone, in the wilderness, with no help.

RIVER: That was the point of the show, wasn't it? To survive.

AMARI: It's one thing to survive on a reality show, where you know that with the push of a button you'll be whisked away to a posh hotel, but it's something else entirely to have to truly survive in the wild. River, I understand your experience as a survivalist was useful to your cast mates?

RIVER: I guess so.

CAM: Without him, we would have died.

RIVER: No. It was all of us together.

CAM: That's true. We needed each other out there.

AMARI: Did you hear that Elizabeth Rojas has recently acquired a deal to produce a documentary about the experience?

CAM: Liza has?

AMARI: Yes. It's called *Fear Itself: Life Lessons from a Survivor of the Cut Off Experience*. What were some of the biggest challenges you faced while lost in the wilderness? How did you handle your fears while you were out there?

RIVER: [shrugs]

CAM: I don't know. You can't really make fear go away, can you? It's always there. You just have to find ways to deal with it.

AMARI: We asked Trip Johnson to participate in this interview, but he seems to have gone into hiding. That's surprising, given his interest in the spotlight before the show. We hear he's developing a series of games that employ virtual-reality technology.

CAM: We don't know anything about that.

AMARI: He's becoming a real pioneer in the industry. But we have sources that say he's on the payroll of the United States military. Do you know if he's working for the military, and if so, what he's doing with them?

RIVER: Trip's a talented programmer. He'll do well with whatever he pursues.

CAM: And I'm sure once it's done, he'll be all over the TV telling everyone about it.

AMARI: How do you respond to the various internet sites devoted to exposing your story as a fabrication designed to shield the show from liability? Is there more to Brandon McCay's death than we've been told? Were you paid to lie to the public, as one of these sites claims? Were you threatened or offered some incentive?

RIVER: No.

CAM: No. We were lost in the wilderness. That's really what happened. I know some people think it was alien abduction, or that we were kidnapped for ransom, but that's all ridiculous. We were lost, that's it.

AMARI: One blogger says you destroyed the cameras yourselves, that you must have hid from the search parties. Another says he has evidence that you entered a parallel universe.

RIVER: [looks at Cam, laughing]

CAM: There are a lot of crazy theories out there.

AMARI: So what's next for you two?

RIVER: I'm working with an outdoor-expedition organization, giving kids from the city an opportunity to be in nature, teaching them skills to survive in the wild or, you know, just have fun.

AMARI: And Cam? We know you've been reunited with your brother. Do you still have plans for him to live with you?

CAM: Actually, we're both doing really well with my Aunt Pam. I was worried because I never really knew my aunt, but it turns out she's been great for him. He loves his new school, he has a bedroom all to himself and a bunch of video games. I'm glad I gave her a chance.

AMARI: And your mom . . . ?

CAM: My mom's doing okay too. With money from the show, we were able to afford a new lawyer to appeal her conviction, and all the publicity I've received has focused attention on her case. I'm told there's a good chance her sentence will be commuted.

AMARI: And what about yourself?

CAM: Everything's changed so much, I'm not really sure yet what I'm doing. For the first time, I'm thinking about college.

AMARI: Any truth to the rumors that romance blossomed on the island and the two of you are an item?

RIVER: No. We were scared, had nothing to eat and no showers, and were eaten alive by bugs. The wilderness is no place to start a relationship.

CAM: [looking at River] But after everything we've been through, he'll always be my friend. I'm sure we'll keep in touch.

CHAPTER 34

The campfire danced in a stone-lined pit. Trip was texting, Cam cooked a hotdog, and River leaned back in his chair, shuffling his deck of cards, feet propped on a rock.

"I can't believe you agreed to go camping, Trip," Liza said. She fiddled with a Skym in her lap—a smaller, less sophisticated version than those that had been used on the show.

"Yeah," Cam said. "Aren't you worried about spiders?"

"You know what? Not so much. A spider here or there—it doesn't bother me anymore. As long as they're not showing up to party in the thousands, I think I'm actually over my fear of spiders."

"That's nice for you," River said. "After the island, I think I've acquired a fear of spiders. Thanks a lot."

"With everything that happened," Liza said, "I wasn't too sure about camping myself."

River laughed. "This isn't camping."

Trip looked up from his phone. "What? This is camping."

"Camping doesn't usually involve tables and chairs," River said. "Or catered dinners. Or actual beds in tents the size of a small house. With electricity, no less."

"Not to mention that we're practically in River's back-yard," Cam added. "I can see the house from here."

"It's a nice house," Liza said. "All this land is really yours?"

"It belonged to my parents. It's in trust with my uncle now, but it'll be mine when I turn eighteen."

Cam twisted her mouth at Trip. "Put the phone away for two seconds. Who are you texting, anyway?"

"Just a guy. The first one I've met who seems to want to have an actual conversation."

"And not just talk about *Cut Off*?" Liza said.

"Yeah, pretty much. Plus, if you think I'm going to stop texting, you're nuts. We're in the middle of nowhere. Somebody has to make sure we're still connected to the outside world."

River shook his head. "We're forty miles from Seattle, Trip."

"Like I said, middle of nowhere."

Liza peered over his shoulder. "I thought you might be texting our friend Dr. Barker. Is it true you're working with her on the multiverse project?"

"My lips are sealed."

"Come on, you can tell us."

"Seriously, I'll never tell. If I did, I'd have to kill you or something. Top-secret."

Cam laughed. "You're not much for the covert stuff, are you? Because that totally means you are."

"The worst part is, I'm not allowed to talk to the media. About anything, even the show! What a waste of fame."

"Then why do you want to work with them?" River said. "What they're messing with, it's dangerous, Trip."

"They're experts," Trip said. "They know what they're doing."

"That's just it, though. There are no experts. They have no idea what they're dealing with, nobody does."

Trip turned to Cam. "Come on, you get it, right? After everything you saw, everything you experienced, are you really willing to shrug your shoulders and walk away? There's so much we don't know. You must want answers. Jacob talked about how the multiverse is like River's cards. If that's true, how can we not give the deck a shuffle? Pick a card, see what happens?"

Before Cam could answer, River slipped his cards together and leaned forward, one card held out and pointed at Trip. "Lose one card in the deck and the whole thing is ruined. Hell, bend a corner and you may as well throw the whole pack away. Are you willing to risk this dimension by messing with another?"

"You know, I'm not sure Jacob was right about it being like a deck of cards," Cam said. "A deck of cards is so countable. The worlds out there—they're infinite. As many as the number of stars in the universe. We can't possibly comprehend the implications of tampering with them. Dr. Barker and Jacob were trying to reinvent virtual reality, and instead they conjured a whole new dimension. They did it by accident. If it's messed up again, who knows what could happen."

"I'd rather be part of the project and keep an eye on them than spend weeks like we did in the woods, having no idea what was going on. At least we'll be on the other side this time, the side of the people who have all the information."

River tossed the box of cards to Trip. "You really want to be on the side of possibly destroying the world?"

"I want to be the one palming the cards, not the one being tricked."

"We're not talking about tricks, though," Cam said. "We're talking about our lives."

"Barker offered you more money than we got, didn't she?" Liza said, rescuing Trip from responding.

"Money is nice, but I'm excited to work on the tech. We can do great things with it, and even though they won't let me talk about it now, this project is going to be huge, and I'm a part of it. You watch—they'll make movies about me."

"Seriously, though," Liza said. "How much?"

Trip mimed zipping his mouth and throwing away an invisible key.

What none of them knew was that Dr. Barker had offered Cam twice the money Trip had received to work with her. She was the only person in the world who had seen the multiverse, even navigated it. She wasn't ready to give them an answer yet, however. There was a lot to think about. It was a lot of money, and money was the reason she'd gone on the show to begin with, but things were different now. She had to figure out what she wanted—beyond money and the safety that money represented. Liza was on her way to becoming a successful producer, and despite Trip's attempts at secrecy, they all knew he was working on cutting-edge technology, breaking new ground in a field that would eventually make him famous. And River was willing to do whatever the rest of them wanted. Cam, Trip, and Liza were more important to him than fame or money.

River was right to be worried about Dr. Barker's project. Even though the others had been there, of all of them only Cam had felt those other worlds hovering just beyond reach, that great expanse of space and time, full of birth and death, love and hate, beginnings and endings, and endlessly full of possibilities. Even now her memory of what it had felt like was fading, dimming under the impossibility of understanding it. When she'd tried to tell Dr. Barker about it, while the woman was desperate to understand, it was clear that even she, with her degrees and her genius, couldn't comprehend it. And it wasn't Cam's fault. What she'd felt, what she'd been through, defied any articulate description. That they had found their way back at all was a miracle.

Sometimes, late at night, alone in the dark, Cam wondered if they'd chosen right. Was this really their world, or was it only a world so similar they couldn't tell the difference? Was their home still out there, missing them? And even if they had chosen right, somewhere out there was a world where they were still wandering the woods, terrorized by their fears, each day closer to disaster.

The more Cam thought about it, the more she knew that the worlds weren't like a finite, orderly deck of cards at all. The multiverse was more like the roots of a tree, constantly growing and branching, varied and unpredictable. What would happen to the tree if, in attempting to study it, the scientists dug those roots up?

"How's the documentary coming, Liza?" Trip asked, pulling Cam from her thoughts.

"Great."

He picked up the Skym. "How'd you get your hands on this? They're not even on the market yet."

Liza winked. "I've got connections."

"Have you started filming yet?" Cam asked.

"I'm in the research stage." Liza took the Skym from Trip and launched it into the air, where it buzzed over their heads. She motioned for the three of them to sit closer and then positioned herself across from them.

Cam wasn't alone in the dark, so she let her worries go, at least for now. She smiled and turned to River. He took her hand and brought it to his lips, then enclosed it against his chest.

The night was cool, but the fire was warm. Almost too warm to sit so close, but they didn't move their chairs. They stayed near, to the fire and one another, their shadows flickering on the ground behind them.

Liza touched some buttons on a controller and the Skym hummed and bobbed until it floated at eye level with Trip, River, and Cam, its green light glowing.

"So," she said. "Tell me what you're afraid of."

ACKNOWLEDGMENTS

Thank you to my amazing agent, Adam Schear at DeFiore and Company. He is a tireless advocate, a thoughtful reader, and a great source of support and encouragement.

My editor, Lily Kessinger, has been an invaluable partner in the creation of *Cut Off*. Her incredibly smart, sensitive, and insightful efforts have made this an infinitely better book. I am humbled by all the wonderful people at HMH who have dedicated their time to making *Cut Off* the best it can be, with special thanks to Jessica Handelman, Mary Claire Cruz, Emilia Rhodes, Mary Magrisso, Erika West, and Cat Onder.

I have endless gratitude to my friends and family for their support. My ride or dies, Leigh'Ann Andrews, Jordan Andrews, Rachel Morgan, and Matthew Weedman. Peg Keller has been both a reader and an Iowa family for our girls. Bill and Rhonda Morgan offered a week of joy and relaxation on Powell Mountain. Thank you to Robert Finlay for being my first reader and editor. Thank you to Caitlin Finlay, Peter Bakija, Conwill Payne-Finlay, Dan and Teresa Schraffenberger, Jonathan Schraffenberger, Carolyn Harlow, Kirsten Faucher-Harlow, Connor Harlow, and Constance Finlay for their encouragement, critique, and enthusiasm.

This book was written while I was on sabbatical; my

gratitude to Upper Iowa University for providing that opportunity. I would also like to thank my students at UIU, who are always excited to hear about my latest project.

I have been lucky to benefit from an amazing community. The Electric Eighteens and Class of 2k18 have been a font of information and support. A huge thanks to readers, bloggers, teachers, booksellers, and librarians. You give this work meaning.

This book is dedicated to Ginny and Hattie, who make my world a better place.

Finally, thank you to Jeremy Schraffenberger, for unwavering support and countless brainstorming sessions. I love you.